# DVARCA

AF555994

MADHAV MATHUR

FINGERPRINT!

Published by
FiNGERPRINT!
An imprint of Prakash Books India Pvt. Ltd.

113/A, Darya Ganj, New Delhi-110 002,
Tel: (011) 2324 7062 – 65, Fax: (011) 2324 6975
Email: info@prakashbooks.com/sales@prakashbooks.com

facebook www.facebook.com/fingerprintpublishing
twitter www.twitter.com/FingerprintP, www.fingerprintpublishing.com

Copyright © 2016 Prakash Books India Pvt. Ltd.
Copyright Text © Madhav Mathur

This is a work of fiction. Names, characters, places and incidents are either product of the author's imagination or are used fictitiously, and any resemblance to any actual person, living or dead, events or locales is purely coincidental.

All rights reserved. No part of this publication may be reproduced, stored in a retrieval system or transmitted in any form or by any means, electronic, mechanical, photocopying, recording or otherwise (except for mentions in reviews or edited excerpts in the media) without the written permission of the publisher.

ISBN: 978 81 7599 385 3

Processed & printed in India by HT Media Ltd., Noida

*'He who fights monsters should look to it that he himself does not become a monster. And if you gaze long into an abyss, the abyss also gazes into you.'*

*—Friedrich Nietzsche*

# CONTENTS

# 1
# DO YOU FEEL THE FERVOUR?

*For the last time, I am not a spy.*
*I am not a Caliphite.*
*I am not a Navmargi.*
*No one will have me. No one is mine. Why?*
*Where do I go in this change-d world?*
*From corner to corner, I skulk and hide.*
*I once had a home, I once had a name.*
*Now all I have is a curse-d leash. I'm a collar-ed man.*

Thoughts of loss darted across his mind as the desperate man moved. Never still, never quiet, ever mumbling execrations to himself. Sometimes the words made no sense. Sometimes he wished he were a mute—he would give anything to quell the chatter. He clung under the belly of a trembling truck, with all the might in his calloused fingers, and looked up furtively at his upturned view of the street. The roads were smooth but for the occasional pothole.

Police jeeps roamed everywhere and surveillance drones swept the night sky in search of people like him. Dirt and pebbles pelted his back as the rock-hard asphalt bounded and leaped, threatening to crush him from above. He pulled himself closer to the variously scalding and freezing machinery of the grimy hulking vehicle. Every menacing gnaw of acceleration filled him with fear. His feet were slipping and he could no longer support his weight. This hiding place was not for him. There was no choice. He had to roll out at the next light.

He felt the rough and unforgiving floor on his back, and scratched his elbows as he tumbled away. He stood up disoriented, between trucks and buses, and disappeared into a cloud of exhaust. He used the nights to get as far away as he could. He hoped he was succeeding.

If only he could outrun the White *Kurtas*.

If only he could find the others.

***

"IS EVERYBODY IN? IS EVERYBODY IN? THE *HOUR OF HONOUR* IS ABOUT TO BEGIN."

Jyoti was slicing carrots in the kitchen when she received the message on her Distant-Directives. She acknowledged the friendly advert-ordinance and wiped a few drops of perspiration off her DDs. The entire family had already gathered in the drawing room. She carried some vegetables out and sat down with them in front of their old grey TV box. A colour-focus-pattern flickered, before yielding to a dark screen and the familiar sound of *nagadas*. The drums of war were special. Their sharp tone signalled enthusiasm, while their ominous tempo warned of an apocalypse.

Jyoti comforted her pounding heart, and rubbed her temples in short clockwise movements, to calm herself. Lately, she had felt more on edge than usual. The slightest sounds would unsettle her. She brushed away a few strands of hair from her forehead and fought back a shiver. No one else in her family seemed perturbed by the percussion. They waited for the ceremony eagerly, grinning, and thumping along.

The show was beamed live from an amphitheatre at the centre of the Centre, and was a very popular daily event. The dark screen birthed a roving bright circle of white light that rose like a hurried sun and lit Shastri *ji's* snowy moustache. Who could deny that it was perfectly coiffed? Who would dare say that it was anything but divine? The word 'PURITY' appeared on the screen, accompanied by the sounds of children chanting. The floating word grew in size and engulfed half the screen, just below the glowing bow of hair on the Great Leader's upper lip.

"Will I have a moustache, Mother?" Jyoti's son, Nakul, was sitting at his mother's feet. He repeated the question without turning to her. His father, Gandharva, was a little offended by the query. He sat at the other end of the couch, his discomfort growing—he had no facial hair and as a result, friends and family sniggered at his stature and vitality. The joke was that Gandharvas were incapable of growing moustaches, that they were timid, effeminate number-crunchers. All the insults came crashing back when his own son wanted to be like another man. The only consolation was that Nakul wanted to be like the best man alive.

"Of course, you will, dear."

"When?"

"In a few years, long, curly strands of uncontrollable hair will grow out and cover your face—under your nose, around your mouth—like the wings of Lord Garuda," she reassured him.

"You will be the manliest man, before you know it," *Baba* spoke up from behind them. His sagely words were based in truth. Nakuls were known to be hirsute.

"I want to be the manliest man! I do! I will crush the Caliphate with my muscles!" the boy exclaimed.

Gandharva got up and went to the kitchen. His observant and thoughtful daughter, Mira, sensed that he was upset. She scurried around him to the sink and poured him a glass of water. He raised it to his smooth mouth for a long draw and thanked her. "Shall we start on dinner early?" he snuck a piece of carrot from the chopping-board and held it out for her. He could tell that she was worried.

"What's wrong? Why the long face?"

"Do you have to go tonight? After dinner?" She looked up at him with big curious eyes.

"Yes . . . I . . ." before he could complete his sentence, she hugged him tight.

"I won't let them hurt you!"

"Hurt me? What makes you think they will hurt me?"

"A girl in my school, she told me that the Visions are very painful . . ."

"Not at all! It is a soothing experience. Deeply moving too! Look at me, I am salivating just talking about it. Very soon, you too will know what it is like . . ."

"Do you really enjoy it?"

"I can't imagine life without it. Come—" They returned to the drawing room to watch the show.

"It wasn't really Shastri ji . . ." Nakul declared his disappointment. "It was just a close-up of a poster."

The spotlight swung away and took the shape of a melting clock from the *Impertinence of Memory*, a great work by the twentieth century painter, Salabdar Daleshwar. Shastri ji loved his works and had brought them back to Dvarca a few years ago. Salabdar was Dvarcan, born and raised in Patna. His paintings were largely ignored in his homeland until he took them to the west, where he gained much fame, under a slightly bastardized Hedonesian name.

To Shastri ji, his works were all glimpses of the same truth. They were imaginative, often anthropomorphic depictions of man's search for God. He liked the series of paintings and sculptures of effete, long-legged elephants. Other works resonated with nationalist ideals. For instance, the *Dream Caused by the Flight of the B*, showed a pair of pouncing tigers, avenging the violation of an ancient and treasured Motherland, against a naked, decadent West. Similarly, *Surveillance* was about the watchful eyes of the State. His works were celebrated and he was a common point of reference.

The spotlight moved to the far right corner of the stage and kissed a brass replica of the Nation's emblem. Four lions looked out proudly, with cameras in their mouths. In Dvarca, for the truth to triumph, it had to be captured. It was mandatory for the idol to be placed at the highest point in all homes. This was in obeisance of the fact that you knew you were being observed, and was one of the fundamental reasons for moral behaviour. Without the scrutiny of machines, how could we ensure the kindness of humans?

With a duster on a stick, Mira polished the feet of the emblem. It hung over the drawing room, on a mantle, above all else.

"That's my girl!" Baba applauded her effort.

Much to Jyoti's discomfort, the drums grew louder and the beats came closer together. The image of a small child smiling and clapping, was followed by a slow fade, revealing two radiant eyeballs with black irises, darker than Sringeri coal. The word 'HONESTY' appeared on the television as children read it out. Nakul and Mira did too. The Great Leader's stern, determined face stretched from floor to ceiling, across a cloth backdrop. His expression reminded viewers that even though the *Hour of*

*Honour* was meant for entertainment, there was more to it, than jubilation and revelry. The word 'STRENGTH' ended the show's introduction. 'PURITY, HONESTY, STRENGTH'.

The master of ceremonies emerged, like a mongoose from a hole in the stage-ground. He was a short man shaped like a tear drop, bottom-heavy with a tiny head. He had a high voice, crisp diction, and the audience responded to his pleasant, self-effacing but Nation-exalting style. He greeted them with his most beloved catch-phrases.

"Do you feel the fervour?"

"Yes!"

"Are you devout without a doubt?"

"Yes!"

"Welcome to the *Hour of Honour*! We begin tonight with a quiz. Let's meet our contestants!"

Emaciated men in resplendent clothes rolled three big podiums up to the stage and placed them side by side, as the three contestants entered and stood behind them.

"Contestant Number One, from Sector 16, a homely and kind *Mata* ji by the name of Jyoti. She has a *Neel kalaava* and she serves her Nation by mothering two young Kubers, and working hard at Dvarca Mills. Jyoti, welcome to the *Hour of Honour*. How many shirts do you make in one day?"

"As many as they need."

"Excellent answer! Next, from Sector 13, we have the lovely and ever-smiling Aditi ji! I don't have to tell you, so you tell me, what does this *Hari* Aditi do?"

The crowd exhaled together: "Obstetrician!"

"That's right, like all Aditis, she is an obstetrician and also the mother of one lovely Samyukta. Tell me, Aditi ji, did you deliver your own girl?" The Aditi nodded sheepishly, playing along with the silly question. Everybody laughed.

"And now, last, but not the least: a wise man. A civil servant, a celebrated two-time Medal of Veneration winner, *Peet* Vidur! How are you feeling, Vidur?"

In a hushed, reverent voice he spoke, "Patriotic and pious."

"Stole the words right out of my mouth. It is time for our 'Patriotic and Pious' segment! You love the game, you know how it works—play along at home! Just switch your DDs to 'Send' and shoot your answers to 3-1001."

The kids shifted their DDs as instructed. These were a compulsory part of the Dvarcan national costume—special goggles that served as communicators between a caring and proactive government, and its wayward, directionless people. From emergency warnings to quotidian work orders, everything came through the all-important goggles. Their red lenses adjusted their hues in response to the brightness of the wearer's environment. They were coded and numbered, allowing citizens to be recognized as 'Valid' by the machines and automatons that guarded the Nation. With smooth metal bands, they were fastened to an amulet around one's neck, and could only be replaced by the Police. As a finishing flourish, a charm embossed with the words, 'For God and Country', hung off the permanent ornament. Baba used to tell the children that DD stood for *Divya-Drishtikon.* This imbued them with supernatural power and made them more fascinating for his impressionable young audience.

Mira's goggles were large for her. She had, just recently, moved into the third head-size group. Nakul's were a bit tight, and would soon need to be changed. He poked and teased his sister about her ill-fitting pair because it hid most of her face. She retaliated by flicking his nose. The fight stopped when the presenter started with the first question.

A giant picture appeared on the backdrop of the stage. It showed a mountain range with a few peaks bunched together.

Shadows hung below them and a stray tree or two, peppered the skyline. 'Patriotic and Pious' always began with a new image.

"What do you see?" led the anchor. "Everyone gets to answer. Jyoti, you are first."

"I love this!" Baba sat up in his chair. It was his favourite kind of question.

"I see Lord Krishna. The middle peak is in the shape of his crown, high and round. I see his attractive, dark-complexioned face smiling at us from the great height. The lone tree is a peacock feather, his preferred adornment."

A murmur of appreciation and approval rumbled through the live audience.

"Judges, take note, the homely and caring Jyoti sees Lord Krishna!"

"One more thing please, the Sun rising behind him is a beautiful glowing halo, filling us, his people, with hope and awe."

"Hope and awe, I like that. Are you sure you aren't a Narad in Jyoti's clothing?"

The lady folded her hands together as the audience clapped for her.

"Aditi ji, what do you see in this photograph?"

"I like Jyoti's answer, but that is not what struck me first. I see a trio of missiles leaping towards the heavens, to bring glory and strategic advantage to our people."

"It is not an act of war if it is carried out in self-defence . . ." the presenter reminded everyone cheekily, smirking into the camera.

"True! And the glow . . . it is from the thrust and rising exhaust below the missiles. Soon, it will become a fiery blanket of death for our enemies."

"A fiery blanket of death for our enemies! Outstanding!"

He danced about excitedly as the homicidal obstetrician took a dignified bow. The cameras and spotlights shifted quickly to contestant number three.

"Venerated Vidur ji, do share your interpretation of this completely random photograph. What is your patriotic and pious perspective?"

The elderly gentleman thought for a moment. It was a Rorschach test for nationalism and holiness, and Jyoti at home wondered how he would respond. Could he outdo the two ladies before him?

"I see an opportunity. We may see God in everything, but we must also *show God in everything!* This is necessary! The beautiful vista is incomplete without a temple and an office for our leaders."

"Bravo!" shouted Baba.

"What is *Navmarg* if it is only in our hearts and minds? All good *Navmargis* should see the face of Krishna and the rising *trishul* of missiles. But we cannot stop there. We must establish a presence to preserve the visions of my fellow contestants, and of those watching at home," Vidur concluded.

"*Har har Mahadev!*", "*Jai Mata di!*", "Jai Dvarca!" Rapturous shouts rang out like cannon blasts.

"People of Dvarca! We hope you have enjoyed the great diversity of opinions on the show today. I thank our participants for their contribution. The name of the winner will be announced later, during the programme." The little fat man spoke with great respect.

"Who are you rooting for?"

"Vidur."

"Vidur!"

"Definitely Vidur!"

There were no dissenters in the household, and the family cheered for the mature gentleman who wanted another temple. Only Jyoti seemed concerned about the need to mark a territory on behalf of a powerful and omnipresent God. A slight sense of redundancy nagged her and the contradictions made her uneasy. Maybe it was something she ate. She steadied her shaking hands and sought inspiration from her happy and committed family. Gandharva beamed blissfully. Baba was as exuberant as the TV host. Her children too, were devoted to the one true way.

The more they hugged and cheered, the lonelier she felt.

# 2
# A SONG FOR THE DEAF

The collared man couldn't shake the taste of dirt from his mouth. The stench of oil stuck to him and the deafening sound of traffic still echoed in his ears. With foggy senses, he continued his search. He found another manhole and bent down to lift it. He tried to slide it out but it did not budge, just like the others. The effort cost him a nail and he gnashed his teeth in agony.

He had heard stories about a place for undesirables in the sewers of Dvarca. But his search for a way into this promised safe haven had proved futile. He tried to catch his breath in an alley, when a dumpster caught his eye. He went looking for old styrofoam containers in the garbage, hoping that someone might have left something edible in them by accident. There were a few boxes that had been thrown out, and he polished them clean with his filthy fingers. Salt. Glorious salt!

There must be a way down, around the residential blocks, surely the Dvarcans in the flats above needed plumbing? There were no openings, risers, or maintenance cabins. To his disappointment, it was all sealed and blocked by cement. He decided to carry on.

In short bursts, he ran from pillar to pillar. A fresh round of posters had just been pasted on them, and he could still smell the wet glue.

'THINK THE SAME
ACT THE SAME
BE THE SAME

—Issued in public interest by the Ministry of
Media Controls and Communication'

He scratched up the revolting wet poster and regretted it immediately. The gummy thick paper lodged itself around his fingers and refused to come off. He bent down to scrape it on the floor and rose up to see an old woman staring at him. Her mouth moved like a hooked beak, her hands rose like talons, clawing at him.

"Who are you? *Hai Bhagwan*, you have no DDs!" She shrieked and raised an official alarm immediately. He caught his reflection in her red lenses and without much thought, pushed her to the ground and ran away as fast as he could, while she shouted hysterically, "A pariah! A *binaaydi!* Somebody help me!" They'd be on his tail in no time.

***

Just a few blocks away, the family stayed glued to their TV box, as the show continued.

"Dvarca, my love, it is now time for the *Hour of Honour*

spectacle. We present a very special performance by an exceptional woman. Many of you must have seen her in the news. She is *Srimati* Shanti Devi and she wanted to be here today, for us all."

"Now who is she?" Nakul asked, bored and disinterested.

"Be patient . . ." Jyoti muttered as she grabbed a bowl of peas to peel.

A frail-looking woman in a white sari was escorted to the stage by an armed contingent. The crowd cheered when they saw their uniforms. They were all *Varaha,* and their famous symbol, the menacing and muscular head of a wild boar with the Earth in his tusks, appeared on the screen.

"We all have our ways of celebrating Dvarca and we all yearn for new ways to honour the Motherland. Shanti Devi is here to show us her way."

"Why can't they just let the Varaha show us their fighting skills? This old lady is a snore!" the children groaned, unimpressed. Gandharva grabbed Nakul and shook him up, ordering him to sit straight.

"Show some respect! Everything that comes out of that box is of great importance." He pointed a threatening finger at the boy and then at the television.

"Dvarcan television is the fulcrum of progress. The fulcrum! You will always learn something from it. Pay attention!"

Shanti Devi's eyes moistened as she began to speak.

"My Arjun was serving with his squadron on the North Western Frontier border. Three days ago, they were attacked by the enemy and he . . . he will not . . . he did not come back." She paused to regain her composure, as they showed pictures of her son and his contingent. He looked young, handsome, and driven. He smiled in the photos. They showed him as a student, in training, and finally in full gear at the battlefront.

"I lost my only son to the Front. He was a good boy. He never had any doubts or questions when it came to God and Country. He just wanted to know where he could go, to protect the Nation. His only goal was service to us." Her eyes were still and centred at her feet. She pulled herself together.

"As a mark of respect for my brave boy and his fellow soldiers, I will do something today."

Jyoti looked on with wide, mournful eyes. She had pulled Nakul into an embrace, unknowingly. His unkempt hair ruffled under her chin as he struggled to free himself from her lap.

"Ma! What are you doing? Let me go . . ."

She was lost. She was still. She looked beautiful to him in that moment. Her firm hold made him feel safe. A sudden funereal calm descended upon them and he stopped trying to get away. He turned back to the telecast.

"We grieve with you. We share your pain. We see the fire in your eyes and steel in your veins." The presenter chimed in with apposite clichés.

The cameras panned forward to focus on Shanti Devi. The wrinkles on her forehead sat motionless. It was called the *bhrikuti,* a mark of learnedness, a characteristic that distinguished the pious and the thoughtful, from the careless and naive. Years of hurt crumpled up as her face contorted into an expression of rage.

"They think they can break us by taking away our children. They think they can terrorize us. They think their guns will silence us. I say no! Never! Jai Dvarca!"

The Varaha guards faced the audience. They shouted in unison, "Jai Dvarca!"

Gandharva asked Mira to scoot back from the television. They had no control over the volume. The *Hour of Honour* had to be watched, heard, and experienced with the prescribed mix and settings. The little girl was defiant.

"Obey your father," Jyoti supported her husband.

Mira climbed onto their ratty sofa and dived in with legs of lead. The cushions were rough and she rubbed her hands on them petulantly. She found a hole in the upholstery, and started to pick and tug at it. The edges started to fray more and more as strings and stitches came undone.

"Stop it, don't do that!"

"The hole is already there Ma, look, it's a lost cause."

The child ripped a strip clear from the covers. Her mother smacked her on the hand.

"I didn't do it—it is already ripped and tatty!"

"Stop making it bigger!"

The *Vanaprasthi* stepped up to a platform. It was a race-winners' triple step-stand that had been covered in gold lace and marigold flowers. One could still see the number '1' peeking out from under the covers. She stood on the winner's box and raised her palms up, joining them in a *namaskar*. She then put them back down firmly on either side of her body and stood at attention.

Two guards stepped up behind her. One of them held her hand and the other pointed his gun up to the sky. It was a modified 47, from the Arms, Weaponry, and Ammunition Zone in Sector 2. It looked big for him. Perhaps they had chosen a smaller looking guard to drive home the message about the giant potent guns. Perhaps it really was an unwieldy mass of deadly metal. He pulled it up and held it tightly under his arm. The old lady turned to him and nodded.

He started to fire. She started to sing.

It was the national anthem. Everyone could hear her, despite the infernal spray of bullets being launched rapidly into the sky above. The frail Mata ji could be heard above the thunderous rattle of the firearm's mayhem. Jyoti wondered if she could really hear her, or whether she was filling in the sounds and words for the anthem in her mind.

"Do you hear it?" she asked everyone in the house.

"I do."

"Do you not?"

"Of course I do."

They could all hear the singing. A blue light started to beep on the emblem-idol, reminding them to stand up. The demonstration had taken them all by surprise. They jumped to their feet and sang out loud. The whole block had joined in. Everyone stood with Shanti Devi. Everyone sang the anthem together.

"Dvarca, Dvarca, Dvarca
God's Dvarca, my Dvarca, Dvarca my love
Blessed like no other
Loved like no other,
Dvarca, my country, I would die for you
From the plains of the north
To the plateaus of the south
From Vaishnodevi to Kanyakumari, I would die for you

You are home, surely
To me and my brothers and sisters
We thank you for your earth and water
We thank you for your bounteous grain
We thank you for your bough of shade
We thank you for our freedom

Holy land, O' Motherland!
Land of the brave Ramachandra
Land of free Parashurama and Krishna
Land of saints and sacrifice
Oh *dharmabhoomi*,
Oh *karmabhoomi*

We live for you, we die for you
Dvarca, Dvarca, Dvarca."

"What is more patriotic than singing the national anthem loud enough to drown out the sound of a machine-gun?" The master of ceremonies took the microphone again and thanked the old lady.

"So much blood has been spilt by our brave martyrs. It is a heavy loss to the country. Let her son's sacrifice not be in vain. Let the Caliphate hear us and tremble!"

The *Hour of Honour* always ended with an emotional provocation. The screen now showed the Death Clock outside the Ministry of Defence and Disaster Evasion. It had replaced a birth clock years ago, and counted losses in the line of duty, defending the Nation. It never stopped ticking upwards.

"A final victory will be born, from the ashes of destruction. Thank you again, Shanti Devi, for making us feel the fervour. For showing us what it means to be devout without a doubt."

The screen faded into a battle scene with charging tanks and marching soldiers. The accompanying voice-over sounded proud and reassuring: "A hallmark of Dvarcan innovation, the cutting edge of the cutting edge, the new Merkava 400."

The tanks spun around acrobatically and sped up, with orange and purple Dvarcan flags, fluttering fearlessly in the wind.

"Silent operation, seamless stealth, give our boys the very best."

The tanks reached the middle of a square, in an arid-looking compound, and started blowing up buildings and towers, as hooded men in black robes ran amok.

"When you think defence, think OMNI."

# 3
# VISION QUEST

He pushed and pulled at the metal collar under his neck. It refused to give. The old lady's alarm had set the Varaha hounds on him, and he was torn between hiding and running. He stopped in a park to rest under a banyan tree. There was activity out in the middle as some *karmacharis* and workers were preparing for a procession. Banners and stands were being erected and arranged. He hid from them and clung to the bark, behind the veil of roots. All his fears came to the fore as a cold, sweaty hand grabbed his neck. He turned around and his dread melted away into sweet relief. He was face-to-face with another man who had no DDs. He almost cried out loud in joy. His hopes and prayers had been answered. Soon he'd be safe!

"Go away, you fool! You—you cannot be here!"

The men knelt down under the danglers of the great old tree as the conversation disintegrated. The collared man did not know what to make of this swift rejection. Still smiling, he spoke, but his words were unintelligible.

Entire sentences were meaningless. Like the disorderly remains of a shredded dictionary, absurd jumbles fell out of his mouth. He did not understand the sounds himself. "I am like you, please give me shelter! Hide me!" he tried to say.

"Are you insane? Shut up! Stop this gibberish."

The collared man covered his mouth with his palms, realizing that words could not help his case.

"Who sent you? What is that thing on your neck? They must be tracking you!"

A voice from the shadows called out to him, urging him to return. "Manyu, get rid of him, there are patrols coming this way!"

Manyu . . . Manyu? Could it be possible that he had found Abhimanyu? The fabled leader of the underground?

"You will get us all caught. We can't help you—"

The frightened runaway acted out with exaggerated gestures. He spoke again, but it was still drivel. He started to weep. Abhimanyu's patience ran thin and the voices from the shadows grew harsh and shrill. It was time to go.

"I am sorry, brother. Please, just go away. Never come back here. You hear me? You did not find us. Just run away."

The collared man nodded, broken in new ways. He had thought that nothing more could be taken from him. He was wrong. He understood why his fellow binaaydis thought him a threat and left. He stepped out into the night again. He would have to keep running.

Only this time, he felt no fear.

***

The family, sat down to a nice dinner of black *daal*, rice, and lady-fingers that had been delivered earlier that evening. Every dinner was a 'State Dinner', but mothers were trusted to prepare their own salad. The only guideline for doing so, was the mandatory inclusion of carrots (a dash of orange was deemed necessary, 'to fight the monotony of green'). This had led to many bumper years of carrot production. Pumpkins too, were in favour, being essential for holy meals.

The food was cooked and packed a few blocks away, by the local Annapurna Division and delivered in cartons of styrofoam. Portions were allocated according to the number of people in a family. There were about 400 families in Sector 17 and dinner was brought in for everyone, everyday. Most of their neighbouring blocks had workers with Neel and *Aasmani kalaavas.* Families with growing children, especially Nakuls, Sahdevas, and Arjuns, were supposed to get a little extra.

"What happened?" Gandharva asked, looking quizzically at the plates before him. "Is this all there is?"

"You can have some of my rice. I am not hungry." Jyoti shifted half her soft white victuals to his plate, before he could object.

"You have to be at the V-lab soon. You should hurry," the dutiful wife added as the family tucked-in.

"Mira, get everyone's medicines please."

The little girl ran along and returned with the pill-boxes. There were two sets of medicines, one for the women of the house and the other for the men. Everyone took their orange and purple pills, and swallowed them with water. They were meant to be taken after every meal and were part of the *Jaivik Vidhi* Kit or JVK. The benefits were too many to list.

"Enough now, it will be bedtime soon. Go wash up, both of you."

The children left the room and the adults sat there in silence, listening intently to sweet musical poetry on the television about Krishna's love for butter and milk. Jyoti carried the dirty dishes to the kitchen and fed them into the washer. They swished and spun as she hung a load of laundry out on the clotheslines. Apart from the hum of the machines, there was peace and quiet. She stood alone and looked out of the window, at the city.

She pulled up a bed-sheet and strung it up on the line, a make-shift curtain for her fleeting private oasis. Baba was preparing for his night-shift and Gandharva too, was getting ready to leave.

There were highrise buildings in the distance and a smattering of work-centres around the residential blocks. Bright lights shimmered all around her and spotlights swept the landscape. Street sweepers scurried about busily below. They were automatons modelled on Venus's Flower Baskets or *Euplectella Aspergillums*: hairy, absorbent little worms that attracted dirt and litter. The designers and architects of Dvarca took inspiration from aquatic life, and many common tools and facilities resembled creatures and objects from the ocean. A novel adaptation of bio-luminescence, the deep-sea evolution wherein the absence of light had enabled beings to develop the ability to glow for themselves, lit parts of her city.

She watched the streets and alleys glimmer, when all of a sudden, a diving disk of light surfed past her window.

"It's just a drone. It's just a drone . . ." she fanned and calmed herself, fighting back familiar waves of panic.

Surveillance drones hovered like airborne electric sting-rays in search of nefarious activity. There were so many of them that one wondered how they did not smash into each other. Eyes upon eyes watched the streets as the perfect city kept winding and unravelling, winding and unravelling repeatedly, on an invisible coil.

All Dvarcans had Visions at their local V-labs, and Gandharva was scheduled for one that night. He was also long overdue for some exercise and had decided to kill two birds with one stone by walking to his appointment, instead of taking the regular bus. Jyoti did not believe that he had fallen short of his steps-quota and he had to project a snapshot of his deficit, off his DDs on their wall, to convince her. She still insisted that he looked as fit as ever. She was kind.

His health deficit, like sneaky sub-cutaneous fats, had accumulated over time and it was coming worryingly close to the threshold of 10,000 missed steps. For every 'Valid' in Dvarca, there was a minimum exercise requirement, stipulated by the Ministry of Health and Healing. Given one's genetic constitution, age, weight, height, BMI, and job-function, there were certain binding guidelines for maintaining good health. If someone fell ill, grew fat or greedy, it was a cost to the Nation. Sloth and gluttony were grave sins.

He left the house in a hurry.

He got into the elevator and pressed 'G'. The rickety doors shut noisily and he found himself alone, inside the dank metal box. It smelt like body odour and jasmine. He tapped the elliptical tubelight that hung above him, and it illuminated one of Shastri ji's video-posters, urging him to 'THINK BETTER THOUGHTS', on loop. The great man's likeness was a permanent fixture across the land. It approved paper-work with a strict expression, watched loo-goers impatiently, smiled radiantly at children in schools, and showed the way in trains and buses. He watched over everyone and everyone looked up to him. He had an avatar for every occasion and every location.

The elevator doors opened and Gandharva stepped out, hunched and tired, lifting a foot at a time as though he were treading through quicksand.

'TAGGED FOR MOKSHA. TAGGED FOR VICTORY.' A lamp-post placard read.

He charted a course to the V-lab on his DDs and walked along as the map directed. He never had to worry about charging his DDs, thanks to the ubiquitous Near-Field Power Ports in homes and offices. The '100%' battery indicator, at the top right corner of his view, was taken for granted. Relentless communication needed interminable power, just as interminable power needed relentless communication.

He crossed the street and looked up at the signs that marked each post:

'REPORT SUSPICIOUS ACTIVITY'

'BINAAYDI = TERRORIST'

"For God and Country, *Mahoday*, where are you going at this hour?" The building sentry rubbed his hands together and shouted out.

"For God and Country, to the V-lab. I have an appointment."

"Take the bus, Mahoday!"

"I . . . I need to walk."

The portly father-of-two tried jogging but could not go very far. He panted his way till the end of the block and stood before a monument to Lord Ganesh. The giant limestone statue of the wise Elephant God stood atop a bed of bright red bricks. One of his arms was raised in instructive rebuke—as a sharp, long finger pointed directly at Gandharva. Words were chiselled into the pedestal and commanded him:

'NEVER START WITHOUT ME!'

He loved Lord Ganesh. All Gandharvas, from an early age, loved and respected the great Tusked-One. He was, amongst other things, the god of auspicious beginnings, academic prowess, and diligent study. To some, he even signified creativity.

*"Vakrutunda mahakaya, suryakoti samaprabha,*

*Nirvighnam kurume Deva sarva kaaryeshu sarvada."*

He prayed with every breath he could spare. The clouds thundered above him and a blustery wind forced him to button up his kurta. It started to rain and he cursed himself—he had forgotten to carry a brolly. He started to run again.

"DETECTION: IRREGULAR PHYSICAL EXERTION. ELEVATION IN VITAL RATES. PLEASE REPORT." A message popped-up on his DDs.

He didn't know if there was an army of people monitoring the DDs, or whether the review process had been automated by OMNI. He responded by reassuring anyone who cared, that he was okay.

"ARE YOU IN DANGER?"

"All good. No danger. Exercising."

He found himself in front of the thick metal bars of a gate. He had reached the inter-sector checkpoint and waited patiently as the skies pelted him. With the sound of a buzzer, he was allowed to enter into a small cage-like enclosure, attached to a guard-house. The scent of ginger tea warmed him as he leaned in to tap a powdered glass window. A crookedly installed mini-speaker above him, came alive with a deep-breathing, tinned voice: "Purpose of visit?"

"V-lab, going for my Vision . . ."

The glass window slid open, and a surly junior Sahdeva looked out in silence, sipping his tea. All inter-sector movements were tracked and Gandharva was used to having this done automatically on buses and in trains. That night, for the first time in a long time, he had to face the sentries as a lone pedestrian. He leaned into the light to get his DDs scanned, and also raised his wrist to show the blue plastic kalaava on his hand. He knew his place.

There were seven security clearance classes, or rings. If you had Violet (*Baingani*) clearance marked by a violet plastic kalaava, you had the least number of privileges and were relegated only to the outermost security rings, a borderline binaaydi. Indigos (Neel) like Jyoti, were granted one additional level of access. Reds (*Lal*) on the other hand, the highest class, could go anywhere. The system had been introduced as part of the *Indradhanush* security reforms of 2064 after the infamous terrorist attack on the Parliament. Gandharva was Blue or Aasmani, lowly despite the lofty heights suggested by the name.

"Tell me, Aasmani Gandharva, is there a higher kalaava citizen who may vouch for you?" The sentry raised his hand, above his head, as though to indicate the stature of the required citizen.

"But I . . . I come here every month. You can check that! I have a Vision scheduled in 20 minutes, for God and Country, please let me pass."

"Yes Gandharva, but you never come through my checkpoint on foot. Especially at this time of night, under what can only be described as suspicious circumstances."

"What is so suspicious?"

A second sentry wielding a *ChaturPad* joined in, "You are suspicious! Everything about you is wrong! Why didn't you take the bus today?"

"Are you too good for the bus? Buses bring people together. They bring people together to places." The double-barrel badgering was quick and relentless.

"They do, yes, no doubt that buses are wonderful. They are the building blocks of modern traffic—" Gandharva stuttered, leaning in as much as he could, to avoid the splattering rain. This worried the first sentry, who quickly covered his cup of ginger tea to protect its aroma.

"Wait! Just wait, we are pulling up your whole record. Then we will see . . ."

Access was supposed to be instant. Only at security barricades and during interactions with the Police, was the network slow or weak. Gandharva grew restless.

"It says here that you have 10,000 missed steps. That's a fat health deficit!"

"Are you trying to become a burden on us all?" The sentry pushed Gandharva back and stuck his head out to inspect his hefty figure in disgust. He then turned back to his ChaturPad.

"You work at the Ministry of Finance and Salvation, and yet you act like a brainless binaaydi."

"Are you an impostor?"

"A Caliphite?"

"A degenerate?"

"A spy?"

They barked at him again.

"I am an accountant, a bureaucrat."

Gandharva noticed that the two Sahdevas resembled each other a lot. They looked like twins but they were a few years apart in age.

"Maybe we should recommend a Dietary Reduction for you! No more carbs!" They declared together, pointing at his wobbly waist.

"Please! For God and Country, don't do that. The stress on my schedule is seasonal. I need to make up just 9,000 steps."

"Ten thousand—Ten!"

"That was before I started out today. I am very sorry. I will be more responsible."

"Have you been eating your wife's share? Or the share of your children?"

"Slob! Fiend!"

"I have done no such thing. Please, trust me . . ."

"Okay," the staccato chorus stopped. His earnest begging had bored the sentries.

"Okay, so may I please go through?"

"You may. But you have just exceeded the time limit at our check point. Unfortunately, an automatic Problem-Log has been generated."

It wasn't his fault that they had taken an unacceptable amount of time to clear him. The Aasmani bureaucrat realized that a new quarrel would only prolong his misery. He came closer to the window, sheepishly, to seek a more private counsel.

"The Problem-Log. Can you please expunge it?" he whispered.

The sentries smiled. They looked at the chubby rube in faux incredulity.

"You mean . . . you want Exceptional Treatment?"

"Yes, please . . . is it possible?"

Since time immemorial, citizens could expedite or prioritize their requests for a fee. Everyone wanted to pay for preferential handling. Some people ended up paying hundreds of *PunyaBindus* for the same work that others had pushed through, for just a quick 50. This was not fair or equitable, and a limit was set on the number of Exceptional Treatment requests that could be handled every day. This became known as the Exceptional Treatment Allowance, or ExTrA.

The Sahdevas had not exceeded their allowance for the day and miraculously, by the grace of Lord Ganesh himself, they had one slot still available. Their demeanour at once changed from terse and unforgiving to motherly, affectionate, and sympathetic.

"Three hundred and fifty, my dear Mahoday."

All payments and transfers of Bindus or PunyaBindus—PBs—the currency of Dvarca, were completely transparent. Of the 350 PBs, 200 went to the State for 'Maintenance'. Fifty were an 'Inconvenience Fee', 50 went to 'Temple Charities', and the final 50 PBs went to the administrator processing the request, who in this case, was a delighted young man. Both their DDs showed confirmations of the transaction, like Diwali decorations blinking in succession. The sentries opened the gates and ushered him through magnanimously. It was still raining and he was very late.

"Do not run, Mahoday! Please be careful."

Gandharva's belaboured half-hearted jogging came to a grinding halt, when a new notification appeared on his DDs.

"Dietary Reduction Recommendation received. Rice rations reduced by 50 per cent for two moons."

He looked back at the checkpoint in disbelief—the gates and windows had been shut. The treacherous sentries had followed through on their threats. He shrugged in defeat, and ambled along the pavement, as the rain washed down over him.

There was no way he would make it for his Vision on time.

# 4
# A MARCH TO INFINITY

They toiled hard under the tropical sun, as it burnt through their clothes, leaving welts the size of beetles on their necks and arms. Gandharva scratched himself, hoping that giving in would somehow snuff the fire out, but it only made it worse. He looked around the beach and saw rows upon rows of his compatriots hard at work.

"Would this do?" his partner inquired.

Gandharva bent down and felt the rock in question. It was smooth and had a nearly-perfect spherical base.

"What do you think?"

The man shrugged haplessly and looked over at the beautiful ocean, splashing coquettishly at the shore. It had been a tiring day, and they longed for her cool and refreshing embrace. Gandharva rolled up his sleeves and dug into the sand with both arms. He heaved the boulder onto their thick red cloth, and the two of them dragged it to join the line. They waited their turn to perform the trial. The line advanced slowly and a couple of pairs walked away, dejected. Only a handful had made it to the brine-y blue.

"Is it just the shape?" His anxious partner poisoned the balmy air with his worries.

They stepped into the trial pond, a man-made hole, about four feet deep. They could see the floor, the moist sand below. Their rock dangled between them in the cloth hammock and rolled precariously to the edge. A pile of failed stones caught Gandharva's eye. They lay nearby and a burly man was hastily gathering them. He was oddly quick for his size. The supervising karmachari blocked out the sun from his high perch and urged them to proceed. He watched over them like a swimming coach for the rocks. Floaters were keepers, sinkers were tossed. Gandharva's hands trembled in anticipation, as they lowered their stone into the water. The rock fell, all the way to the floor. His compatriot cursed, raised his arms and backed away with the affected gait of a failed athlete. Gandharva fell to his knees. He could not remember the last time he found a natural buoy for the cause. He had let them all down. His failure had held up the armies of Lord Rama himself.

"Are you praying?" the karmachari asked.

"Yes." Gandharva barely replied.

"Are you lost in prayer?" the supervisor bellowed like a captious teacher.

"I am!"

"No you are not! For God and Country, you are not."

"I am, Mahoday."

"Prove it!"

Gandharva joined his palms, shut his eyes, bent his head, and thought of all the gods he knew. He started with Lord Ganesh and went on to see all the others. He tried to shut out all distractions. He wanted not to think of his job. The files, logs, puzzles, and submissions disappeared. He wished not to be reminded of Baba,

Jyoti, Nakul, or Mira. He only sought the divine. To his amazement, even the gods disappeared from his consciousness. He felt that his soul was engulfed in nothingness. All the powers filtered into a converging beam of white light and drew him into a wormhole. He felt a strange heat, a delicious tingle in the middle of his forehead.

He could touch, taste, and smell the glow. His knees weakened and his eyes cried rivers of joy. He felt a real, physical pull towards this radiant vortex as it changed colours and towed him, flying over a rocky terrain. He could see the divine. Nothing else mattered. Only God and Country! He felt a nudge and came back to the trial pond. He opened his eyes, and saw that his rock had risen to the surface. It bobbed and floated proudly. It was a dud no more! The onlookers cheered and so did the karmacharis, with an air of satisfaction.

"Bless you Gandharva! You are one with God and Country! Take your rock to the army at the shore. Lord Rama has blessed you. You are a worthy devotee!"

They wrapped the spherical rock in their wet, red cloth and lugged it away. Gandharva felt that he was finally of use. He was loved.

He woke up at the same spot, but it felt new to him. The sound of the Vision Lab apparatus had grown familiar with time. He sat up slowly, still weeping, profoundly moved by his Vision. His head, arms, chest, and legs were all still connected to the machine in the 'tank'. He knew not to start pulling away. He looked up, still in bliss, grinning like a buffoon. The room was a bluish-grey blur.

His pills were on a table within arm's reach and he took them quickly. They were essential book-ends for any visit to the V-lab. You couldn't start or finish without them. Sounds became clearer and contours grew sharper before his eyes, as he slowly exited his trance-like state. The room smelt vaguely of soap and he was conscious of all the points where his body touched the bed.

Goose-flesh. The tank door opened with a clang and the V-lab assistant entered.

"That was . . ." Gandharva tried to speak.

"Euphoric?"

"Yes," he wept.

"You've had a great epiphany, for God and Country."

"I have had a new Vision. I saw the divine," he mumbled and repeated rapidly. He was unable to walk.

Shastri ji believed that regardless of one's *karma*, irrespective of one's *dharma* and kalaava, all Dvarcans were connected to the divine. This connection came with frequent communiques and teachings, delivered through the channel of Visions. God spoke to us in our dreams. The V-lab greased the rails and prepared Dvarcans to receive and understand His messages, serving as a direct conduit to the inner depths of one's soul. Sleep was the best state, for a holy message, to circumvent one's difficult intellect. People were blissfully unaware of factual limitations, inconvenient rationality, or cumbersome logic. Everything that was *seen* in the tank, was recorded for analysis and interpretation.

"My body sleeps, my spirit awakens . . ." Gandharva stuttered the V-lab motto unknowingly.

Citizens started their V-lab sessions at the age of 12. The lab had recorded each and every one of Gandharva's Visions. Some recurred, while others were unique one-time experiences. The more avant-garde Visions usually accompanied a celestial shift or a significant astrological event. These phenomena affected the entire population of Dvarca, and an incredible discovery was made. The people's Visions were identical. Many had helped to build the bridge to Lanka. Many had fought in Kurukshetra, scaled mountains with the Pandavas, and even witnessed the cruelty of the Caliphate through haunting, scarring nightmares. People dreamed alike. God spoke to everyone in the same way, to show them their place and purpose. Visions were amongst the strongest pillars of Dvarcan society.

Through the miracle of modern technology, they were able to make films out of the dreams and show them on television and in cinemas. DGI, short for Divinely Generated Imagery, had powered some of the greatest blockbusters in recent times. A ticket usually cost 700 PBs, but who could put a price on inspiration? The films were beautifully visualized, narrative-driven, hyper-realistic spectacles. Most importantly, they were 'based on a real dream'. They were a celebration of us 'not being alone', or of there being a 'shared cause'.

Gandharva and the V-lab assistant went into the Review Suite. It was a small chamber with screens and displays that covered the walls from floor to ceiling.

"I have only just seen the rushes and it . . . well . . . it looks stunning."

"Thank you."

The first capture was always a bit jumpy and erratic in terms of colours and order.

"Inconceivable beauty! Look, the screen whites-out for a few seconds."

The left panel re-played the Vision. The right side was split into a few sections, and a small square on top showed a video of Gandharva's face, while he was in the tank during the dream. Below it, in horizontal strips, were his vitals. They raced along like the view of a hill-range from a fast train.

"Your heart-rate went off the charts," the assistant stated with some concern.

"I have never felt better."

"Do you remember choosing to seek the divine in your dream? Or did it just happen?"

He had no answer. He wanted to say that the divine chose him.

There was a degree of machismo associated with being able to handle certain dreams and ideas. He secretly gloated in his racing heart.

"Who is the karmachari, the silhouette? Was there such an inspector checking the rocks for their buoyancy when they built the bridge to Lanka?"

"I don't know . . . I do know that the *vaanar sena* carried the rocks for quite a distance. They must have had some sort of quality control."

The V-lab assistant tinkered with the screens and focused on an image of the karmachari who had graciously watched over Gandharva.

"Usually in these cases, the supervisor turns out to be your father, grandfather . . ."

"No, it is not them. I have seen them in my Visions before. It is someone else."

"Could it be? Hold on!"

They highlighted portions of the screen, enhanced the image and zoomed-in. The magnification revealed a light coloured moustache. The two men turned to each other. The karmachari, who till a few seconds ago, had only been an indistinguishable authority figure, started to resemble none other than the most distinguished Shastri ji himself! Gandharva was delighted. He could not believe his luck. The pleasure that this brought him, led to a rather vain question.

"Have you ever seen such a Vision before?"

The lab assistant was crestfallen and ostensibly jealous. He did not try to hide it.

"Do you think that this dream of mine . . . could someday be a film?"

"I don't know. It will compete with all the dreams of all the people in Dvarca. I can't say which ones will make it to the Film Council."

"What are my chances? This is extraordinary . . . you said so yourself."

"I will flag it to my supervisors as a long-list selection, but that is as far as I can push it. There will be countless reviews by several boards and they will make the final decision . . . whether or not to take it to the people."

The assistant was getting uncomfortable and he saved the Vision in Gandharva's cache, with all his previous recordings. It was a tapestry of providence, a warehouse for old dreams and spiritual messages. There were lessons that Gandharva had learnt, affirmations of faith and some stunning images of the other worlds. The proud bureaucrat felt a sense of longing, and in his biochemical haze of enlightenment, his inhibitions seemed to vaporize. He leaned over and asked to see one of the old Visions again. The lab assistant was appalled at this most unusual request.

"No Gandharva ji, it is forbidden. There is no room for selfish nostalgia. What will you gain?"

"I'll remember who I was . . . how I became who I am. They are my dreams after all."

"I beg your pardon Mahoday, but it is no longer your dream. Once we've imaged something through the DGI process, it belongs to Dvarca. For you to see it again, countless approvals from several boards will need to be sought. I will have to raise an official request and obtain permission, Gandharva. This is most irregular!"

"It is right there, we can both see the thumbnail. Just click it, please. It changed my life. I must see it again!"

The lab assistant pointed to the poster that hung over his workstation.

'COMPLIANCE IS ITS OWN REWARD'.

"My hands are tied. Procedure is procedure and compliance is its own reward."

"It came from me, out of my mind. Did it not? It rose out from my soul! Here, I am willing to pay you."

A quick ExTrA PB transaction was made, and Gandharva inched back into his seat, raising his arms behind his head to recline and enjoy the hard-earned replay. It was confounding to wonder why a simple combination of moving pictures and sounds had become so important to him. Was it because it came imbued with astrological meaning when he first saw it years ago? Or did it just seem to answer his questions and show him the way, at that time in his life? All he wanted, really, was to feel the same rush again. He felt like he craved the epiphany, even though he had just lived through a great one.

The replay began. It was an edited version of an old Vision. He watched the screen, as a dance of light and colour commenced. He felt that he was flying above the surface of a different planet at great speeds, towards an ever-changing horizon. Textures and hues changed rapidly. The morphing landscape was intercut with shots of a rally, of marching Dvarcans. These interspersions were of a different quality, and seemed raw when compared to the sublime astronomical expanse traversed through the rest of the Vision. He felt blessed and sat up, tilting his head towards the screen, hoping to somehow enter it.

"Was this . . . was this not a film once?"

"This was used in a film, yes. Many people had this Vision."

"What did they call it?"

"*Dvarca: A March to Infinity*, Mahoday. I think you have seen enough. Please . . . until next time, take care."

With that, the assistant switched off the monitor, returning Gandharva to his pallid, aching, insipid routine.

# 5
# SHAHTOOTI ANJEER

Gandharva came out of the V-lab. Thunder and lightning signalled a stormy resurgence and he crouched under the thick branches of a road-side tree, as it started to pour. He huddled down and squatted, shivering in the cold. He had just missed the last bus home. Some men were born fit, some achieved fitness, and some had fitness thrust upon them.

The way home, looked arduous, even though street lamps lined the path like sparklers. Their soft yellow light crackled under impetuous torrents from a bursting sky. He looked at his ratty and torn slippers. His feet disappeared into a muddy puddle, and he feared leeches and other vermin. He hopped back, like a slippery frog, to the pavement. He stuck out his feet and let the rain wash them clean.

An unusual sound arose from the mysterious abyss around him. It was a thumping noise and it grew louder, bounding, beating. He strained foolishly to pull the curtain of water apart. A blur of beige and black was coming right at him, leaping down the sidewalk in enormous steps. Was it a beast? Gandharva tried to move out of its way, but they both chose the same side.

Like a goalkeeper in a penalty shootout, Gandharva caught the bounding object in his chest. It had a head, arms, and legs. It was a man! Their heads bumped into each other. He was all bones and metal, harder than one would expect. The clap from their collision rang out like thunder.

They both fell and the rushing man lay on top of him, struggling to find his feet, caring little for how he crushed and pushed Gandharva. The twitchy beige-black-blur stood up. It was the collared man.

"Son of a *kela, shahtooti-anjeer*!"

Gandharva was still reeling and did not understand the growling man's blurry, beige-and-black twaddle. He was a tall wiry figure with screaming eyes. His emaciated legs hung out from under a ripped pyjama. He had no DDs. He shouted over the pounding rain.

"Shahtooti-anjeer! *Narangi gajar!* Narangi *kaddu!*"

Gandharva noticed that the man had some kind of a shiny collar under his chin. His weathered face stretched out into new angles as he went to pieces. His kalaava was Red. Before Gandharva could speak to him, or ask him where he was from, the man let out a pained howl and started to run again. A jeep nearly knocked him down, and two men in impeccable Varaha gear jumped out.

They caught him and proceeded to beat him mercilessly. Gandharva feigned unconsciousness and folded his arms to cover his face. The White Kurtas dragged the man by his metal collar as he shouted in agony. His screams were punctuated by the punches and kicks that rained down on him. He whimpered and begged as his voice grew hoarse and piercing.

Lights were switched on, in the flats of adjacent blocks, and soon half-silhouettes hung from window bars, watching the action unfold. The Varaha men waved them back to sleep; shining torches at their faces. They knew that they had been seen. Darkness prevailed in the apartments again and cloaked the curious figures in obscurity. Gandharva assumed that they were all still watching, just like him.

Varaha never acted wrongly, and were guided by Navmarg and the State. The beige-black-blur must have been a criminal. His crying stopped and the attackers turned their attention to Gandharva, who was still in a foetal position, on the wet sidewalk. They pulled him to his feet and scanned his DDs.

"Do you know who we are?"

He looked at them and their saffron arm-bands with golden sequin work. Gandharva leaned in, wide-eyed, like an awestruck infant. He had never been this close to them before, and could not help but admire the big boar on their shiny arm-bands.

"Of course, you are Varaha—protectors of Dvarca!"

One of them padded Gandharva down, checking him for illicit substances and weapons. They found only a *laddoo* wrapper. They waved it in front of his face before crushing it and throwing it at him.

"Do you know this man?"

"No!"

"Why were you talking to him?"

"I . . . I did not talk to him . . . he crashed into me . . ."

They stood on the sidewalk, soaking. One of the guards grew agitated. He was looking up a report on Gandharva's activities that night.

"So, you assaulted a sentry and his Pcet Sahdeva at an inter-sector booth today . . ."

"Assaulted?" Gandharva gulped.

"After that, you harassed an assistant at the V-lab."

"Harassed?"

"It is in his report. You committed a most despicable crime. An SUI—Seeking Unauthorized Information, it says. Quite a busy night you have had!" He reached behind and pulled Gandharva's ear.

"What were you looking for, Gandharva of Sector 17?" The ear-pulling was followed by a sharp slap.

"I am sorry. I did not mean to cause any trouble . . ." Gandharva offered to pull his own ears, as rain water crept into his mouth and nose, mixing with tears.

The Varaha man spat in disdain. The collared beige-black-blur who had been captured, beaten, and cuffed to their jeep, started to wail. He let out more pained whimpers about fruits and vegetables.

"What is wrong with him?"

"That is none of your concern, Aasmani Gandharva of Sector 17, Block 8A. The question is, what are you doing with him?"

"Like I said, I don't know him from Manu really, I don't know him at all . . ."

"What did he say?"

"Something about an anjeer, kela . . . maybe shahtoot," Gandharva laughed uncomfortably.

Another jeep pulled up and two more men joined the investigation in a huff. One of them was also in a white kurta. He marched up to Gandharva, pulled out his gun and pointed it at his head, ready to shoot. The Aasmani weakling shrieked.

"Is this the fugitive?"

"Stand down, Nakul ji. The runaway is in our car."

"Then who is this quivering piece-of-shit?"

"A bureaucrat having a bad day. Isn't that right?"

"Y-Y-Yes, absolutely."

The gunman went over to the jeep. There was a lot of

kicking, shouting, and clenching of teeth. They put the gun in the prisoner's mouth and yanked him around. Gandharva could not stand the sight and looked away. A new message flashed across the investigators' DDs and halted the torture. The beige-black-blur caught some respite as he lay in the gutter.

"Does he have it? Check—" They pulled him up and inspected the electronic collar.

"Yes, Nakul ji!"

They turned him around and saw that it stretched all the way up the back of his head. There was an unruly patch of coarse hair that concealed the device. They pulled it and rummaged around to see that it had three tentacles stuck to different parts of the convict's scalp. The man in white started a voice-call.

"Please may I go home? My work starts in a few hours," Gandharva implored.

"Shut your mouth."

Only one side of Nakul ji's conversation could be heard.

"Do you want it back, Mahoday?"

"Wait, the device or the prisoner? Why can't I take it off?"

"What do you mean it is attached? Attached to his what?"

"Okay. As you say . . ."

He held out his gun and waved it casually in the prisoner's direction.

"Do you need him alive? Sure . . . that would be great. I will hold . . ." he cupped the DD speakers with his right hand. "They are checking if they need him alive," he whispered.

The prisoner slumped down. He would know his fate in a few seconds. He tugged at the contraption around his neck. The beatings had jammed it deeper into his skin.

"Please Mahoday, my wife and children will wake up . . . I should really be home with them," Gandharva pleaded.

"Do you feel safe, Gandharva?"

"Yes, yes I do," pat like a laser came the reply.

"You people want to feel safe. You want to go for your 8:00 a.m. shifts, but you don't want to see what makes it all possible."

He pulled Gandharva along and held his face close to the bleeding prisoner.

"This is Dvarca being protected. Your country's finest military intelligence team is capturing a dangerous terrorist. You should not be begging to leave. You should be thrilled and grateful for the privilege of seeing us in action."

Gandharva looked into the eyes of the enemy of the State as he drooled uncontrollably.

"I am honoured Sir! I am truly honoured and glad!"

"Nakul ji, anything for this Aasmani Gandharva?" the Varaha sneered.

The voice-call continued.

"Understood. There is another person. Just one. The bystander . . . I sent you his coordinates. Some low-level Gandharva. Yes. Of course Sir. Completely useless. An impediment. I will. Okay. For God and Country. Jai Dvarca."

They lifted the prisoner by his arms and threw him back into the jeep.

"Aasmani Gandharva of Sector 17, Block 8A, you will have a Disciplinary Committee Review at the Central Command."

"But I have done nothing . . ."

"Expect an IM with all the details. Don't be late."

They got into their vehicles and sped away. Gandharva felt sick. A chilly wind blew into his back and he rubbed himself to keep warm. The Instant Message, as promised, appeared on his DDs to warn him of a Disciplinary Committee Review later that day. He was doomed, he thought. They had not let him go, this was just their way of shifting responsibility to another department.

He sneezed, coughed, and sighed as he trudged back towards

his sector. The sentries gave him a hard time again, but there was no ExTrA quota left and they let him pass, eventually. He stumbled down the road, away from the checkpoint and stopped. He felt a burning sensation welling up in his chest and staggered into an alley, stood over a garbage bin and vomitted violently. Undigested remnants of laddoo and rice, in familiar balls and grains sprayed across the wall like gastronomic graffiti.

He sat down to regain his composure. He remembered how his mother used to rub his back to comfort him as a child. He had a habit of eating too quickly. He rubbed himself against the wall, but it wasn't the same. Drops of rain pattered all over him. He felt something soft in his left hand.

It was a discarded, bunched up blanket, but it seemed to be in good condition, barring a few greasy stains. It smelt dreadful, but the bitter odour was not enough to put him off. He wrapped himself in it and decided to lie there till he felt strong enough to walk. The exhausted, wayward Dvarcan fell asleep in the alley.

# 6
# ARCHITECTS OF BEAUTY

The *Vaigs* were baffled. The senior Dr Vishvakarma was a neuroscientist, while his junior was from the robotics programme. Together, they had produced many electronic interfaces with the human body, but most of them were still faulty or incomplete. Like everyone else at the Ministry of Science and Theology, both of them were named Vishvakarma.

It led to less confusion than you'd imagine as the bands and associated colour codes served as distinguishing marks of one's identity. The Doctor was a Peet, as was clear from his bright yellow kalaava. The young Vishvakarma was a very self-conscious and lowly Neel, obsequious and sweaty, constantly dabbing his brows with a cloth. Like most underlings, he was eager to please.

"Are you sure he was naming fruits?"

"Yes!" All four of the Varaha men spoke in unison, as though it was a Sanskrit class, and they were practicing their pronunciations. They were seated in uncomfortable plastic chairs, one behind the other.

"Why has this beast been kept alive? He is worth less than the price of his hand-cuffs!"

"Something intriguing has happened here. You see the machine, this collar, is a very early prototype. He is one of the lab's oldest patients . . ."

"He is a convict, not a patient. He should still be considered a dangerous pariah."

The doctor walked towards the trembling prisoner and wiped the spumescent refuse from his open mouth. He patted the bruised man on his forehead and examined his collar before announcing, "It has stopped working. The machine is damaged!"

It was a rough and heavy contraption that clamped together at the back, like the hooked pincers of a crab. The knuckle-swinging Nakuls were confused.

"His Speech Sentinel, the SS6.2 is dead. But this beast, as you also reported, still says nothing but the harmless names of fruits and spices. It is fascinating."

"What is the Speech Sentinel meant to do?"

"Shahtooti anjeer. Shahtooti anjeer," the poor prisoner muttered, as though he were joining the conversation to illustrate the senior Vaig's point.

"It corrects . . . mistakes. Would you like to see?" even before his audience could ask for any kind of a show, the pompous scientist reached into his pocket and extracted a plastic box.

"You Mahoday, you will make a great volunteer."

"What are you crazy Vaigs doing? You had better not stick a collar on me."

"Don't be afraid. We've made a lot of improvements." He pulled out a disk shaped red dot from a box, using a pair of tweezers. He then planted it gently behind the sceptical Nakul's hairy ears.

The Neel Vishvakarma pounded his keyboard passionately, hoping to impress his superior. Passion meant promotions. The scientists giggled like naughty schoolchildren as they powered-up a bulky contraption in the room.

It was an enormous block of levers and wires, weaving in and out of each other, connected to miniature monitors, oversized oscilloscopes, and dreary decibel meters. All the paraphernalia seemed to arrange itself like a wreath around an all-important conical funnel. It stood there with its mouth open, shiny, made of brass, as though they'd fashioned it from an old gramophone. Their messy workstation was a synecdoche of the entire lab. Heaps of hardware lay about in disorder, in all corners of the room, while the most important work continued at the centre of it all, under the warm glow of a hanging lamp.

"Is it receiving?"

A sweaty thumb was raised in confirmation.

"Now, my good Nakul, please, say something . . . inflammatory."

"What?"

"Say something . . . beastly, vile, and repugnant!"

"I don't understand."

"Yes, of course, we Dvarcans have been raised to be polite. You probably don't know any words from the Forbidden List. Here, why don't you read from it?"

He handed him his ChaturPad and urged the horrified man to call out from it.

"Where did you mad Vaigs get this?"

"It was given to us . . ."

Even though the Forbidden List had existed for a long time, all the legalese and directives that accompanied it, were meaningless without proper enforcement and execution. One thing led to another, and soon it was discovered that machines were uniquely capable of implementing the difficult task of censorship. Who could be more impartial? Who could be more consistent? Who else could ensure the sanctity and cleanliness of language, without bothering with petty distractions like context and intentions?

"I must admit that when we first got the list, we were quite surprised. As you well know, it is illegal to utter or write the unmentionable words on this list. But this is for a good cause. We have to know the filth, in order to curb and correct it."

The list was truly dangerous. The clerk who typed it had been found guilty on 1,786 violations. He was never heard from again. One could not make *kathal-ki-sabzi* without ripping open a few kathals.

"Do it! I assure you, you are cursing for Science. There will be no repercussions."

"I must not! Please do not make me."

"What kind of a warrior are you? Do it! Strong, accurate, swift, show us!"

The scientist enjoyed this rare moment of power over the brawny, boorish brute. He leaned in and goaded him with an innocent, questioning expression on his face.

"Kesar anjeer! Kesar anjeer! Kesar anjeer!" The Varaha almost fell off his chair. He cupped his mouth and shook with anger.

"What have you done?! What happened to my voice?"

The doctor was calm. "Yes, the screeching, well we are still working on reducing that. It still makes that unfortunate noise . . . did you see what it did though?"

The muscleman shook his head.

"The first word became a herb and the second a fruit. What were you trying to say?"

"I . . . I cannot repeat it."

"Stop censoring yourself. What horrible words were you trying to say?"

He pointed it out on the list, apologetically.

"Ah, you went for gold there. Wise choice. It's a tricky word, or word-combination really. The first one is a kind, soft, normal word, most often invoked by children: 'Mother'. The second half, well . . . that has been on the Forbidden List forever. It is particularly hard to pick up this ugly combination and correct it, mid-transmission."

"That is remarkable."

"It is. This device, in its next iteration, will be a durable, bio-compatible implant. We have come a long way from clunky collars, to bugs, the size of insects. No Dvarcan shall ever hear an unkind word again. No more profanity, no more sedition. No more conspiracies."

"We are the architects of a beautiful new world," his junior declared with pride.

"Never forget that I am the Aryabhatta of this operation. You are a mere zero, Neel Vishvakarma."

"Of course, Peet Vishvakarma ji. Of course."

He removed the little red disc. Orderlies arrived and took the prisoner away.

"We will watch him for a few days. After that, it is Project L for SS6.2."

"Is he named SS6.2?"

"Yes. He's a . . . he's a troubled pariah. He had a name, but he stopped responding to it. He had a serial number, but he took a knife to it. Did you see the scars on his collar-bone?"

"No, we did not."

"He did that to himself long ago. Didn't like the number. Ever since then, we decided to name all our patients after the devices and treatments we tested on them. Makes it a lot easier to know them by what we have done to them, as opposed to who they . . . used to be."

"Elegant."

"Was he a terrorist?"

"A Caliphate sympathizer. He never learnt to assimilate with civilized society."

# 7
# CHICKEN AND EGG

Jyoti was fast asleep in their bedroom. Baba was out for his night-shift and the children lay still, contorted and bent away from each other like the hands of a clock. It was ten-to-five. Gandharva shut Mira's mouth and stopped Nakul from sucking his thumb. He watched them for a moment, before carrying on.

He didn't want to risk waking Jyoti by using the toilet attached to their room, and decided to use the small common toilet next to the kitchen to clean up. Rain had found a way to bounce off the window-shutters, and wet everything, from the lights to the floor. He looked at himself in the mirror. He was still wrapped in the foul-smelling cloth from the street. It had saved his life. He took it off and flipped it around to fold it away. His face went deathly pale when he saw the other side of his new-found vestment. Something was written on the cloth. He leaned in close and read the words. They looked like scratches after a desperate fight.

'WHAT CAME FIRST? POLITICS OR RELIGION?'

How could he have been so careless? How did he end up with a cloth that clearly came from the pariahs? He crumpled it into a ball. He panicked and splashed his face with water to make sure it wasn't some sort of lurid Vision. Had he been seen with it? Would they believe that he had nothing to do with it?

He tried to wash off the unholy letters but they were stitched on. He looked around frantically for a way to get rid of the cloth. He could not burn it on the stove, all gas supplies were switched off after 10:00 p.m. for energy conservation. He could not carry it out and throw it away; it was too risky. He tried to flush the ball down the toilet, but it was too big. There was nothing in the bathroom of use, just some of Baba's toiletries.

Gandharva rushed out to the kitchen and found one of Jyoti's scissors. He hurtled back into the bathroom and pulled the door shut. He lowered the toilet seat-cover and sat down to cut the cloth into smaller pieces. The scissors had thick, blunt blades. He made some headway with them and then decided to rip the cloth with his hands. He was no Nakul or Arjun, but he tried his best.

"DETECTION: ELEVATION IN VITAL RATES. PLEASE REPORT."

The veins of his forehead popped out like new hill ranges after a deep seismic disturbance. He quickly responded with the first thing that came to his flustered mind.

"Stomach upset. Recovering."

He sat atop the commode with the stinking shawl in his hands. There were words stitched all over it. Some portions of the writing were illegible because of the indelible grease stains. He read a sentence.

'YOU'VE FALLEN FOR THE OLDEST TRICK. THEY KNOW WHAT YOU WILL DO, BEFORE YOU DO IT. THEY'VE

DRAWN LINES IN THE SKY AND LINES IN THE SAND, TO MARK GOD AND COUNTRY.'

Who were they addressing? Who was speaking? Why?

'DO YOU FEEL FEAR? ARE YOU SAFE NOW? THE PRICE OF PROTECTION IS LIBERTY. ARE YOU A SLAVE TO NAVMARG? ARE YOU DVARCAN ENOUGH? YOU'VE BARGAINED AWAY OUR HUMANITY, AND BECOME WHAT WE SET OUT TO FIGHT.'

He tore the venomous pieces from the rag and held them tightly in his fist. He felt more righteous with every rip.

'IF THERE IS A SCORE, WE DO NOT KNOW IT. NAVMARG IS A LIE.'

The pariah propaganda continued.

'THEY TELL YOU WHOM TO TRUST AND WHOM TO FOLLOW.

HOW TO LIVE. HOW TO THINK. HOW TO HATE—AND WHOM.'

He lifted the toilet seat and threw the scraps in, before pulling the flush triumphantly. He saw the grey-brown cloth whirl in the white bowl before disappearing. It made him think of the collared prisoner. The tank drained and filled up slowly, as he waited to drown more words of dissent and blasphemy. The stitching was jagged, with ill-shaped letters. The strings were of many colours. His DDs grew misty from the exertion. He flushed again.

There was a knock on the bathroom door.

"Is that you, Papa?" Little Nakul had woken up and wandered out.

"Yes son, go back to sleep, Papa is not feeling well."

There was a moment of silence.

"Stomach?"

"Not exactly . . . yes . . . stomach . . . yes."

"The *amrut-dhaara* is in the kitchen, shall I pour you some?"

"No, just get some sleep, please."

The boy walked away as his father hung onto the last remnant of the scornful rag. He pulled two pieces of it apart and it came undone.

'IS THIS THE NATION YOU SET OUT TO BUILD?'

His DDs sparked up with a new message. It was a simple, terse instruction. They were moving his Disciplinary Committee Review from 5:00 p.m. to 7:00 p.m. that day. He did not know what that meant. He felt uneasy. A familiar, burning sensation grew at the back of his throat. He lifted the toilet seat and heaved hard with his face down. Nothing came out. He held onto the bowl to steady himself.

He had never been hauled up for a review before, but like all good citizens he had heard much about them. Mythical, legendary, urban folktales about 'restored righteousness' and 'realigned moral acuity' came screeching back to him. How could he show them that he was patriotic and pious, even after reading the pariah propaganda?

# 8
# MORNING IN DVARCA

Jyoti stood for a moment and inspected the floor she had just swept. She gathered stray clumps of dust and hair, and shovelled them into a bin. The lid closed with an odd thump. She feared she might have woken up the family before time.

She turned her attention to the table-tops and proceeded to wipe, scrub, and rub-out stains with her duster. Her eyes kept drifting towards the clock on the wall. She had about 15 minutes before the Song would burst through the radio at 6:45 a.m. sharp. She checked on the *poha* in the kitchen, simmering, steaming, and smelling of love. There was too much turmeric. She liked it that way.

The door opened and Baba returned from his shift. They'd replaced his walker with a wheeled-model and he constantly complained that it was harder to manoeuvre. He didn't really need it but it was mandated outside the house, as a precaution. She helped him to his chair in the drawing room. He touched her tired face with his wrinkly hands and thanked her. He rubbed his legs and looked at the clock.

"What have you been doing? You look worse for wear than usual . . . did you not sleep well?"

Jyoti did not reply. She went to the common bathroom with a plunger. The commode appeared to be backed-up. She pushed and pulled with all her might, but the inscrutable plumbing refused to give. On one spirited thrust, she slipped and the handle of the plunger rammed into her DDs. The blunt wooden stick slid off her sturdy goggles and struck her in the forehead.

A small cut appeared and she rose to the mirror. She was more concerned about the lenses and looked down in horror at a tiny red crumb of plastic on the floor. She picked it up. It was the size of a pebble and had broken off from her left lens, which was thankfully still intact. Blood oozed from the cut above. She washed it and moved on, dabbing it with her sari. Over the years, her night clothes had started to resemble the duster. Grey, worn, and unclean, even after a wash. The small splotch of red added a bit of colour.

"Is everything alright?" Baba asked.

"It is this toilet. There seems to be a blockage."

"Oh dear . . ."

"You can use ours till it is fixed."

She returned to the drawing room. The old man was visibly upset by the prospect of sharing their toilet, he was used to the one by the kitchen. Their eyes met and before he could ask her again, she blurted out a statement that was more of a plea.

"I can't fix it . . . !"

"Then we will need to call someone—how much would it cost?"

"I will speak to Gandharva."

"What happened to your glasses?" the old man was worried

now. He didn't ask about the blood on her forehead, or the crimson spot on her sari.

She continued, as though nothing had happened. She dabbed the spot above her eyes again, and made her way to the children's room where Nakul and Mira slept like little angels. Radio static erupted ceremoniously and alarms rang out with the loud Song of Prayer.

*"Sarva mangal mangalye,*
*Shive sarvaarth sadhikay,*
*Sharanyetrayambakey Gauri,*
*Naraayani namostute."*

It was a melodious voice and a beautiful chant. She knew how powerful and important it was, especially first thing in the morning. It had been the State alarm forever. The children woke up saying the prayer with the Song, and stood up almost immediately. They were still groggy, feebly shaking the sleep from their faces like new-born foals, shrugging off placenta. They walked into her arms. She kissed them and patted them both on the bottom, nudging them along to start the day's work and prayers. Nakul rubbed past her and she turned to see a small hole in his pyjamas—they were due for a change. She'd have to speak to Gandharva about that too.

And there he was, her haloed husband, wiping yellow crumbs of dirt from his eyes, struggling to reach them under his DDs. He had a habit of inspecting the crust before throwing it away. It gave him great satisfaction. He looked exhausted as he continued with his morning rituals and pulled his pyjamas up. She had no idea what time he had come in. Some things about him truly repulsed her, and she took strange solace in that fact that neither Nakul, nor Mira were *his* children.

He looked at her with the same benevolent gaze one would bestow upon a cow, or other harmless bovine that had accidentally wandered into one's home in search of food and shelter. He stopped short of patting her on the head. She was disgusted by his odour, and dragged the children between them. The family stood together, facing the sensors in the drawing room. DDs scrubbed and in position, red lenses gleaming, spines straight, chests out, and palms firmly together.

"Smile, children."

The house alarm was set at its peak volume. It was an ancient prayer, immortalized in the voice of the Nation's nightingale, Lata Mangeshkar, long gone but never forgotten. There were four chants for everyone to get into position. By the fifth chant, all members of the family had to ready themselves under the sensors and out-sing Lata ji. Only in terms of loudness of course, anything else was unthinkable. The house sensors were state-of-the-art and had been installed with all the other *ChaturGrah* machinery. They detected DDs as well as recognized all the voices in the mix. The alarm had a screen that lit up with names as attendance was taken. The laser scan, like a curtain of red light, swept the room from top to bottom, then from left to right.

Gandharva jerked Nakul out of his stupor; he was still half-asleep and needed to be more effusive about his devotion. The little man sang louder and clearer, to be acknowledged by the red-eye in the room, and much to everyone's relief, finally, his name too appeared on the screen. Attendance was complete. The children had learnt the same prayer at school, and had practiced it a million times. It was a personal chant and a community slogan, all rolled into one. The Ministry of Media Controls and Communication believed in concise, easily repeatable messages for the folks. Wisdom had to be the size of a jingle, for it to be consistent, effective, and permanent.

The tower bell struck seven times, marking the start of another day. The entire block was up and about. Efficient showers were taken, *dhotis* were tied, well-ironed, crisp kurtas were worn, and fragrant hot poha was cradled lovingly into plates.

"Is everyone eating the same poha, Mother?"

"Yes darling, more or less, now please don't play with your food."

He had already separated his mound of gooey, savoury goodness into two cones. He was driving a spoon between them, towards the speck of chutney that he was allowed. Gandharva wiped the foggy clouds from his DD lenses, and took another big bite.

"Listen to your mother, Nakul," he slurped.

The boy sat up straight and ate quietly. Mira was not at the table yet. She was in the children's room, a precocious little pony-tailed 12-year-old, ready in her blue *salwar kameez*. She sat on the bed and was about to put on her black shoes. She'd found gravel in them, and had poured the dirt out on the ground and spread it with her feet. The children shared their room with Baba, and she tried to make the mess less obvious. Jyoti shouted for her.

"What do you think you're doing?! You will miss the bus!"

She popped the shoes on and ran out promptly.

"You should wake up early and learn to cook with your mother," her grandfather bellowed. "You must help out around the house . . . you will be a grown-up soon," he warned.

"Baba, do some snakes think they will grow into elephants one day? Do they think they are lost, wandering trunks?" She had taken to asking him questions that were immediately dismissed as silly childish ramblings. He rubbished her nonsense and wagged his finger at her. She was learning to tune the old man out. She didn't care much for the school uniform, nor did she appreciate the tight pony-tails pulling her hair. She was not interested in schoolwork and was unconcerned about the impending exams. They always seemed too close and too frequent. She looked down at the thick, yellow mound in her plate. The radio in the room sparked up again.

"All sector school buses will arrive in five minutes."

"There, now you'll be hungry till lunch!" Jyoti forced a spoonful into Mira's mouth and pulled the children out of the house with her. It was quite a gallop to the bus-stop from Block 8A in Sector 17. They trotted along with the other children being guided out of their houses, and were led to the bus-line.

"Mira, will you take Nakul with you? I need to talk to your father."

Mira nodded and took her brother by the hand. He was not too pleased about this. The other boys would mock him for being his sister's doll. Jyoti pecked them both on their cheeks and asked them to run along. She watched them disappear round the corner. A hawkish Vanaprasthi Watcher lady with binoculars sat on a perch atop the opposite building. She gave Jyoti a judgmental gaze that was a mix of contempt and pity. The young mother returned to her apartment. She managed to catch Gandharva just as he was about to leave the house.

"I need to talk to you—about the toilet—"

"What? What about the toilet?"

"The outer toilet is clogged, it won't flush and it won't fill up any more."

Gandharva adjusted his *khaadi* satchel and kept walking, feigning not to know the reason for the sudden obstruction.

"Did you try to fix it? Use the plunger, that's what it's for—"

"Of course I tried! It's no good."

"What do you want me to do, Jyoti? I am not a plumber."

"I am going to place a complaint with the PUB office. Is that alright?"

"Let me . . . let me take a look at it this evening. Okay?" He was sweating bullets.

She searched his face for concern but found only fear. He sought a little reason but saw only demands. It was hard for them to read each other. The windows to their souls were forever masked. He held his palms together in sarcastic deference and made his way to the elevator landing.

She went back into the house and sat alone for a moment. Baba had gone to sleep. He worked the night-shift as a Watcher and rested through the day. He had a strange habit of sleeping with his report register clutched tightly to his chest. She went to his room and shut the door. The snoring was continuous and sounded like a broken electric-saw, jamming its way through the stubborn trunk of an old Deodar.

She stepped into the bathroom to start getting ready, and looked at her face again in the mirror. No one had noticed the cut on her forehead. She touched it, cleaning it softly with some wet cotton. The antiseptic-oil dispenser squelched out more air than liquid in the first few plunges. Finally, the off-putting off-white ointment blew out, more up her arm than on the cotton ball. She collected it all and tried to clean her wound. It was a deeper cut than she had earlier thought.

She heard the sound of jangling outside their front door. Then she heard the twisting, turning rattle of a key. Cotton ball on her forehead, arm held up like a dancer, she went to see who it was. Someone was trying to enter their house.

They kicked the door open and stood in front of her, six men decked from head to toe in blue-and-white combat uniform, armed with guns and a familiar silver suitcase. She knew them well. She knew why they were there.

"No!"

# 9
# FOR GOD AND COUNTRY

The entire squad marched in. The Commander stepped forward to the sensor and registered his presence. The others went straight for Jyoti. She pushed one of them away and managed to squeeze herself into her room, shutting the door behind her.

"No! Please, I beg you! Leave me alone . . . there has been a mistake!"

"Mata ji, please open this door."

Jyoti sank to the ground. She was inconsolable. She cried for help. The old man stopped snoring.

"Baba! Please Baba, stop them!"

She sat huddled at the door, balling her knees under her chin. She could hear a muffled conversation outside. They started to beat the door and it shook behind her. There was nothing in the room that she could use to defend herself. There was a mesh on the window that blocked her escape. She got up to try and pull it down, but it was welded to the frame. There was no ledge outside anyway, just an eight-storey dive.

"Help me!" She banged and pulled at the window frame like a caged animal. The pounding on the door became louder. She cried in defeat and hid under her bed. The door was forced open and giant black boots appeared at the base of the bed, and she could smell the dirt under them. They lifted the bed clean off the ground.

"Mata ji, please cooperate!" the Commander spoke to her.

She begged and pleaded. He crushed her arm in his hands and pulled her.

"It is your duty."

She fell to her knees, sobbing.

"We must all do our part. Can you imagine a world where we stopped doing our jobs?"

The bed was put down behind her and she was pushed on top of it. With fastidious precision they removed her sari. She lay on top of the bed, a sweating, quaking ball of anger and anxiety. She tried to cover herself with her hands, hiding, praying softly.

"Please . . . please don't . . . I beg you."

"Send in the Aditi."

A woman wearing a white lab coat, accompanied by a nurse, entered the room.

"There's been a mistake!" Jyoti pleaded as the guards slipped coir and jute shackles onto her and pulled her arms and legs into an 'X'. She lay stretched tightly across her bed. The nurse went about her work quietly, wheeling in a tall, shining apparatus in the shape of an anti-aircraft gun. The silver briefcase was quickly connected to it and with the click of a button, two stirrups popped up on either side, like the raised arms of a boxer. The guards helped her position it between Jyoti's legs. Everyone in Block 8A must have heard her screaming. She was not going quietly.

"It will all be over soon, Jyoti ji, just breathe deeply. Try to calm down." The nurse moved one of her legs into the stirrups and asked a guard to help. She kicked them away. The Commander climbed on top of the bed and slapped her across her face. He pushed her legs apart and they were quickly latched into the stirrups of the IMP machine. Her struggling was of little use now. She turned to look her oppressors in the eye but none of their faces could be seen. He threatened to slap her again if she didn't look away.

"Can we please get a blindfold?"

The nurse looked inside her bag and pulled out a black patch with a band around it. They strapped the blinders on, as she cursed them. She screamed herself hoarse. The nurse was distracted by this violent outburst and turned to the doctor again.

"Should we just sedate this Jyoti?"

"Most definitely not. No sedative has been authorized, she has to go to work today."

"About turn!" the Commander continued. The guards held her arms firmly with the shackles, but turned their backs to her. This was a deeply private matter, after all. The nurse pulled Jyoti closer to the IMP machine and adjusted her remaining clothing to displace her underwear.

"Mata ji, you have to calm down. If you do not, this will be much worse than you can possibly imagine."

"I already have two children, please . . . please . . . stop!"

"Calm down Ma'am, please . . . the UET is ready now." She was sweet and measured.

"I am already a mother! I am already a mother twice over!"

The Aditi stepped in and tightened the stirrups, pulling them further apart to immobilize their terrible and unaccommodating patient. The guards too, took a step further away, tightening the harnesses to pull her apart like a spread-open spider.

"Here it comes. Ready?" The Aditi's intonation was cheerful and musical.

The probe of the IMP machine inched forward and made a sound like a dentist's drill. The pistons pushed into Jyoti, opening her. She gasped in pain. She stopped fighting. She knew that the machine could hurt her and she held still, in submission.

'UTERINE EMBRYO TRANSFER IN PROGRESS. SEARCHING FOR MOTHER WALL>>', the cold screen of the silver case read.

And then, just a few painful seconds later: 'TRANSFER COMPLETE>>'.

"Congratulations!" the doctor rejoiced.

"Hopefully you'll provide a hospitable environment, for the baby at least."

"Schedule her for a full Post Transfer Follow-up."

"You know how this goes Mata ji. No heavy lifting or strenuous activity, no douching, no pelvic thrusts. You hold the promise of the Nation inside you now. Take good care of it." The nurse covered her with the traditional cloth.

The guards removed their harnesses. The stirrups loosened their grasp. Jyoti climbed up to the head of the bed and covered herself. The nurse walked over to her and tried to comfort her with soothing tones and gentle bedside manner, greatly in contrast with the surgical violence that had just been inflicted.

"You are not alone, Jyoti. We are with you. We will see this through together."

They started to leave.

"What is it?" Jyoti mustered enough strength to whisper her question.

"I'm sorry?" the doctor stopped.

"What . . . who am I having?" the mother-to-be looked up

with a piercing glare, speaking through waves of rage crashing behind her eyes.

"A Vidur," the Aditi read it off a chart and grinned.

Jyoti turned her head and sobbed uncontrollably.

"I thought that would make you happy. Vidurs are our most intelligent men."

With that they left her alone. Baba came to the door. He had seen the same sight twice before. He hoped it got easier with time, he hoped that she'd found the strength to cope.

"She should appreciate her place in society," he thought. He didn't dare say it though. He closed the door and went back to his chamber, to massage his knees and then fight to fall asleep.

Jyoti rubbed her wrists; they still hurt from the harnesses. She felt herself. She was cold and dry, just as the machine had been. It did not get easier. There was no pride in being a State Mother or Mata ji as they were called. She turned to the medal on her bedside table. She'd received it at a Republic Day function from the Minister of Community Development and Animal Husbandry. She remembered shaking his hand as he stood angled away from her, smiling for the cameras. He never really acknowledged her. Three hundred other Mata jis were celebrated that day. She remembered receiving the bouquet from a lady as she got up on the stage. She had to return it backstage on her way out.

They used 20 bunches for all 300 mothers. Funnily, that was the only part of the ceremony that she clearly remembered. Shastri ji cared more for flora than other things. She'd never met him. Perhaps after giving birth to a healthy baby Vidur, she might be celebrated at another function, receive another medal, and shuffle another set of stale flowers. Perhaps this time, the Great Leader would be there himself. She wiped her tears.

The silence was broken by the flashing sensors in the bathroom. She had to start getting ready, in order to make it for her shift.

She crawled quietly on all fours, stopping at the entrance of the bathroom. She looked up. The curtain of red light swept across and registered her. She was present. She wondered if it might be easier to run away than to stay and bend down to a system that treated her no differently from cattle. She questioned herself again, for having these questions. She cursed herself and her fate.

She pulled herself up to the sink and reached for her toothbrush. The tiny television in the corner of the mirror started to play hygiene instructions for her benefit.

"Away from the gums, up and down. The State toothpaste is produced using the best natural and chemical ingredients. Neem, tulsi, peppermint, fluorine, and iodine. Away from the gums, up and down. When you think oral hygiene, think OMNI."

The instructions came complete with animated diagrams showing a mouth opening backwards, like a bear-trap, to be cleaned thoroughly.

"Remember to work over each row of teeth at least 30 times. But be careful now, we don't want to damage those lovely gums."

For the most part, Jyoti was an obedient and responsible young mother. She quite enjoyed her rituals and costume. Women were to be in saris at all times. There were three approved colours: grey, pink, and white. This made life a lot easier. People cared very little for their *shringaar*, as there was no room for vanity or tailored appearances. She had never, in her life, worried about what to wear.

No one had ever commented on her looks, not even her husband, the mild-mannered and gentle Gandharva. Like most Jyotis, she had pronounced features, a long nose and big eyes. She felt that her hands were disproportionately large for her body, but had never shared this with anyone. The big round *bindi* never left her forehead and the *sindoor* marked her as a married woman.

She peeped into Baba's chamber before leaving. He was asleep. She locked the front door behind her and fixed her sari as she walked towards the elevator. All the other women from Block 8A were assembling there too. They greeted her with a knowing look. She showed no sign of hurt and they took the elevator down in silence together like any other day. They climbed into the buses and sat side-by-side. Another beam clicked on and attendance was taken. The side of the buses read, 'For God and Country'. The bus monitor powered on for a chanting session and all the women sang along, in a low din: "*Om namoh bhagvate Vasudevaay namaha.*" They would soon be at the factory, ready to plough through the day, for God and Country.

# 10
# NOIR TIMES

"Listen, just repeat after me. Okay? Just try to say the words that I am saying to you now: 'Namaskar, my name is SS6.2'."

"*Shakarkand ajvain* shahtooti anjeer!"

"It is hopeless. You are wasting your time with him."

"It still baffles me . . . how could this have happened?"

"For all you know he could be doing it on purpose. Our project is in excellent shape, we don't need to dissect the ramblings of a stray mental patient." The Peet Vishvakarma did make sense.

"Why would he do it on purpose? I am convinced, that inadvertently, we have replaced his entire vocabulary with, well . . . garbage."

"You can keep him here for a few more weeks. After that, there will be no more of your parallel experiments. In case you haven't noticed, all other subjects are doing just fine."

"Understood . . . yes," the younger *Vaig* sounded despondent and lost.

"Don't tell me you are feeling bad for this degenerate-skinny-crow."

He did not answer. The truth was—he did not know. Somewhere deep down, he might have felt responsible and guilty for the collared man's condition. He passed off his 'parallel experiments' and tests as scientific curiosity. In truth, he was worried about the man's plight and sought to postpone further mistreatment, as much as possible.

Even though the binaaydi had cut and scratched away his barcode tattoos, the lab records still had his old number. His face had changed over time. It had grown thinner and bonier. The photographs in his files showed a fitter man with a strong, triangular jaw. Most other fields were blank or incomplete, and there was little else to go on. Except for the dates. This bit of detective work did shed some light on SS6.2's origins, though they were still largely shrouded in mystery.

Vishvakarma concluded that he could have been enrolled in the programme for one of two reasons. Based on the dates, he might have been involved with some of the late purges, a part of history that people knew little about. It was referred to as the 'Noir Times' for a reason. SS6.2 was either a genuine pariah who had refused to recant his beliefs, or he was a Dvarcan soldier who had renounced the righteous path. Either way, his will was strong. He was not one to bend easily and submit to coercion or bullying.

The scientist observed the rambling man through the glass panel in the door to his cell. The private investigation had made him think about his own beliefs. Was he certain of his ways? Could anything ever make him change? As a scientist, he knew that new evidence, experimentation, and facts could shape his views. As a dedicated Dvarcan and a devout Navmargi, he saw little that could change his mind, let alone raise questions. For long, he had thought that he had found a tenuous balance, between the two extremes of reasoned flexibility and unreasonable intransigence. It worried him to find that the dissonance still persisted. It haunted him.

# 11
# AN EQUAL MAGIC WITHIN YOU

*"Tvameva mata, cha pita tvameva,*
*Tvameva bandhush-cha sakha tvameva*
*Tvameva vidya, dravinam tvameva,*
*Tvameva sarvam, mama Deva Deva."*

The prayer ended and after a moment of silence, the Principal got up to address the entire school at assembly. One of the last few bald men left in Dvarca, he spoke softly with a soothing baritone that his students knew well. His bright eyes surveyed the auditorium and stopped on little Nakul in the front row. The boy was a bit restless. Vidur Chaturvedi, the much-loved educator smiled at him.

"We are all gifted. We are all experts at something. This is a fact. Through the science of divinity and the divinity of science, we have created a perfect world. Every Dvarcan child knows, from the day that he first opens his eyes, that there is a place for him. A vital place! What am I to do? Who am I? Why am I here? What am I good at? What do I lack? The need to discover these things about ourselves is paramount and mankind has struggled with this since the beginning of time.

My dear students, I am here to remind you, that thanks to Navmarg, your revelation was bestowed upon you at birth! There are special abilities, skills, and strengths that each of you possess. There are also some limitations, some things wanting. This is the way of nature. We need each other.

What good are the great designs and creations of Vishvakarma the engineer, if he has no Arjun or Nakul to protect them? How will the next army of strategists and academics be born, how will we have more Vidurs, if we do not have our caring Miras? We all serve a purpose. We are all brothers and sisters of the same faith, under the same flag, working towards the same great ideal. Look to your left, look to your right. You will see a willing compatriot. You will see exceptional talent, fortitude, and determination in each other's eyes.

None of you are superior or inferior. You are not competitors. You are parts of a bigger whole. Can a poet look down upon a labourer? Never! Should a Mata ji scorn a Sanjeev? No! Should an Arjun bully a Kuber? Unthinkable! The very purpose of having you all here together, my lovely children, is to bind you as one.

For every weakness you see in your neighbour, there is a shining strength in them. For every ability of theirs that you envy, know that there is an equal magic within you. We are here to learn and hone that magic, to become the best students we can be. Onwards!"

There was a brief round of applause, leading into the uplifting rhythm of soft bells, *tablas,* and harmoniums. Three Narads, teachers of devotional music, played the instruments. It was a Ganesh *vandana*, and the children sang along. There hadn't been a new batch of Narads for the past two years and that had brought the existing lot closer. Some feared that they were to be made redundant. It was just a smaller profession needing fewer candidates. The teachers turned proudly to their contingent, approving their flawless pitch and tune.

The morning assembly ended and students started out in orderly lines. The Shastri Mahavidyalaya was an enormous school serving all disciplines. Most of the Kendriya Vidyalayas and neighbourhood schools had been driven into extinction by the strict requirements imposed by the Ministry of Enlightenment. Each institution had to serve all kinds of students, from classes I through XII. There were nine kinds of students to teach:

Miras (mothers, factory-workers handling light machinery), Samyuktas (mothers, artisans), Arjuns, Sahdevas, and Nakuls (warriors and enforcers), Aditis (obstetricians, dentists, ophthalmologists, nurses), Sanjeevs (all other medical practitioners, pharmacists), Vidurs (strategists, academics, mathematicians), Kubers (accountants, bankers, traders), Vishvakarmas (researchers, engineers, contractors, builders, factory workers operating heavy machinery), and last but not the least, Narads (journalists, musicians, painters, writers, and artists).

There had been a few sub-groups in the past with different names. Most of them had been discontinued after a generation of testing. For instance, no new Gandharvas or Jyotis were needed. Their best qualities had already been assimilated to create brighter Vidurs and more acquiescent Miras. Only certain high-achieving and privileged Dvarcans of appropriate rank and position, were honoured with a surname.

The nine student groups filtered off into different wings of the school, each a massive structure connected to the Central Auditorium by long walkways. Nakuls and Arjuns raced along in typical boisterous fashion. The Vidurs spent a little extra time, discussing what was just said, only to be hushed by a teacher in the corridor. The Kubers were waiting for everyone else to leave. They didn't like mixing with large groups—the sweat, dirt, and noise were unbearable to them. They were quite meticulous about their uniforms and didn't want them to start looking worn at the very start of the day. The Vishvakarmas, often considered the awkward nerds of the mix, kept to themselves too. It was interesting to see that these distinctions and divisions took shape more in the higher classes and less so, when the kids were still, well, kids.

Little Nakul ran along with the rest of his legion towards their block. A few of the larger Arjuns from higher grades decided to have some fun and tripped his classmate. This would prove to be quite unwise, as a slight on a Nakul was a slight on all Nakuls.

'YOU ARE YOUR CONTINGENT!'

'UNITY THROUGH ONENESS!'

Little Nakul took it upon himself to avenge his brother. It was a one-sided fight and the teachers did not intervene immediately. They stood back in admiration of his courage. The bigger boys pushed him and he fell. They wanted to punch him, teach him his place, but they stopped short. A teacher stepped forward.

"Why have you stopped?" said Arjun Virdi, the gruffest one of the lot.

"He is my junior, I can't hit him . . ." he hesitated.

Little Nakul kicked the big boy who had pinned him in his shins and got up from the ground, ready to brawl.

"You are an Arjun. You must fight."

"Crow! First you push us around and then call a truce?" Nakul was not taking prisoners that day. His teachers stood behind him, in awe of his willingness to take on those so much bigger than himself.

"Come on! Come on, Caliphate spy! Traitor!"

"Sir, are you sure? I might hurt this squirt . . ."

"You cannot hurt him, he has already won by challenging you," the Principal had arrived. They all stood and watched, urging the warriors to destroy each other.

"You are born to it. Do not suppress your instincts."

"Embrace your dharma!"

Nakul threw the first punch. He jumped at the burly, shaggy boy in front of him and clung onto his leg, biting, snarling, and finally pulling him down. He climbed on top of him and smacked him around, viciously enjoying the ignominy of his victim. The teachers exchanged a knowing look and they pulled the boys apart. They raised the tiny pugilist's hand and patted his back. Some of them would have shed a tear, but it just wasn't in their DNA. The boys were brought together in a huddle. Arjun Virdi spoke, every syllable strident with pride.

"Now forgive each other and apologize."

The boys were reluctant.

"Aggression is important. Strength is important. But we must learn how and when to use it."

Little Nakul listened carefully.

"We must defend the weak and stand up for our brothers. It is only natural that we spar here. It is okay. We must sharpen our teeth on each other, to uncover the mettle in our bones." Bucolic wisdom, shared with gravity.

"Now you must forgive each other and vow to work together."

The elder boy examined the bite marks on his leg and hands. Every fibre of his being was focused on preventing tears from streaking down his cheeks. They were a sign of softness and would bring his already damaged position into greater doubt.

"I forgive you. And . . . I am sorry," he gathered.

Nakul smiled triumphantly.

"Both of you, forgive each other, or I will make you do it!" Arjun Virdi was losing patience.

They shook hands, albeit half-heartedly.

They marched along, happy little soldiers, to their classes.

Along the walkway, there was a recurring motif celebrating the legendary warrior, Arjuna. Their insignia depicted the head of a fish with an arrow through its eye. The image was designed to celebrate and commemorate one of Arjuna's best known feats. He had once shot a model fish target rotating on a ceiling, with only its reflection in a pool as a guide. Their motto was 'Strong, Accurate, Swift'.

The boys changed into their Physical Training uniforms. For them, the first two hours of the day before lunch were devoted to exercise and training. The young ones were engaged in mass track-and-field exercises. The older children were in tactical training and special courses like shooting, archery, and hand-to-hand combat.

Nakul completed his rounds before everyone else and decided to take a celebratory walk around the sports centre, surveying what he thought of as *his land.*

"Eh, hero!" someone called out to him.

"What is it?"

"Come, join us . . ."

A couple of senior Arjuns were sitting behind a tree. He sauntered up to them.

"What are you doing here? What is all this?"

"It is a map of the Caliphate." They held up a piece of paper on which they had drawn the enemy region. It was crudely sketched, with jagged edges.

"What are you doing with that?"

"Do you know where the capital is? You want to lead the air raid? Come . . ."

They were lighting the tips of *chandan-bels* on fire and using the wax to 'bomb the map'. Nakul sat down with them and with great relish took the smoky bel in his hand. It was warm and little globules of hot lava oozed out from it. He swung it over the page slowly as though he were toying with the foe. He flung three big drops in the heart of the hated territory.

"Make sure you hit some civilian targets too, come on now . . . don't be a softie . . ."

He obliged and poured more wax across the map. The boys laughed as the paper melted. Black craters swallowed it slowly.

"That'll teach them. I can't wait to get out there."

"Me neither," Nakul agreed.

The bell rang and it was time to return for classes. The afternoons were spent studying language, history, strategy, and mathematics. Students, who showed a better understanding for strategy early on, were put in the 'Officer' stream. Little Nakul was one of them.

## 12
# AN ACT OF WAR

Images were unstable and refused to snap into place. New messages opened with great difficulty. The ordeal with the valiant and virtuous IMP team, seemed to have worsened the condition of Jyoti's DDs. She pressed the corners into the arms to try and stabilize the feed. It did not work. Just as she got off the bus, Advance Directives announced that there had been a surge in demand for poly shirts.

"What are you doing here? Shed 7, you're needed at Shed 7," shouted a karmachari.

The women started out and one keen lady pushed Jyoti to get ahead.

"Keep moving . . . please. Mata ji, get up and keep on moving!"

Jyoti cupped her ears and bit her tongue to apologize for her clumsiness. She had lost control of her DDs, and distracting messages kept opening and closing at will. At Shed 7, karmacharis outnumbered the workers and pushed them through a series of check-points towards the main entrance. Jyoti ducked through the security arches, being scanned by each sensor. A guard stopped her.

"I was just checked back there . . . must you also—?"

Her questions were ignored and she was pushed in front of a T180, an early iteration of an outdated scanner. It was like an octopus with joints and it moved like an old man with arthritis. It creaked and always reminded Jyoti of her father-in-law. The long arms of the law danced from left to right to register her as a 'Present-Worker'. A deafening alarm started to blare and a rickety camera rested on Jyoti's face.

The women in line behind her shuddered and tried to leave the machine's review radius. Jyoti did not move. It was too late. The chip in her glasses had been noticed. The screens lit up and instructed her to 'SEEK GUIDANCE NOW>>'. The karmachari smiled at her and ushered her to his superior officers. Two of them were seated at a desk in the middle of all the chaos.

"What happened to your DDs?"

"House work . . . It was an accident."

"Are you sure?"

"Yes . . ."

"How did you have this accident?"

"I was trying to unclog the toilet . . ."

The officer got up from his chair. He stood inches from her face, looking at his reflection in her glasses.

"It's a nasty little crack."

"Yes, I am very sorry *Sriman* . . ." Jyoti nodded.

"You cannot work like this. You must go to the Monitoring Cabin."

"The MC—is that really necessary?" She was meek and her resistance was timid at best.

It was a huge industrial complex and reaching the cabin

without strict adherence to directions was almost impossible. A map showing her the shortest route was downloaded to her scratched, malfunctioning DDs. It kept slipping in and out of its folder and shook like a leaf in a storm. The busted device had been entrusted to guide her to her destination. She walked away, past piles of trash. It was unclear whether the dumptruck, parked beside the stinking rows of fetid heaps, was there to remove or deposit more refuse. She covered her mouth and walked along.

"God and Country . . . God and Country . . . *Jai Shri Krishna! Om namah Shivaya!*"

The route was almost indecipherable. She figured she'd go straight down past the cafeteria, turn left into the First Sub-quadrant and then walk towards Circular Road B, until she was in the Administrative Section. After that, it was anybody's guess about the MC. The letters and numbers on the grids of her map, shivered and blurred. Bs looked like As. She felt nauseated but walked along, saying her prayers before the interrogation. Everything still hurt, but she was a strong woman of Dvarca. Nothing would stop her from fulfilling her duties.

The Administrative Section was quiet. She stopped at a crossroad and consulted the unreliable map again. It showed that she needed to be at BB5, Room 12. Or was it AA6? She figured it was just down the road. There were no guards or sentries. No T180s to scan and check her identity. She walked through the main entrance and went straight to the lobby, where a lady sat behind the reception desk.

"Good morning! Do I need to register or take a number here? I think I need to go to Room 12."

The receptionist strangely stayed quiet. Jyoti tried again, but there was no answer. The wall behind her had a grid of the premises, and Room 12 was at the end of a long main corridor. Three big brass lamps burnt bright at the other end. A sentry sat in the middle of the walkway. His steel chair was angled away from her and she could not see his face.

"Good morning Sriman. For God and Country!" She greeted him and he too ignored her. The silence and stillness grew with every step. She peeked into one of the waiting rooms. There were about 30 people seated inside. Their chairs were angled away bizarrely in the same direction and they faced the far corner of the room. They were all irregular, but in the same way. Did that make it regular? Jyoti wondered as she pushed the door open and entered. She looked down to see that she stood in rose petals that were strewn haphazardly across the floor in the doorway.

'OMNI WANTS YOU TO BE PRODUCTIVE' read the banner at the back of the room.

"*Pranaam . . .*"

They all seemed to be asleep. One lady had almost fallen off her chair and Jyoti tried to wake her up.

"Mata ji! Mata ji?"

Jyoti tapped her shoulder. She held her arm and shook her slightly. Her body was cold and limp, and she slipped and fell to the ground with a great thud. Her mouth struck the floor, and teeth smashed and sprang out. With the spray of shattered incisors and cracked bicuspids a wet, green ball of spit also flew out.

"Wake up! Please!"

With great difficulty, Jyoti pulled her back into her chair. She looked down at the fragments of teeth and saw that the floor was sprinkled with brown seeds, grains, and husk. Dvarcans of different ages, professions, and gene-tags sat in the room like the entranced audience of a spell-binding show. Were they drugged? Had they been poisoned?

Regular consumption of the JVK should have made them all immune! She covered her mouth, fearing a nerve-gas attack or some kind of chemical contaminant in the air. She looked up at the surveillance cameras and waved for help. Somewhere in the building, a door shut loudly. She heard it and shouted: "Help! Is anybody out there?"

Something sinister was at work. She did not want to abandon her compatriots, and tried calling and sending messages to the Terrorism Helpline. Her DDs looped and failed—all the applications were out of control. Old saved messages interfered, maximizing and minimizing without reason. The map, unstable as ever, flickered green and black. She was blinded by the flurry of activity.

She decided to leave. Just as she reached the door, she heard an explosive crack behind her. She turned to see a series of detonations, one from each room on either side of the corridor, bursting like the rounds of a linked firecracker. She ran as fast as she could. She could feel the heat from the raging fire. Pieces of ceiling had broken and rained around her. She felt as though the earth was swallowing her, and in the middle of a prayer, she blacked out.

# 13
# THE MEASURE OF A MAN

"Alright boys, it is my honour and my privilege, to ask you to turn to Appendix 5 of your notes for today. Nakul, please read the heading."

"It says: Rate your parents. What is this, Guru ji?"

The teacher smiled and got up from his desk.

"Apart from being a band of keen warriors, able sportsmen, and strong-willed stalwarts, what do you all have in common with each other? Anyone?"

"We are patriots?"

"We are devout?"

"We are full of energy?"

"All true. But I was looking for a simpler answer. You see, you are all 10-years-old. From your eleventh birthday, you will have a say in measuring the performance of your parents."

There was a chart that adorned the walls of all classrooms in the Arjuna wing of Shastri Mahavidyalaya. It depicted the different life-stages of a typical Nakul or

Arjun. Starting with an inch-high infant, it went all the way to a prostrate martyr. There were four basic *ashramas* that marked the main life-stages: *Brahmacharya* (0–20 years), *Grihasta* (20–40 years), *Vanaprasthi* (40–60 years) and *Sanyasa* (60–85 years).

Within each of these key stages, there were specific milestones and targets. For instance, at age five, they were to receive their first DDs, and also start memorizing and reciting important scriptures from the ancient texts. At the age of 11, the children would be asked to start evaluating the true contribution of all citizens. This started with the tracking and valuation of their relationship with their parents.

"You are familiar with the fact that the Dvarcan financial system is a unique one. It links the progress of your soul with your savings. Yes?"

"Yes! PunyaBindus measure our wealth spiritually as well as . . ."

"What's the word, can someone else help young Nakul?"

"Fiscally."

"Yes, excellent. Spiritual ascension and fiscal progress are one and the same in our beautiful system. Let me take you through the chapter. This is one of the most basic principles of Navmarg. Every Dvarcan, through various activities, work, and output is in a position to earn PunyaBindus or Bindus as they are commonly known. These can be exchanged for goods and services, or they can be stored in a bank account at the Peoples' Omniscient Savings Bank of Dvarca. Has everyone heard of POSB?"

A resounding affirmation followed that question.

"Does everyone here, know what they have earned already?"

There was pin-drop silence.

Guru ji elaborated, "Ah, you see, each one of you must have some amount, some small amount in your accounts, already in there, waiting for you to start adding to it."

"What if we are not able to add to it? What if we are unable to save?"

"That is a great question, my son. You see, everyone needs a certain level of Bindus in order to achieve *moksha* and break the cycle of death and rebirth. Based on the time of your birth and various celestial measurements, your Target PBs were determined."

"Who figures out this 'Target'?"

"This wholly important holy task is in the hands of the Bureau of Astrological Mensuration. All of us, Dvarcans, are born into PB debt."

He pointed at his students and made eye contact with them, one by one.

"You are in debt. So are you. All of you have different amounts of debt acquired over possibly many previous lives. Your purpose in this life is simple. You must acquire enough Punya, to clear that debt and free your souls."

"What if we save, but not enough, Guru ji, what happens then?"

"Simple, if enough Punya has not been earned, one can expect to return in rebirth. One can only pray that one is reborn in Dvarca. Most of the world, inhabited by the likes of Hedonesians and Caliphites, lives in darkness. They do not even know how to earn more Punya. They are as self-aware as fungus. To learn these important facts about one's *aatma*, one has to accept Navmarg as the way."

"Can we convert them? Can we show them that Navmarg is a better way?"

"Yes, we can. Of course there are penalties for late-comers and taxes based on origin. You see, for them, we have no clue what they have done with their lives until the point of conversion. Even their starting coordinates are not tracked in a meaningful way."

Young Nakul raised his hand to ask a question.

"How do we measure the Punya of our actions? Is this known to all?"

Guru ji smiled before turning to the board to write a long formula. The marker squeaked along, as he emphasized certain letters. His entire body curled and curved to produce the calligraphy.

"Your parents, like all Dvarcans above the age of 18, receive statements on a monthly basis. In these statements there are three important numbers. Bindus Earned-To-Date (B-ETD), Bindus Required-For-Salvation (B-RFS), and the difference (D). This D, is one's personal Punya Deficit."

"Can we borrow Punya?" the class laughed.

"It is not a funny question. One can borrow Punya, but only from POSB. This is necessary in order to manage a citizen's worthiness and to track his or her position, in a complete way. Of course you can only take a loan for a few permitted reasons, up to a very limited amount. You would owe it back to POSB with interest...it is not recommended. Fortunately, most Dvarcans manage to live within their means."

"Now pay attention. These are the different ways in which you can earn Punya. It all boils down to a comparison between what you are meant to do and what you have actually done. This is, in basic terms, called the KDR, or the Karma-Dharma-Ratio. Let us look at the full formula for monthly Punya pay-out calculation:

$$\mathbf{(S) \ X \ (0.6K_w/D_w + 0.4K_H/D_H) \ X \ (M) + (B_W) + (F) + (C) + (G)}$$

Who can tell me what (S) is?"

"Salvation?"

"Sample-set?"

"What? No. Children, **(S)** is the base Salary for your job function and your kalaava. This is known to all. The thing that requires tracking and control is the variable component . . ."

He pointed to the two ratios $\mathbf{(K_w/D_w + K_H/D_H)}$.

"These two ratios are a measure of Karma at Work versus Dharma at Work ($K_w/D_w$) and Karma at Home versus Dharma at Home ($K_H/D_H$). At work, supervisors compare the impact of your Karma (deeds) with the essence of your Dharma (essential duties). Dharma is predetermined and transparent. It changes from band to band, and clearance to clearance, within the different job functions. As you all know, you are genetically pre-disposed to be able to perform your Dharma."

"Sorry, can we go back? Why is there a 0.6 and a 0.4 in front of the ratios?"

"Because the two ratios have different weightage. In Dvarca, your work has 60 per cent contribution and home life has 40 per cent contribution, to your performance as a human being. For women, it is the other way round, though. Let's look at ($K_H/D_H$). We measure the respect, balance, love, and affection in all households. The home-sensors watch families and track whether they pray, eat, sit, and watch television together. The most important aspect of a successful family life, is to physically be there for one another. The second aspect looks into how one behaves, while in the presence of one's family."

He stepped out to the front of the class again, and looked at their fresh young faces. Some made notes in their books and others listened carefully.

"This is where you come in. Parents are already watched quite closely. Elevated heart rates and tension at home for a sustained period of time are indicators of an unsuccessful parenting style. But to really rate their performance, you, the children of Dvarca must fill out a parent-child evaluation form every quarter."

Young Nakul flipped back to Appendix 5 as Guru ji continued to speak. He wondered how he would rate his father.

There were two sections, one for each parent. He had mixed feelings about them both and wondered what it would say about him and them, if he were to be truthful. He glanced over at the eight-point questionnaire and the scoring system for each facet. If the sum-total of all responses turned out to be less than 35, an explanatory note would have to accompany the submission.

| **S. no.** | **Rate your father's parenting style:** | **5** | **4** | **3** | **2** | **1** |
|---|---|---|---|---|---|---|
| 1 | Respect for the Great Leader | | | | | |
| 2 | Patriotism | | | | | |
| 3 | Piety | | | | | |
| 4 | Kindness to family | | | | | |
| 5 | Care for you and siblings | | | | | |
| 6 | Teachings about Scripture | | | | | |
| 7 | Teachings about Dvarca | | | | | |
| 8 | Secrecy | | | | | |
| | **GRAND TOTAL** | | | | | |

"I would encourage you to start thinking of your parents in this light. Think about how they measure up, with these attributes in mind."

Little Nakul thought about all the times that Gandharva had tried to teach him something. It all started to fit nicely into the boxes on his evaluation sheet. Teachings were usually book-ended with terse declarations that they were in fact, 'teachings'. There was always talk in the house about how Dvarca was superior as a Nation and how lucky they all were to be Navmargis. Credit had to be given where credit was due.

The lesson continued with brief introductions to the other ways in which a Dvarcan might gain additional Punya. A workplace bonus **($B_w$)** was discretionary, only due when the ($K_w/D_w$) ratio exceeded a value of one. This meant that a citizen had gone beyond the call of duty.

Charity **(C)** was another way to earn some extra celestial goodwill. Everything from helping out the Annapurna Division with food delivery, sweeping temples, donating blood, and speaking at schools had a PB value tagged to it. Most menial tasks had already been automated, but it was the principle of putting oneself in a position to do them, that constituted the act of charity. It was easy and transparent for people to choose their supplementary sources of income. The State revised the Charity Incentive Structure from time to time, to ensure that different types of donation methods received attention.

Fasting **(F)**, too, was considered a great way to raise PBs. There were personal fasts, which were quite common since they could be started and concluded at any time (in a pinch). There were specific fasts on recommended days that served a certain deity, or were in lieu of a particular objective. And lastly, there were mandatory fasts that served both God and Country. These were quite important and ensured by non-delivery of food by the Annapurna Division. Nakul had seen his mother do this regularly. It was one of her favourite ways to practice her faith.

"Can we also fast at will?"

"Only after you turn 18. Till then, only the occasional mandatory fasts apply to you."

"How is that fair? I would like to fast now," Nakul challenged the teacher and received only a conciliatory nod as an answer.

Citizens were also free to receive a gift **(G)** from anyone, including the State, up to a maximum of 75,000 PBs for men and 50,000 PBs for women.

"Children, I hope you have understood the basic building blocks of our system of remuneration and recognition. There is, however, one letter in the formula that we have not discussed as yet. Which is it?"

"M!"

"Indeed. **(M)** signifies 'Multiplier' periods of special significance. During these windows of opportunity, all work and activities stand to earn double or triple the normal amount of Punya. This may happen during festive seasons and on holy days on the calendar. It may happen at different times for different citizens. There is a profound science that helps determine when these events of fortune occur. Everything has to do with one's time of birth and place in the universe. This information too, is controlled and communicated by the Bureau of Astrological Mensuration to each Dvarcan citizen when necessary. It is up to citizens to make the most of these chances."

"You must have all heard the saying: Fate is fair. The stars and heavens know best. All our attempts to do their bidding can only hold us in good stead, for this life and the next."

Nakul sat back in his chair, wondering how much Punya he needed, in order to never be born again. It was an unsettling thought at first, to know that the aim of life was to escape its trappings, but it sat well with the mind of a young soldier. He wanted to sacrifice himself for his country. He had always wanted to go out with a bang.

"Is there a way that we might lose our PBs?"

"Most certainly. Through constant monitoring and surveillance, all crimes or acts against God and Country are known to the State. These result in PB demerits and directly eat into a person's balance of Punya. All infringements, in addition, will be handled within the jurisdiction of the penal code and legal system."

"What if I have more Punya than I require? What if I become unnecessarily rich?"

"That usually does not happen. There are a lot of things to purchase and maintain for a decent life, for you and your family. Even at the end of your life, 50,000 PBs are required for the *antim yatra pujan,* or final prayer ceremony. After that, whatever is left, is matched against your Target PBs for Moksha. A maximum of 75,000 PBs could be left to each son and 50,000 PBs to one's daughter or wife."

The thought of the final calculation left the entire class quiet.

"Don't be burdened by this knowledge, my brave Nakuls! Be liberated by it! You are on your way to becoming men. Now please, take the mock test and see how you might rate your fathers and mothers. Let's see where they stand."

# 14
# ZERO TOLERANCE

The Ministry of Finance and Salvation did many important things. Gandharva's job, as an Aasmani bureaucrat, was to track and review the PBs earned and spent by citizens. He was the Assistant Financial Analyst for Sectors 11 through 13. It was an important function with very real implications on the lives of men, women, and children too. He went about his business in a dispassionate and clinical manner, scanning through a new set of PB demerits. He did not have to care which infractions had been committed by whom, he just needed to assess and confirm the demerit amount.

He had finally forgotten about the Disciplinary Committee Review and was getting into a productive rhythm when a new test popped up on his work screen. The yellow font on the red background was a welcome change from their usual black-on-cream reports. As usual, the test asked him to identify the outliers in a sea of numbers.

The definition of 'outliers' changed every time, from test to test, puzzle to puzzle. There were no set formulas or equations to check against. One had to study the patterns and decide. These little games of detection were frequent. Gandharvas were prompted with puzzles to break the monotony of their work and to alert them to the 'charm of numbers'. It kept them thinking.

At their fanciest, the interruptions were a form of code-breaking. At their lowest, they were no tougher than basic numerical intelligence tests. Gandharva had taught himself to 'seek the stranger' over the years. His training as an engineer, sort of over-qualified him as a quantitative analyst. It was another matter that he had studied civil engineering and perhaps understood city planning better.

Nevertheless, he was a Gandharva. He had a duty to perform and no puzzle was going to stand in his way. The yellow numbers on red sheets appeared as images, and most of the time, he had to type them into an accounting software. Sometimes he made mistakes and he'd have to scroll up, down, left, and right to check the digits he had copied out.

As he tried to glean a pattern, he remembered the most complex relationship he had ever uncovered. He had solved it by representing all the numbers on a graph. It won him a medal. That was also the day he went from a Baingani Sub-Analyst to a Neel Analyst, ages ago. He looked around the office and saw that a few of his colleagues were also in the midst of a puzzle. It was not uncommon for them to get the same test at the same time.

The bureaucrats had never quite figured out where the numbers came from. They were just happy to set them aside quickly and get on with the business of accounting. He cleared report after report. Most of the demerits were under Code 76 for non-compliance through negligence. Surprisingly, there were a few 295As, which he recalled, pertained to disrespecting Navmarg. Why were people questioning the State religion? Was there a recent change in standards that he had missed? There were three 124s also on his report. That was a dangerous code, and had something to do with sedition.

The number of people falling into high-risk buckets was increasing. There were many reasons for this, but he was not required to go into that level of detail. It was a mystery for the higher kalaavas to ponder. He submitted another report and went to the tea dispenser for some hot Darjeeling. He took a big sip and kept the burning hot liquid at the back of his mouth. He breathed in deeply and swallowed. A Peet Gandharva walked past and expressed pleasure at having received some of the more complex reports in record time.

"By the way, that last test that you solved, brilliant effort! What was the solution?"

"A sietic polynomial, Sir."

"How did you figure it out?"

It had just sort of come to him. He could think of no way to deconstruct the source of his inspiration, so he shrugged to shake off the burden of the compliment.

"Good work, anyway."

"Sure Sir," as soon as he spoke these words, silence spread across the office. The screens hanging from the ceiling at the centre of the great hall at the Ministry of Finance and Salvation stopped showing pictures of aquatic life. The soothing fish were gone. Narad Vedshankar, four-time 'Excellence in Broadcasting' winner appeared, speaking solemnly into the camera.

"Good afternoon. Now hear the news. Two acts of war have been committed against our great Nation. First, at 4:45 this morning, the Caliphate shot down one of our Patrol Guardians stationed on the North West frontier. Second at around 10:00 this morning, on our very soil in the heart of the Dvarcan Industrial Complex, a bomb explosion killed hundreds of peace-loving Dvarcans. Here is the Minister of External Affairs and Defence, Shri Lal Arjun Walvarkar."

Lal Arjun Walvarkar spoke from a podium in front of a giant poster of Shastri ji at the Pushkar auditorium. The towering image of Shastri ji's face showed his bright white moustache, Nehru cap, trademark red-*tilak*, and his raised wagging finger. The minister's soft-spoken demeanour grew into passionate outrage as he spoke. The Varaha men standing around him were unmoved and stern as ever. He spoke directly into the camera.

"In retaliation for this heinous attack, we launched surface-to-surface OMNI Bhimadev missiles, destroying three Caliphate watch-towers. We have warned our treacherous neighbours many times in the past. Our policy of zero-tolerance is widely known and internationally respected. For every attack against us, we will strike back with three times the force. This is justice. This is necessary. Dvarcans, let us not flinch in the face of evil! Let us protect what is ours, with an iron fist, and the trident of Goddess Durga guiding us. Jai Dvarca!"

Narad Vedshankar took over the broadcast.

"Minister Shri Lal Arjun Walvarkar there, making an important point about national defence. To discuss this further, we have our distinguished panel of experts. Professor *Santri* Vidur Giriraje from the Shastri University of Public Policy and Defence Studies, my senior Shri Lal Narad Vedshankar the revered Minister of Media Control and Communication, and Srimati Peet Samyukta Mishra esteemed artist, writer, and philanthropist. Shri Giriraje, let's start with you, what do you think about our response to the attacks this morning?"

"It was necessary, it was just. I am in complete agreement with the actions taken. We have to teach the aggressors a lesson. We are not the weak Nation that we used to be. We will not tolerate any attack on our soil."

"Srimati Samyukta ji, what are your thoughts? Is the triple-impact zero-tolerance policy adequate?"

"I mourn the loss of Dvarcan lives. I cannot understand why these cowards keep attacking our civilians. It was a mill, was it not? They attacked the Administrative Sector of a mill. Through my years of volunteer work at animal shelters, I know that dealing with beasts is always tricky. They learn through repetition. I feel that the triple-impact zero-tolerance policy is effective. It is just and it is quite necessary. We are not dealing with human beings on the other side. They hate us and have little, or no respect for anything other than strength and anger."

"Thank you Ma'am. You always bring such colour and perspective to our discussions. Let us now turn to my Lal superior, the Minister, Shri Vedshankar, what is your take on this whole brouhaha?"

The Minister of Media Control and Communication was a learned man. Everything about him was round. His face, his tilak, even the logo for his Ministry was a circle within a circle. He was fond of *paan* and was rarely seen without one in his mouth. He mumbled and hissed while speaking, and always tilted his head back at an angle to stop the *paan* juice from dripping out of his gaping curved mouth. It pooled behind his lips and coloured them maroon. His grey hair bobbed behind him in a bushy ponytail as he spoke. Subtitles appeared on the screen, for the benefit of the audience.

"We are in complete agreement, we must band together behind Shastri ji and Walvarkar ji. In an armed forces survey, there was 100 per cent appreciation for our triple-impact zero-tolerance policy. It goes a long way in creating a just and necessary deterrent against future aggression. The Caliphate seeks new pastures to ruin. Their goal is to proselytize the rest of the world, and force us all to submit to their false and treacherous 'God'. We must stay together, stay vigilant, and help the administration protect us."

Someone started a cheer in the office: "Jai Dvarca!"

Men in all colours of kalaava stood up and shouted: "Jai Dvarca! Shastri ji ki jai!"

Gandharva stood up too. He shouted with the rest of them. He looked all around to make sure that his vehement support was registered. His eyes opened wide, his mouth spat the words, and his fists reached for the heavens. He was one with the crowd.

"Kill them all! Destroy the Caliphate!"

# 15
# THE DHARMIC MIRA

All courses were State prescribed and all examination certificates were centrally awarded. The language of instruction was Sanskrit. It was considered much more than just a language, and was taught as part of a subject called 'Way of Life' that covered scriptures and their meaning. Mira pondered the recent lesson while most of her friends gossiped about their first ever V-lab session. She felt left out of the conversation as the girls around her, raved and gushed about it. Even though some of them claimed to have been devastated by the experience, they could not wait for the next one. The thrill of horror was irresistible.

"When do you think they will take you?"

"I don't know . . . my parents have not spoken to me about it."

"Your father's just an Aasmani Gandharva, right? Probably doesn't know much anyway—"

The teacher walked in before Mira could defend her father.

"All right girls. I want you to take three deep breaths before we start the lesson."

The class obeyed and straightened up.

"Now, what was the most important thing that Principal Vidur ji said today?"

"We are all special?" Mira mumbled.

"Excellent. That is correct. What makes a Mira especially special? What makes a Mira good? Start calling out from the last chapter. I will write the words on the board."

There was a flurry of activity as the girls flapped open their textbooks to their previous lesson: 'THE DHARMIC MIRA'.

They started blurting words out of order, without permission, as their teacher hurriedly penned them on the board.

"Kind"

"Nurturing"

"Tactful"

"Gentle"

"Emotional"

"Very good! Keep going. How about you, do you have an idea?"

"Not an original one, Guru Mata, but I can read one from my book . . . 'Submissive?'

"Carry on!"

"Mathematical?"

The teacher was not impressed.

"Who told you about mathematics? It is a waste of your time. Mathematics, sciences . . . these are all things that come naturally to Dvarcan boys. You cannot compete with them. I thought we learnt this last week. More! Give mc some more words for the board."

"Home-oriented"

"Dependent"

"Passive"

"Sensitive"

"Okay, that's better." She wrote them down and stepped back.

"I think we have enough examples here. As we learnt the last time, Miras have a predestined place in Dvarca. You are all preordained to be mothers. Physically, you are fit. But, are you the best Miras you can be, to support your husbands?"

There was a brief chuckle. The girls covered their mouths and giggled naughtily.

"It is not funny. You must think about your future. Are you home-oriented? Do you put family before self?"

The 12-year-olds grew pensive again.

"Let's work on this from both sides. Let us look at the parallel qualities that our men exhibit, to complement the attributes we just discussed. Yes?"

She scanned the classroom and picked on a girl who seemed lost.

"Let's start with you. 'Kind'. What is the male response to that?"

"Unkind?"

"Not exactly. It is 'ruthless' or 'tactical'. We must give our men all the kindness and nurturing they require, in order for them to be the best they can at their jobs. They have to do better and get ahead in their streams."

"Let's try another one, what is the corresponding male feature for 'submissive'? Who will venture an answer?"

"Dominant. My mother always agrees with my father."

"She is a real role-model. Now, what about children? All these attributes will also make you a better mother. You have to be a home-maker who cooks and cleans, apart from doing a full-time job."

Mira wrote all of this down. She was growing tired of being 'submissive'. She was a long way from being 'passive'. She wondered if it meant the same as being indifferent.

"Guru Mata, what does it mean, for us to be 'passive'?"

"It means, accepting or going with the flow. Letting your man be the 'active' one. Let him lead and shape your lives. You are there to support him—sometimes guide him—but never actively. Does that answer your question?"

She nodded and tried to make sense of the words. In her book, she saw diagrams of Miras with their children. Pictures of doting mothers and testimonials about how babies had fulfilled them, and made them feel complete. She ached for that sense of achievement and validation, though she was unsure if she could ever earn it.

# 16

# XX

"Where am I?"

"For God and Country! She is awake! She is awake!" A nurse shouted.

Jyoti came around slowly, regaining her senses one by one. It felt quite like recovering from a V-lab session. Had it all just been a bad dream?

"Am I dead?"

"*Shubh-shubh bolo* Mata ji, you are alright . . ."

She was in an ambulance, but they were not moving. The back doors were open and she could see dust and rubble outside.

"We have been attacked, Mata ji. This time they have gone too far. They blew up an entire building."

Her eyes were still adjusting to the light and she felt giddy. There were scratches on her feet and her head felt swollen.

"It is a bloodbath. We found you lying in the street. How do you feel?"

"I . . ." she suddenly realized that her DDs were no longer malfunctioning. They were stable. Messages came in and opened up normally, there was no disturbance but the crack in her lens was still there.

"Your Personal Activity Log shows that you had an IMP visit this morning and . . . I see that you were visiting the Monitoring Cabin for your damaged DDs."

"The baby . . . my baby . . ."

"Everything seems to be alright. There are no signs of internal strain. The Doctors have looked you over. They will be back shortly."

She looked at herself and prayed out loud, giving thanks.

"Please concentrate all your energies on feeling better. Shall I notify your Gandharva?"

"No please don't. There is no need. I will tell him myself."

The sympathetic nurse gave her a tonic and asked her not to get up. The doctors came by to check up on her.

"You were very lucky, Mata ji. There is a minor injury on your back, but other than that, you are all right. It's the lower lumbar vertebrae. I see from your records that you have had some history of back pain?"

"No, nothing to complain about."

"You've been using *ashwa-boswellia* for some time, Mata ji," he looked at her with suspicion. "Tell us the truth. Are you in pain?"

She didn't really know how to answer that question. She was so unaccustomed to concern that she started to tear up.

"I'll take that as a 'yes'. We will keep you on the ashwa-boswellia and the next time you go in for an examination with your Aditi, we will schedule a full check-up."

"I feel fine, Doctor Sanjeev ji, I am alright," she was doing the calculations in her mind, estimating how much more this would cost her. She did not want to ask Gandharva for his hard-earned PBs.

"You were very lucky. No other survivors have been found. Where exactly were you when it happened?"

A message popped up on her DDs. It did not have the usual prefix associated with messages from the State, family, friends, or colleagues. Even the font was different. The sender was marked as 'XX'.

"JYOTI, YOUR LIFE IS IN DANGER."

She stared at the doctors, dumbstruck.

"Maybe she is still in shock. Mata ji, can you hear me?"

"SAY YOU WERE GOING TO THE MC. YOU SAW THE EXPLOSION FROM AFAR AND FAINTED."

"Yes . . . I can hear you, Doctor . . ."

"DO NOT TELL THEM WHAT YOU REALLY SAW. THEY WILL MAKE YOU DISAPPEAR."

"I was down the street, from BB5. I was going to the MC when I saw the blast."

"MEET ME. 6:00 P.M. GRAND PARK. SOUTH WALL, MANICATA BUSHES."

She looked behind the doctor and saw a dharma-*sevika* lady waiting for her. The medics and nurses left them to talk.

"Pranaam Jyoti, I am a Mira." She climbed into the ambulance and sat down.

"I have a Mira of my own."

"Oh that's wonderful, how old is she?"

"She just turned 12."

She looked up at the lady and saw her serene face, her kind soul laid bare for anyone who cared to see it. She looked tired and slouched, though her spirit remained radiant. She spoke in short, fast clips of sentences.

"I have a Nakul too."

"Oh that's a matter of pride! Nakuls are in great demand. Your son may someday get to be a martyr," her disposition changed from warm and caring to stern and imposing. She held Jyoti's hand.

"Tell me what happened this morning."

"Nothing . . . the streets were quiet . . . everything was normal," Jyoti tried sitting up. She could still see flashes of the people in the room—the silence of the corridor, and the broken teeth.

"You were sent here, first thing in the morning, because your DDs were broken."

"Scratched . . . yes, I came looking for the Monitoring Cabin. I think I got lost along the way. I can't really remember . . ."

"We have footage of you, turning at the cafeteria, stopping down the road."

"Yes . . . yes . . . I had not been to the MC before, never had the need . . ." Jyoti started to sob.

"What's the matter?"

"I've let them all down—my husband will be furious when he finds out about all this."

"Finds out about what?"

"I do not know how it all happened, I just stumbled down this way and then it all went up in flames. None of this would have happened if I had been more careful."

"Careful?"

"About my DDs . . ." she felt the chip on her lens. "All of this could have been avoided."

"Calm down, Jyoti." the dharma-sevika caressed Jyoti's head lightly. "I believe you."

"Can't our surveillance show us what happened?"

"The cameras inside the building are all burnt. We have some coverage of the area outside, but . . ."

"But?"

"But it malfunctioned too. There was a disruption and we have a gap of a few minutes, before and during the blast."

"Oh . . ."

"It has happened before. The enemy seems to have a way of scrambling our sensors and cameras, but only in short bursts . . . did you see anyone? Anything?"

"It was terrifying . . . I feel . . . I feel that the blast is still happening, do you understand? The haze. The smoke, the bursting bricks . . ." her panic was real. The dharma-sevika saw that there was little use in continuing their conversation.

"For your own safety, we will keep you out of the news. If you ever need to talk about it, you can reach me." She sent her DD coordinates over as she got up to leave.

"Speak to no one else about this. Stay safe."

# 17
# A BETTER GANDHARVA

It was almost 12:30 p.m. at the Ministry of Finance and Salvation. The noisy commotion that accompanied milling crowds in the cafeteria, was gradually giving way to a more relaxed and familiar din. Famished colleagues pushed forward, jostling for space. People cut in front of him, grabbed their *thaalis*, and moved along. Gandharva was not particularly hungry and stood quietly in the line. The impending Disciplinary Committee Review ruled his thoughts.

Waiting in the queue, reminded him of his Vision, and the divine, glorious communique he had received. The Gandharva in front of him, made his choices at the food counter, as the vending robots scanned the trays and made necessary deductions automatically. It was difficult to spend more than 120 PBs for a hearty lunch. He stared at the options in the glass case.

Daal was mandatory—that day it was *urad* with *tadka*. He took a big whiff as it was ladled into his tray with precision. The duct connected to the roti-maker opened up and four hot bulbs of steamy Lucknow flour slid into his plate. The left lens of his DDs came alive with the notification of an incoming voice-call. He answered it in a dulcet tone. An unknown number usually meant that it was a senior Gandharva calling.

"Yes, how may I help you?"

"This is your Peet Gandharva. Come to meeting Room 7, in five minutes."

"I will be there."

He had no choice, but to complete the walk through the Annapurna archway. He quickly selected the *kaddoo* ki *sabzi*, *bharta*, *aloo chokkha*, and salad. He had a penchant for chillies, and requested the moustached pundit behind the counter, for some extra green *mirch*. Shastri ji believed in mirch. He didn't trust anyone who could not take chilli with their meals. It was believed that he had an iron stomach lining, holding the world record for eating the most chillies in a single sitting. He had also mandated that all food served in cafeterias be mashed, pulverized, or presented as some kind of paste. It was easier to digest in that form. Gandharva loved it. He sat down with his thaali and rushed through his meal, sucking up spoonful after spoonful, like a scoop-wheel. In less than two minutes, it was all gone.

He bolted across the bright and cheerful office. He ran past the screens showing videos of loggerhead turtles swimming with gorgeous Picasso Triggerfish and Powder Blue Tangs. He turned a corner past tall mirrors, pillars, and potted plants on his way to the meeting room. The floor plan of the office was meant to resemble a *yantra* and was a bit confusing. But they had all grown used to it. The *vaastu* of every office had been calibrated to facilitate its key functions. The Ministry of Finance and Salvation was designed to trap light, preventing its passage from one side of the building to the other. It symbolized the concentration and direction of wealth at the Centre. As a result, even some of the 'corner-offices' were windowless. No one seemed to mind, since it seemed to be working.

He took his slippers off outside meeting Room 7 and felt the spotless, warm, jute carpet under his bare feet. He enjoyed its gentle massage as he walked to the door. The air purifiers puffed moist clouds of Tulsi and Sandalwood. The Peet Gandharva was already present. He stood with his back to the door, looking at a poster of Shastri ji.

"Have a seat, Gandharva."

"Thank you."

"Had a good lunch?"

"Yes."

"Good. It has come to my notice that you have been summoned for a Disciplinary Committee Review this evening. What did you do?"

"It's a simple case of being in the wrong place at the wrong time. The Varaha were apprehending a criminal, I just happened to be there."

"They apprehended a very dangerous runaway."

"I have no clue who he is . . . was . . . he looked like a pariah."

"What do pariahs look like? Have you ever seen one before?"

"Only in training videos and school books. I did not talk to the man. They caught him and took him away."

"I see. I am a bit concerned for you, because Disciplinary Committee Reviews are usually quite serious and onerous."

"I have heard about them. I am not sure what to do in preparation . . ."

"Just tell them what happened as plainly as you have told me."

"In case I need someone to . . . you know Sir . . . to vouch for me, would you mind speaking to them?"

The Peet Gandharva turned around but did not answer. He played with the controls at the table in front of him and spoke.

"There is something else . . . of consequence . . ."

Gandharva moved closer to the edge of his seat.

"I have two pieces of good news for you. You might be wondering why we have steadily increased your workload over the past few weeks."

"It has not been that bad . . ."

"It will get heavier. We believe that you are performing well. The reason for this increase is that you will soon have another addition to your family. You will have a Vidur." The Peet Gandharva referred to his ChaturPad and looked up.

The sudden review with his grand senior started to make more sense now, as did the fresh workload.

"Oh . . ."

"Yes. Your wife Jyoti was visited by the IMP this morning. You have been picked as part of a pilot program to have three different children under the same roof. You will be the new, model Dvarcan family."

"I see—very good Gandharva ji."

"There is some more news, my diligent Aasmani Gandharva. The blast at the Industrial Complex this morning . . . your wife . . . she was near the bomb site."

He sank back in his chair. The shock was overwhelming. His nonchalant senior had just taken him through a dramatic sine of deep emotions, from fear to joy and then back again.

"Is she alright?"

"She is well."

"She never told me anything . . . she has not contacted me . . ."

"It is your duty, Gandharva, to look after her. Only real men are tested and I think the next year or so of your life, will be telling."

"Thank you Sir, is she really all right?"

"Yes, did I not mention that? She is perfectly fine. She was far away from the actual blast."

"Praise Krishna."

"Praise Krishna, yes!"

"I want to do better, Peet Gandharva ji. I want to be a better husband and a better father. I want you to know that."

"I am sure you do. Listen, if you manage to complete and submit all your pending reports by the end of this week, you will receive a bonus of 10,001 PBs. On top of that, we will award you another 5,001 Bindus. We also want you to step up and be the father you need to be."

"Will my kalaava be upgraded as well, Sir?"

"In due course, Gandharva. There is much to do before you go from Aasmani to *Hara*."

"Thank you Sir, thank you for the opportunity."

# 18
# RENDEZVOUS

"My time is extremely valuable, Vishvakarma. I hope you have a good reason for dragging me away from my work," Arjun Virdi sneered. The two men met in his office.

"I apologize, it's just that I needed to speak to you about a patient of mine." Vishvakarma was unaccustomed to surreptitious meetings. He had come to the Mahavidyalaya without the permission or knowledge of his superiors. He carried a small folder with him that he guarded with his life. He reached into it and handed the teacher a file.

"Do you know this man?"

Arjun Virdi casually looked at the contents and stopped at the photograph of SS6.2.

"This man! Why is he still alive? I tell you . . . these bureaucrats and their procedures. What is he doing at your lab?"

"He is being used as a subject in a trial for a new scientific breakthrough. They first brought him in before my time."

"He shouldn't be there. Is he cooperating with you?"

"That's the thing, Sriman. I don't know what to make of his behaviour. We've . . . how should I put this . . . we seem to have damaged him. Now, most of the time he's impossible, but once in a while he shows us glimpses of humanity. He won't say a word, not a lick of sense left in him. But he did do this—"

The scientist took a picture out from his pocket and held it out between his middle and index fingers. It was crisp card-paper like an old-school photograph. Ripped up bed sheets had been arranged in a pattern on the floor of SS6.2's cell. They spelt out the following message: 'Get Arjun Virdi S19 2083'.

"Were you at S19 in 2083?"

"I . . . I was."

"I guess he wants to see you. Is he an old student?"

"Something like that. I wasn't always a teacher, Vishvakarma."

"Will you visit him?"

"Why do you care?"

"The only sensible, clear, or intelligible thing he has done, is ask for you. Meeting him might benefit the experiment. It could change him—possibly make him more useful . . ."

"People do not change."

"How exactly do you two know each other?"

"Do you want me to report you—you snivelling parasite? This is of no consequence to you."

"I apologize. Please do let me know if you can see him. I will make the necessary arrangements ahead of your visit. Yes?"

"I'll let you know." The teacher kept the picture but had to give up the file.

Vishvakarma continued to yammer nervously, as Arjun Virdi walked him off the school-grounds. The pensive teacher ambled back to the sports fields, thinking about the young ones around him.

Dvarcan children started to show signs of their nature early. By the age of six or seven, the Vidurs were performing prodigious mathematics. This was expected. They were training to be innovators and thinkers. Those with a penchant for the humanities were guided towards working for the bureaucratic superstructure in the realm of public policy, advisory, and execution. They had to have their young minds opened at an early age, and were given all sorts of problems to think about, decipher, and solve.

The Kubers were more crass and transactional in the understanding of their subjects. They were much better at arithmetic and algebra. They were being taught to complete their sums, zeroing-in on definite 'answers' and 'quantifiable benefits'. Everything they learnt, had to have a known end, or use. Some of their tasks included monetizing and interpreting the first, second, and third degree impact of changes in industrial processes, in terms of PBs.

The Nakuls were gifted athletes. Watching them during their physical training sessions was a treat for any fan of sports. Arjun Virdi stopped at the sidelines as two teams slugged it out on a patchy football field. The ball was harder to control on the wet surface. It skidded through the muddy grass till a Nakul passed it with a single touch. It was a blistering counter-attack. A swift lob over the mid-fielders' heads, landed with a crack at the feet of an advancing striker. He fended off a close off-side call, and sprang quickly from the defenders' trap. No whistle. The other forwards followed in line and the goalkeeper steadied himself, starting to guess their next move.

"He won't shoot till he's closer . . . he's barely at the D," the fidgety keeper thought to himself.

"He will cut you!" the coaches bellowed from the washed-up benches.

A defender slid in under the attacker, he barely kissed the ball but managed to destabilize his mark into a pile of shin-guards and shrieks. There were no calls for a free-kick or a foul. There was no such thing as 'dangerous play'. The boys had to play like men and histrionics were not tolerated. The ruthless defender taunted and kicked his victim in the leg before re-joining the game.

The line between sport and war was blurry. Both were forms of organized aggression. Both followed some rules, required skills, strategy, and training. Both war and sports crowned winners and scorned losers. Little Nakul saw his opportunity and ran in to take the ball. He had eyes only for the goal. The keeper did not matter. He took a shot. It was a fluid, precise movement, like a musical interlude, a thing of beauty in the midst of carnage.

The ball flew like a rocket, inches away from the outstretched arms of the diving keeper. It pushed the net behind him outward, till it could extend itself no more, and then returned, bouncing across the slushy pitch. The keeper punched it away quickly, hoping to dispatch with it, his shame.

The coaches made a note of Nakul's performance. Arjun Virdi smiled as he added more tales of heroism to his records on the promising young prodigy.

"Good job, Nakul!"

Twenty-two little boys turned their heads to acknowledge his praise but only one of them knew it was for him. He kicked ahead like a little trooper and did a celebratory wave, as the mesmerized spectators chanted their name.

## 19
## FATHER TIME

Jyoti was not answering Gandharva's voice-calls. She messaged him back to say that she was all right. The brave Mata ji had gone right back to work.

"There is no better way to beat them, than to work harder than ever before." Gandharva was so proud of her. He beamed as he read her message. It was a quote from the Great Leader himself.

He felt the weight of the world on his feeble shoulders as he too, tried to put his mind and body to work. A puzzle appeared on his screen. He tried to focus on it but struggled. He decided to take a break and took the elevator down. He paced nervously around the office lobby.

It would be four weeks before he could mention the pregnancy to anyone. He knew that the next immediate phase was sensitive and complex, even though he had never been invited to be a part of the preparation. Even though he had two children, the entire pregnancy and birthing process was opaque to him. That was not what bothered him though. He was unsure if he wanted another son, let alone a cerebral and calculating Vidur. He'd known a few in his time and had never seen eye to eye with them.

Who was he to question the State, though? Planned pregnancies were the only pregnancies. Schools were mostly paid for and food was greatly subsidized, but it was still a decision that he would have liked to have made. The disconsolate parent-to-be wandered out of the office.

Giant walls of glass stretched from the floor to the heavens behind him as he arrived at a small square patch of grass. The Ministry of Finance and Salvation had a marvellous garden. He sat on a rock as notifications and report-requests flew in on his DDs. He tried his best to ignore them.

All his life, he had been an island, and unknown ships would sail up to him without the slightest warning. They'd dock and new folks would come ashore without seeking his permission. He'd never really felt close to young Nakul—they were too different and this made him strict and terse with the boy. Sometimes, he tried to be more like an Arjun to gain his son's respect. These endeavours usually devolved into awkward competitions. Even their most inconsequential discussions were now coloured with a tinge of resentment.

He felt that his sweet daughter's affections were more out of pity than love or respect. They had some nice times together and in her appraisals of him, she had been mostly kind and generous. But he still felt like a fraud. Could he really teach her anything? Soon his son too, would have a chance to assess and rate him. He was not looking forward to the results.

He wanted to ask Jyoti how she was. He almost called her again, but decided against it. His avid concern could be misconstrued as interference or disturbance. He empathized with her and felt sorry for her troubles, but there was not much else between them. He thought back to the day when he found out he was marrying her. The instruction was to show up at a temple hall at 3:00 p.m. No reason was given in the communication and he did not know that he was about to get married.

He showed up, in office attire with his satchel in hand. In his younger days, he fancied himself as an intellectual and a leader. Back then, quantitative analysts were comparable to Vishvakarmas and scientists. They were the cream of the crop, until the next generations were born. The Ministry for Community Development and Animal Husbandry was constantly perfecting their gene cocktails, picking and enhancing the best traits to produce the best Dvarcans.

At that time, Gandharva fell a few ranks in the hierarchy, and became a simple accountant in the eyes of the State. Assignments involving code-breaking and mathematical analysis were given to the new generation. School children were being raised to replace him and annihilate his legacy. But it was all for the greater good. With time, his career had lost some of its sheen and his hopes of being betrothed to a brighter lady had diminished. He had imagined long discussions on the meaning of scripture, happiness and love with an equal, but it was not to be. He stood in line with the other men who had been called to the temple that day.

None of them knew what was in store until a *pagdee*-tier showed up and set up his kiosk at the head of the line. He started wrapping grooms in long, red headgear. Gandharva waited patiently and braced himself for the experience. He had been taught that his wife would become his better half. He was to share everything with her. They were to work together to build a home suitable for children, suitable for a harmonious society. These teachings had been part of Civics, Moral Science, and Way of Life lessons from as far back as he could remember.

He had never felt any passion for a woman before, and sexual contact was out of the question. *No one in Dvarca felt any sexual urges.* They had been eradicated and outlawed, curtailed through piety, discipline, and surveillance. Society had evolved, and temptations of the flesh had gone the way of polar bears. Private parts were to be kept private at all times and they were treated with some degree of contempt.

Shastri ji had once said: "All carnal pleasures are impediments to salvation. The filthy West has failed because they are a gaggle of debauched, oversexed, distracted harbingers of bestiality, and other perversions." The *Kama Sutra* had been reinterpreted as an ancient but state-of-the-art lesson in group aerobics and exercises. Children were taught balancing acts, pad-locks, bridges, crouching tigers, ploughs, and lotus positions to improve flexibility, teamwork, and agility.

Relationships between men and women were all about respect. They demanded that every household ought to be a caring place. The closeness of sex had been substituted by other recommended activities. This was necessary to maintain a clean and *satvik* environment at all times. Guidelines were published to show couples and families how to show each other their love. The breeding of future generations no longer depended on fickle human passions of 'longing' or 'lust'.

On his way to the head of the line, to have his pagdee tied, Gandharva recalled being accosted by a very enthusiastic priest. The man had handed him a flier and proceeded to explain its contents.

*HOW TO SHOW YOUR NEW WIFE*
*THAT YOU LOVE HER*

*a) Set aside a monthly allowance for her (not more than 500 PBs to prevent excess).*

*b)* *Encourage her to fast for you (at most once or twice a week to maintain productivity).*

*c)* *Memorize and recite scripture for her.*

*d)* *Compliment her on her mind and soul.*

*e)* *Compliment her on her child-bearing ability.*

*f)* *Go to the temple together (at least twice a week).*

*g)* *Hold her hand in private (palm-on-palm only, not beyond the wrist).*

*h)* *Help her cook and clean (only if time permits and it does not interfere with your dharma).*

*i)* *Gift her flowers (only white jasmine).*

*j)* *Thank her and acknowledge her for being your partner.*

He read the primer a few times and before he knew it, he was at the head of the line. Three photographs were taken while he was having his pagdee tied. It was an unbelievably long cloth that the expert had wrapped around his head in just a few minutes. It was too tight and pushed his DDs down into his ears like knives. The turban covered his ears rendering him deaf, before an additional veil of jasmine flowers robbed him of his sight. He stumbled out of the chair, flier in one hand, zealous priest on the other, and walked slowly to the temple's *mandap*.

Other weddings were already underway. They performed the rituals in tandem and eight different holy men sang the hymns together. They were loud and their piercing *uchchaaran* soared over the hisses and eruptions of crackling fire. He adjusted his veil up and looked at the mandap. The ceremony before theirs was almost over and the *pheras* began. Fumes from the fire, chaotically tossed flowers and rice, loud relentless chanting, the thick scent of incense and the perambulations of the newly-weds hypnotized him. There were seven other men waiting in line with him and eight young brides stood sheepishly on the other side.

He wondered if the State had assigned a specific woman to

be his life partner. He wondered if it really mattered at that point. They were all strangers but they believed in the same things. He tried to see the bright side of the situation and hoped for the best. He was no longer considered a special talent; he was no longer going to be at the forefront of discovery and analytical reporting. Perhaps he was best suited for an average life after all. There would be nothing special about that day. He was just one of many.

Tiny robots attacked the mandaps immediately after the ceremony was over. They cleaned it up swiftly, removing all traces of dirt, renegade petals, and *samagri*. Even the furnaces at the centre of the circular mandaps were put out before a new flame could be lit for the next cohort. Gandharva and the other grooms were ushered in and asked to sit down on the floor. He looked about anxiously to see which woman would walk over and sit down with him.

He grew impatient as the women entered the area and walked about quite slowly. They were in thick and unwieldy marital dresses. They looked the same to him, a homogenous mass of red, gold, and glitter. One of them shuffled her way to his mandap and sat down. The priest spoke to her. Gandharva could not hear a word and leaned in.

"Sit up straight and fold your legs. We will start shortly." The priest's assistant ordered. Gandharva put the flier in his pocket after folding it carefully.

"There has been a mix-up. This is not the Jyoti for this Gandharva." The priest announced for the benefit of all present.

"Excuse me?" the nonplussed groom spoke out of turn, hoping to be added to the conversation.

"Sit straight. This is none of your concern. We are looking for the right Jyoti." The nosey assistant reprimanded him.

"Jyoti, Sector 16, Block 5B, #20-02, where are you?"

A slight woman from a different mandap raised her hand.

"What are you doing there? Your Gandharva is all the way over here!"

"I can go to her . . . she will not be able to get up and come over . . ." the gentleman offered.

"Stay where you are. There is a reason for our arrangement. There is a reason for everything. You do not know, because it is not your business to know. Come here, *suputri*, please, come and sit at this mandap."

She came over and they looked at each other through various veils and red-tinted DDs. That was his wife. She was the one he would live with, for the rest of his life. True to form, he could think of nothing clever to say at the moment, and ended up making a sound reminiscent of a yelp from a frightened street dog. She did not reply or reciprocate.

The first impression was a disaster. He did not know if he had managed to redeem himself through the years, and believed that that yelp, had in fact been the most meaningful thing he had ever said to his Jyoti.

# 20
# RUDRA MANICATA

Jyoti sat alone on a bench. It was the northernmost point of Grand Park. A gust of wind carried an orange-and-purple banner down the garden path towards her. The cloth had escaped the grasp of the grounds-men and now sprang and jolted at the mercy of a temperamental gale. They chased and shouted after it, as though it could hear them, struggling to end the drape's inconvenient adventure. Their efforts amused her at first, but they were getting too close for comfort.

There was no sign of her mysterious benefactors. It wasn't easy to keep a secret in Dvarca. She tried to calm herself by breathing deeply. The scent of sandalwood filled the night air like an invisible shroud. Marvels of modern botany crept up around her, moving busily.

Bright yellow climbers crawled over one another, squeezing their hosts, ridding the bushes of dirt and scum. The climbers, or *bel*, were originally parasites. With new research in the field of Utilitarian Biology, they had been improved to become protectors. They also secreted the scent of *chandan*, hence the name chandan bel. Jyoti pulled one of them up from the hedge behind her. It danced like a headless snake before writhing and falling dead in her hands. She caressed and studied its soft knots. Its intoxicating odour became too much to bear and she tossed it away.

The flying drape had found her. It wrapped around the far side of her bench and fluttered madly. It reminded her of a scene from the *Known Soldier*, a blockbuster film in which a fatally injured, young, handsome Dvarcan warrior cried out for his countrymen. A panting worker called out to her.

"Mata ji! Please, grab it . . ." He stopped and started.

"Hold it please!"

She sat still, looking up at the sky. There was another storm coming. The grey and pink clouds moved slowly and she tried to make sense of them. She thought she saw a giant solitary lotus morphing gradually into the shape of a quadruped. Perhaps, it was a bull. She took a photograph on her DDs. She was a picture of calm beside the chaotic, rapping, beating cloth that looked as though it were trying to engulf and swallow her. It was almost 6:00 p.m.

"RAINFALL IMMINENT. RETURN HOME." Her DDs flashed with the friendly warning. *They* were watching and tracking her.

Orange and purple streamers too, darted about all over, like electrocuted serpents fleeing their abode. A metal ladder fell down in the chaos, and some of the bamboo poles that had been installed seemed to be next in line. The makeshift gazebos were dismantling themselves. Hoardings for sponsored messages on standees and roller-banners lay strewn about.

'ONE NATION! ONE LANGUAGE!'

'NO MARG BUT NAVMARG!'

'EARN TRIPLE* PUNYA WITH OMNI'

She tugged at her plastic kalaava nervously as the gardeners and workers came closer. Six bars on it announced to the world that she was a Neel who could easily be ordered to assist in menial maintenance work.

"Why are you not helping us, Mata ji?" said an irate, sweaty man, wielding a hammer. He wrapped up the banner and glared at her angrily.

"I have to return home soon," she implored.

The site had been a checkpoint for the annual *Goumedha yagya*, a procession that featured a sacred white cow marching from one end of the country to the other. A frightened cow, decked out in flowers, paint, and shimmering gold accoutrements, made her way through the cordoned streets and roundabouts of Dvarca. Everyone greeted the beautiful emissary, making way for her to pass and mark Dvarca's territory. In the news-coverage, everything had looked bigger and cleaner.

Jyoti had to make her way to the narrow path and reach the south wall, to get to the Manicata bushes. The park was circular in shape, with four quadrants of greenery. High lamps left very little unseen or uncovered. She walked along the north-south trail. Surveillance cameras, attracted by motion, were distracted by the hardworking groundskeepers. A silicon broadsheet flew and wrapped itself around her. She peeled the *newspatra* off and saw the headline. "RECORD YEAR FOR . . ." something. She did not care and threw it in with the other celebratory scraps. She tried to act natural.

"YOU'RE ALMOST THERE." Finally a message from XX!

She looked over to see if there were people hiding, waiting for her. The shrubbery contorted and swayed into a *parivritta utkatasana* as she looked at the plants at her feet. Enormous grey leaves dangled and dipped under their own weight. She stroked them, their rough pores stuck to her fingers and she pulled away immediately. The roots were bulbous, growing out of the soil, as though they would burst at any moment. They were dark blue in colour and looked like a drenched sack of rotten potatoes. They twitched, expanded, and contracted, as though they were breathing. They'd been around for a long time, but she'd never seen one up close.

The *Rudra Manicata* were named both for Lord Shiva, the remover of sins, and the original *Gunnera Manicata* plants that were known for their untamed expanse. They had been genetically modified to use the fan-like spread of their enormous leaves as filters for the air.

They pulled filth and harmful chemicals straight from the atmosphere, stored them and broke them down into useful nutrients, before releasing them into the soil to enrich it. They also happened to be the largest middle-height plants in the world and much to her delight, Jyoti realized that she could be completely concealed if she hid under the leaves. She crouched and crawled under. It was like a punch in the face, a rude, sudden change from the overbearing perfume of chandan. The roots smelt like death.

"Thank you for coming," a man spoke from the shadows. He moved closer to her, to reveal his gaunt face in the sliver of light that broke through the thick foliage above them. Two others were behind him, one of them moved closer to the opening, peering out at the Park. He wore a pair of strange looking DDs.

"Who are you?"

"You probably have a lot of questions, Jyoti. We have many questions too," he had a wispy moustache and his teeth were crooked.

"My name is Abhimanyu. This is Dhruv. Faiz over there will warn us if we need to cut this short."

"What kind of a name is Faiz?"

He pulled his kurta collar down and revealed a serial number tattooed under his neck. She knew at once that he was a pariah. Her mouth and eyes widened.

"Do not scream. I saved your life. I was at BB5 when it blew up."

"Did you do it? Did you blow it up?"

"Is that what you think?" Dhruv spoke.

"I don't know."

"No"

"Then what were you doing there?"

"Watching."

"Who blew it up?"

"Them, your Government. The Varaha . . . we have footage of this. But it will take some effort to retrieve it. We had to save you and in the process, we lost some of our equipment."

"How convenient that your proof is damaged."

"It's the truth. The Varaha planned and carried out the bombing."

"Why?! That is absurd. Why would they do such a thing?"

"To keep fear alive. To continue to control you."

"Everything they do is to protect us . . . from animals like you! Are you not a Caliphite? You're clearly not a Dvarcan . . ."

Manyu hung his head and looked back up at her. Dhruv sighed.

"We are Dvarcans forced out of Dvarca."

She realized that they were sitting in slush. The stench of the Manicata roots choked her, curling in her lungs, giving corporal form to her growing discomfort.

"What did you do to my DDs?"

"We fixed them. We also took down your coordinates, to be able to message you. You can message us too," Dhruv reminded her.

"Why would I want to do that?"

"You may need to," Faiz turned and looked at her.

"I don't understand . . ."

"What did you see in there?"

She hesitated. "They were . . . they were all unconscious. Had someone poisoned them?"

"In a manner of speaking."

"I don't know . . . I don't want to know any more . . ." she started to rise.

Dhruv stopped her and thrust a parcel into her hands. She pushed it away. He leaned in and spoke in a menacing whisper.

"You saw what was in there. More than a hundred people died. You almost died with them. No inquiry, no evidence, it is blamed on shadows serving the Caliphate. Are you not the least bit curious to find the truth?"

She looked at the parcel in her hands. It was neatly wrapped and quite compact.

"Keep it safe. It is for your eyes only."

"What is it?"

"Contraband. Be careful."

She watched them walk out on the thin trail along the edge of the park. With quick and deliberate steps, they soon disappeared into the black night.

# 21
# FIVE WISE MEN

'GIVE YOUR BODY TO WORK. YOUR MIND WILL FOLLOW.'

A popular poster flickered over Gandharva's DDs as he pondered over the printout of his last puzzle. There seemed to be a large number of primes in it. He exhausted all arithmetic and geometric progressions. Trigonometry too, was failing. It was a sequence he had not seen before and in frustration, his grip on the piece of paper tightened. Perhaps a change of scenery would help him clear his mind.

He went to the window and looked down at the people outside. The new Central Karma District was still under construction and his Ministry was to spend a few more months at the old Parliamentary quarters. The massive grey edifice in front of him was covered in memorabilia, posters, and pamphlets. The administration had decided to leave the old buildings as they were, as protected monuments. The national colours, orange and purple, found favour with the masses and had been splayed generously everywhere. Slogans of troth and truth in pithy language adorned the walls with the most prominent words, forming an arresting image of their own: 'MULTICULTURALISM IS DEAD'.

It was time for him to make his way to the Disciplinary Committee Review. He took the printout of the puzzle with him, hoping to solve it later. He picked up his khaadi satchel, said a prayer, and walked out of the office.

"Dvarca, my Dvarca. Oh Dvarca. Dvarca dear." His mind ran riot as he worked through his explanation for the events of the previous night. He was walking fast and before a single rehearsal of his sad but true story could be completed, he had already reached the main boulevard. He stood at the third junction on Shanti-path, facing the Central Command offices. The media had been reporting on the construction and development of the new offices in assiduous detail. Every new foundation, floor, and lamp post was described and celebrated. No development went overlooked and everything seemed to be going as planned.

The hope was to build skyscrapers that disappeared into the clouds. Red bricks the size of buses, and cement vats the size of homes lined the streets. It was unclear why they had already shifted some functions to the new offices, in the midst of all the commotion. He walked across the street and sentries started checking his identity. This was the Central Command. They were expecting him, and he was waved in by three chirpy robots and a gruff human guard.

He was a tough greying Arjun, slightly hunched over with years of duty. He still looked like he could have snapped Gandharva in two, like a biscuit. Arjuns were an early iteration of modern day Nakuls. The main improvement, as per public records, was that Nakuls were designed to be better team-players and seemed to be content with blending into a crowd. Individual glory meant little to them.

He walked up the staircase and entered a hallway of bright-white light. He smiled into the photo-log and received a number on his DDs, before heading to the room assigned to him. There was a queue to see the Disciplinary Committee and two men sat outside, waiting in the corridor.

One of them was in a bad way, shifting and sliding in his chair, whimpering as he stuck his head between his legs like an overstrung ostrich. The other man was the exact opposite, a picture of calm, staring into space, like a preoccupied pelican. For some reason, he reminded Gandharva of one of his old Visions. What was it? Was he trying to convince this man to do something? Were they in the midst of battle? "Pardon me, Mahoday, but have we met before?" Gandharva asked.

"I doubt it . . . but then again, I have a very common face," the man chuckled.

"What do you do?"

"Hara Narad, thespian, pleased to meet you," he offered a half-hearted namaskar.

"Aasmani Gandharva, bureaucrat . . ."

There was a moment of silence, in which the two men contemplated the need for further conversation.

"Why are you here? If you don't mind my asking . . ."

"Apparently I talk too much," the actor said, with a smile.

"Good, you are on time. Come with me please." A man had emerged from the DC chamber with a ChaturPad, they had not noticed him until he stood right beside them. He asked the unnerved ostrich and the unflappable pelican to wait. Gandharva looked up at the eye in the sky. There was a well-advertised PB demerit for jumping a queue.

"Are you sure, Mahoday? These men have been here longer than I . . ."

"Please Mahoday, don't lecture the Disciplinary Committee

about the rules," he slapped Gandharva on his back and urged him forward like a contestant on the *Hour of Honour.* Gandharva entered the chamber with caution.

Disciplinary Committees comprised of five wise citizens, picked from different walks of life. They were keepers of the law and representatives of the people. Gandharva was asked to sit down on a low wooden stool. He found himself at the centre of a circular room, as though he were at the bottom of a well. A thick white light hung over his head and on the side, like a lazily conferred consolation prize, sat a potted Tulsi plant. He folded his palms in a gesture of benediction, and bowed his head as a mark of contrition.

A shutter rose above him, close to the top of the well. It peeled upwards with the sound of a mechanical elephant trumpeting its master's arrival. A hall behind glass windows stretched all around the round edge of the room. It was filled with red light and he could not see much inside it. He wiped his DDs and strained his eyes to make out five torsos silhouetted behind the glass.

No matter how he moved, at any time, there would be at least two of them watching him from behind. One of them was possibly a Varaha. Two had thick bushy moustaches. The fourth gentleman leaned to one side, forming a judgmental triangle with his body. The last person, a mysterious man with no telling features, sat like the portrait of a sage on a hill-top. He turned to the others and they exchanged a nod.

A microphone curled out from under Gandharva's stool and he was instructed to make all his statements directly into it. He adjusted it and brought it closer, holding it with his left hand.

"*Adarniya* DC Mahoday, pranaam."

"Pranaam Aasmani Gandharva of Sector 17, Block 8A."

"Thank you for being punctual."

Gandharva was disarmed by their politeness. The two men,

who had spoken until now, sounded identical. They were the moustached twins. They both sounded old and were possibly Watchers in their final ashram. He felt jealous of the mysterious man, who at such a young age seemed to have climbed so high. He had such poise and command, without uttering a single word, even the elders seemed to follow his lead.

"We would like to ask you a few questions about last night."

"Am I in trouble, Mahoday?"

"Should you be?"

"No, I was not told the subject of this review. I know what triggered it and I was concerned . . . that is all."

A holographic reconstruction of the previous night shot out above him. Gandharva saw himself step out from under a tree in the pouring rain. It was like a terrifying documentary film and he almost called out to his thin and wavy avatar, to not do anything incriminating. The footage was a bit shaky on account of the heavy rain. Gandharva's milky figure stopped after walking a bit and looked up as though he had heard something. The demonstration was paused and it flickered between two adjacent frames.

"Were you expecting someone?" a voice bellowed from the red chambers above.

"No Mahoday, not at all."

They allowed it to play on. The binaaydi ran straight into him while making his escape. Gandharva felt the pain of the impact all over again. In his mad rush last night, he had forgotten all about the bruises on his chest and knee. The two men fell on top of each other in a clumsy ball.

"Did he say anything to you?"

"As I mentioned to the esteemed Varaha last night, I had nothing to do with that man."

"The binaaydi."

"Yes, the binaaydi. There was no sense in his words, just fruits and vegetables."

"Did he give you anything? A letter, a code, perhaps a piece of cloth? Why did you not raise an alarm on your DDs at this point? Why did you not report a man whom you could see, was a pariah?"

"Beg your pardon Mahoday, I did not know that he was a pariah. I could barely see his face."

They froze the video-hologram above him and spun it around. They enhanced and magnified their faces. It was all still: block-like and pixelated.

"Did you not see at this point that he was a beef-eater? A pervert? He had no DDs? Did his tattered clothes not arouse suspicion?"

"Were you temporarily blind? O' Gandharva?"

"No Sir, I did not notice anything . . . it was pouring and I was . . . disoriented . . ."

"Have you read *My Road to Navmarg*?"

"Of course Sir, many times."

"Can you tell us what it has to say about vigilance?"

"The dharmic man must forever be vigilant, watching over his shoulder for signs of terror. Evil manifests itself in many ways, most commonly as pariahs. They are everywhere and they are out to harm us. It is therefore, the duty of every able-bodied man and woman to be on high alert at all times, and look out for signs of these demons."

"Well said. What is the easiest way to identify a pariah?"

Gandharva struggled. There was a common mnemonic, but it escaped him. He knew he was in trouble now.

"I apologize. I cannot claim to remember all the signs of suspicion off the top of my head."

"Then what kind of a citizen are you?"

"Weak!"

"Yes! He is soft."

"I am weak . . . I am soft," the bureaucrat agreed.

"Yes. At least you admit it." The committee saw this as a victory.

The holographic reconstruction sped along to the capture of the pariah. The Varaha started to beat him, and now Gandharva could see what he had missed the previous night. He looked away in disgust.

"You seem bothered by their actions. Why is that, Gandharva?"

"Mahoday, I am a bureaucrat. What would I want from violence? I know the pariah deserves it. But . . . I can't bear to see it."

"The violence is in your name. To save you. You must support and cheer."

"I agree. I apologize for not cheering when they broke the pariah's face."

There was a moment of silence. The holographic recreation continued to the point where they started questioning him. They had pushed him around too. He remembered it, now that it was in front of his eyes.

"Why were you in their way?"

"I was not, they came to me. They had to, being good investigators. They asked me why I was there."

The Committee was losing patience. "We know why you were there. We will not go into the other irresponsible, rash, and harmful things that you did last night. I think you know what we mean . . ."

"Yes Sir . . ."

"I have heard enough from the bureaucrat."

"I agree, this man is not a threat. He is just weak, overweight, and slow-witted."

The five wise men discussed something inaudibly. They shut the hologram with a swift gesture and the shutters started to come down, as they announced their judgement, over the sound of the mechanical elephant trumpeting in reverse.

"Aasmani Gandharva of Sector 17, Block 8A. Here is your penance: 12,501 PBs fine for being a nuisance during an investigation conducted by the esteemed Varaha Brigade, 7,501 PBs fine for harassing Inter-Sector sentries and V-lab assistants, 2,501 PBs fine for being soft, bloated, and ignorant. You must also undergo a compulsory re-training on Pariah Identification, the cost of which shall also be borne by you. You must schedule it at the earliest possible time. That is final. We thank you for your cooperation and hope to never see you again." With the end of that damning and costly imprecation, the shutters too, came to a halt.

On his way out, Gandharva pressed the button to call the elevator. The doors opened and he got in quickly. It was going up instead of down, and he found himself stuck with a pretentious Vidur who was reading a newspatra. Not to be outdone, Gandharva pulled out his printout of the puzzle and started circling numbers randomly, as though he were solving some important problem. The doors opened and the Vidur left. It was the twenty-first floor. Gandharva had never seen the view from that high and stepped out for a quick look.

Vast windows framed the ever-growing metropolis below. It was going to be another rainy night. He felt small and insignificant, and leaned his head on the glass, breathing condensation on it. He quickly pulled the sleeve of his kurta into his hand and rubbed the surface clean. It shone, and he could see the streets below, making zigs of zags.

He then had one of those rare, inexplicable moments of inspired insight. He held up the piece of paper with the puzzle and pressed it against the glass. He had always been so focussed on unravelling the mathematics and discovering functional relationships that he had never realized that the puzzles themselves, resembled the bird's eye-view of a street, or even an entire city. It was just a strange hypothesis, but it opened up his mind to a host of possibilities that he had never considered before.

# 22
# ARE YOU DEVOUT, WITHOUT A DOUBT?

*The images of men toiling in military fatigues took to the screen.*

"Who built the bridges on our mission to take the North? OMNI."

*The shadow of a drone inched towards a bearded man wrapped in flowing bedouin garb as he raised his hands in surrender.*

"Who created the X360, the world's greatest inspection drone? OMNI."

*Footage of a temple in the middle of the Ganga River.*

"Who rescued the *Mahakali* temple in Kanpur? OMNI."

*Annapurna men delivered food in stacks of packets.*

"Who ensures the food and drinking water supply for all our citizens? OMNI."

"Who puts God and Country first? OMNI."

*Their logo was simple: just the Om symbol within an Ohm symbol.*

"OMNI, proud employer of over half-a-billion Dvarcans. We serve with pride."

The famous blatherskite continued after the short ad break in the broadcast. He was in the middle of the stage with the giant OMNI logo behind him. An interview was underway.

"Welcome back to the *Hour of Honour*, I am speaking with Doctor Vidur Ramanathan, Chief of Research and Development at OMNI. Tell us Doctor, what is nationalism to you?"

"It means putting God and Country first, in all our thoughts and actions. Through these two, we are stronger. Through them, we can fight any threat. Even lone tigers have little sway with hordes of jackals."

"Who are the jackals to our tigers?"

"The Caliphites and their cronies, of course. They want to overrun the world and establish their flag as the masthead for a dark new dawn. I believe Shastri ji was chosen to protect us from them. Had we not united, we would all be subjects of the Caliphate, converts, and slaves with no home or culture. We would have been orphaned."

"What new measures have been put in place to help us put God and Country first in all that we do?"

"We have recently introduced the polling method to seek citizen reports about suspicious activities. We are also working on a new form of therapy that will transform the nature of even the most hard-nosed fundamentalist Caliphite. It is designed to show them that Navmarg is the one true way."

"That sounds very interesting. How does it work?"

"I am not at liberty to say, our top minds are still working on it. I can only tell you that the preliminary tests have been very promising."

"Doctor Vidur Ramanathan, I thank you deeply, for sharing your thoughts with us, you have certainly put God and Country first in your life and you are an inspiration to us all. Viewers, that concludes our opening segment for today's *Hour of Honour*, we shall continue right after these messages from OMNI."

***

*Darkness swept across the screen and the voice-over began.*

"Who brings you unstoppable electricity, 24 hours a day, 15 days a cycle? OMNI!"

*Smiling, happy faces of a Dvarcan family revelling in the joy of glowing tube-lights and sleek hanging bulbs. The scene changed to a view of three giant, metallic cylinders towering over the horizon, in the middle of a desert, shimmering in the sunlight.*

"Who made the Sun the backbone of Dvarcan energy? OMNI!"

*The last scene-change revealed hard-working professionals laying integrated chips, pouring colourful liquids in and out of test-tubes, yanking enormous levers, and typing together in front of screens.*

"For God and Country, who is constantly innovating new ways to keep you smiling? OMNI!"

It was one of their shorter advertisements. Jyoti wondered why OMNI needed to advertise: they were as pervasive as the slogan, 'For God and Country'. She worked for them too, and they were already inseparable from the welfare of the citizens of Dvarca. She realized that Gandharva was staring at her, instead of watching television.

"I am alright, really."

He smiled at her and wanted to hold her hand (only at the palm). The children leaned back between them and he turned his attention to the *Hour of Honour.* The programme resumed with a *Patriotic and Pious* quiz. The three participants were a farmer's wife Sharmila, an Aasmani journalist Narad and an army man Arjun. The orotund anchor began in earnest.

"What makes Dvarcan culture the greatest in the world?"

"Our ancient customs, our traditions," answered the farmer's wife, to a round of applause.

"Our adherence to values and a clear definition of culture makes us great," said the journalist with a knowing smile.

"We protect our people from evil influences. This has made us great." The stadium erupted with applause. Arjun was immediately a crowd favourite, with his broad chest and impressive moustache. The other two contestants looked small, standing beside his towering presence.

They then proceeded to reveal an image on the screen. It was a white woman, wearing a top with narrow strings holding up a thin cloth that squeezed her breasts, tight pants that hugged her and enormous dark glasses that were partially obscured by her unkempt hair. She held a cigarette in one hand and a bottle of brown liquid in the other. She was laughing.

"What do you see?"

A barrage of statements followed like a volley of grenades.

"*Haw ji haw!* Shamelessness."

"Promiscuity."

"Disrespect for the right way. Women should not dress like this. It is deplorable. In the West, they are all like this, you see. They have no values and they have no morals. They are addicted to pornography, alcohol, drugs, cigarettes, and they worship fame and fortune. Their lives are complicated by unnecessary things!"

"Does she have any values?"

"She thinks she is free, but she is actually a slave to consumerism and fashion!"

"From her smile I can tell she has done dirty things, very dirty things."

"She most likely has no family values. You know how they address their parents by the first name? You know how they leave their parents to die in old-age-homes? They are a disgrace to the human race. I almost wish the Caliphate had wiped them out."

"What else, what else can you infer from this picture?"

"Those pants! *Apchaaram! Paap!* Where is the modesty? Why must we all see the roundness of her behind? She must be a prostitute, to advertise herself in this shabby manner!"

"I have seen these people before, being a journalist. She is most likely, some kind of demonic succubus who dances for the pleasure of men, luring them into submission and then stealing their life essence."

"Why is she wearing dark glasses? She is perhaps ashamed to look at us. She knows in her heart that her life is empty," said Sharmila through her DDs.

"Maybe she is hiding from someone? Her ex-husband?"

"Yes, yes, divorce is a major part of western culture. There is no basis for marriage but lust. How can you base your life decisions on whimsical longing?"

"I think it is absurd that we are even giving her that much credit. As if she could get a man to accept her as a wife!" the farm-lass sneered again.

"It is possible. They have no governance, no long-term thinking. It is all about instant gratification. Marry now, alimony later. In every field of life, their passions are unchecked. What will happen then? Men will become animals, of course!"

"I think you are right. She is definitely a divorcee. There is age in her arms, see how they sag? No one needs to see that, but she is right here in front of us, flaunting her semi-nude cow-stranglers."

"She is overweight. See how she has let herself go? It must be all the Texan beefs. Is that right? Beefs, plural?"

"I have no way of knowing, but I see how everything about this picture is linked to excess."

"The liquid she is carrying, is that alcohol?"

"Yes, yes I believe it is alcohol."

"Demon piss!"

"Mind altering *madira*!"

"Filthy, fetid, ugliness!"

*"Why is it such an important part of western culture? This demon piss, as you call it?"*

"It all goes back to the same problem. Why do they drink? Why do they smoke? To forget about their empty lives! To free themselves from concern for a few hours! With no guidance and no purpose, would you want to be lucid all day? It would be excruciating, not that I am defending her behaviour," the journalist presented his theory.

"She might have been drinking for some time. It is night time in the photo, maybe she is looking for someone to intercoursalize her and then leave. Is that right? To intercoursalize?"

"It is wrong to intercoursalize."

"No, I meant the word, is that a word?"

"The time of the day does not matter to these people. They do anything they want, anywhere, any time."

"Even at the time of morning prayers?"

"Let me check. I now request the research team to assist us with this query. Do the people of the Hedonesia, intercoursalize each other, at any time of day?"

A clock appeared on the screen, to show that the research team was working behind the scenes. The anchor was ecstatic.

"Yes! It is true. We do have reports stating that these people may indulge in carnal pleasures at any time of the day. There is no stopping them from doing it. I am being told that the technical term is horniness. This will have to be taken with a pinch of salt, it is just off their own dark-webs."

"Horniness. How apt! Makes them sound like mindless faunae. No different from goats, or rhinos."

"At least animals do it to reproduce. The horniness of Hedonesians does not always mean the continuation of life. It may well just be a revolting romp of passing desire."

"Filthy, filthy, filthy."

"Look at her lipstick! She must have had many abortions."

"It is bright red and shining, though one side has been smudged. Do you think she fell down?"

"She might have fallen down, she might have mouthed a man earlier. Who can say about this creature? This abomination! Am I right?"

The crowd had been gasping and clapping with delight all along. The 'astute observations' were met with widespread approval. The picture had probably been taken from one of those public electronic forums where people from the West shared their private lives. It had provided fodder for the *Hour of Honour* before. Jyoti imagined what it would be like to be silly for some time. Perhaps she was still shaky from the explosion. It was remarkable how the contestants on the *Hour of Honour*, with some helpful nudging and winking from the host, had reduced an ordinary woman to a representative of cultural failings. They had envisioned her entire background and future with a single image that would have lasted less than a second of her life. Then it became clear to her. To them, pariahs were just walking-talking representatives of stereotypes, whether they liked it or not. It continued:

"How would you cure her?"

"Oh there is no cure. No cure for this. We would have to go nuclear."

"Nuclear! There's a thought."

"Whatever you say about the people of Hedonesia, the entire north-western hemisphere has been unfriendly to us. If you look to recent history, they did try to be strategic allies to us and Canaan. God give strength to our brave brothers on the other side of the

Mesopotamian ugliness. The Hedonesians tried to support us, but they grew weak. They lost their way and their bags of money and the 'beacon of hope' started to diminish."

"They overspent on the wrong fronts and even fuelled a lot of the 'uprisings'. Back when the Caliphate was still inchoate, they tried to buy friends. It did not work because radicals only used the 'new commerce' to drive their own agenda. They may befriend you at first, but eventually they will stab you in the back. The Hedonesians never attacked us, but they did appease the enemy at our expense. I see no reason to save them from themselves."

The army-man's message of merciless blame struck the crowd like a lightning-bolt, and they rose up in ovation. The host too, clapped and cheered. The journalist however, had this to say: "I think there are ways to cure them." The crowd was shocked by this rare divergence of opinion.

"I judge and ridicule them the same way as you do—I think that is abundantly clear. But I do believe that we are a compassionate Nation. If someone comes to us for help, we will offer them our hand in friendship. But, they have to be willing. They have to take the first step to start a new life. In the recent few months, I have written three articles in the *Jagran*, about ways in which outsiders and pariahs can be reformed.

These ways were mentioned earlier on this very programme too, by the esteemed Head of our Research and Development wing, Dr. Ramanathan. We can save this woman, but she has to be willing to learn about Navmarg. She must submit wholeheartedly to the one true way. Only then can we find out what sins she has committed in the past, weigh her current life in the same balance, and learn how to correct her heavenly debts. There is a way." He had won them over, they felt pity for the woman in the photograph, and with the warmth of their hearts, managed to make place for her appalling choices and errant ways.

"I suppose we will hear more about this way in the near future?"

"I hope so."

The Government had always claimed to be at the forefront of science and technology, leading the charge with OMNI. Jyoti looked over at her family and saw how pleased they were with the way the show made them feel. A sense of superiority had become part of the one true way, perhaps unofficially.

They waited for the final act of the show, where an elderly Vanaprasthi gentleman with diabetes, was about to demonstrate his love for Dvarca by eating 64 different types of sweets, spanning all Sectors of the Nation. As a reward for his feat, he had been promised a new pancreas.

# 23
# DOMESTIC BLISS

Jyoti walked around the room, and went about her usual chores and ablutions before bed. Gandharva was already lying down, with his back to her. He felt her eyes on him and turned around to see her enter the bathroom. He adjusted his cold pillow and mulled over the different ways in which he could talk to her. There was so much he wanted to say.

How was she? Was she hurt at all? Did she want to be left alone? She looked fine, peaceful as ever. He wanted to reassure her that she was a good mother and a model citizen. It was quite obvious, given the faith the State had shown by giving her a third baby. Gandharva's words would add very little. In most ways, he was the third wheel.

"Would you like some water?"

"Yes, please."

He answered quickly and shifted about on the bed awkwardly. She had spoken to him with such ease.

"Would you like some water?" she had asked, while he'd spent hours thinking of ways to break the ice. It was nice of her, he thought. She brought a bottle from the fridge and placed it on his bedside. Her expressionless face matched her steady and calm demeanour. He didn't want to upset her with talk about his Disciplinary Committee Review or the fines. That would only make her more anxious. The refresher course in Pariah Identification too, would only worry her about his status as an Aasmani Dvarcan. Even his prospects at the office, after the discussion with his Peet Gandharva, were not worth sharing. He didn't want her to know that he was up for a promotion. Not yet. What if it didn't work out?

"Is the fridge okay?"

That's all he could muster.

"It is."

"And the TV?"

"It's fine, why?"

"No I was just . . . thinking of . . . just be careful with the remote."

"Be careful with the remote?"

"Yes, it's a delicate piece of equipment."

"The remote is fine!"

"I know I know, it is fragile and one needs to keep it properly."

She looked at him incredulously, before huffing and turning her back to him. She curled up like a knot around her pillow at the far edge. He couldn't help thinking that he had pushed her there. His efforts to be a good husband had all come to naught. Once again, his personal dictionary failed him and even simple compliments seemed inconstructible. The nebulous cloud of unspoken, half-spoken, and misspoken words between man and woman grew larger. It swallowed him whole and churned him around, leaving him confused and disappointed with his attempts to communicate with his partner for life.

"I might get . . . closer."

"Closer?"

"To the Lal kalaava."

She stayed where she was.

"Congratulations."

"Yes, I heard only this morning. I could have gotten a big bonus today but I could not finish all my work."

"Why?"

"Had to . . . had to come away."

"You'll do it tomorrow."

"Yes."

"Are you . . . ?" the incomplete question hung in the air like a lobbed ball between two reluctant fielders, each one hoping that the other would commit and go for the catch.

"Am I . . . ? Familiar with the TV remote handbook and manual?" Jyoti quipped.

"No . . . Are you feeling better?"

"Yes."

"After this morning . . ."

"Yes."

"Good. I am glad nothing happened to you. And . . . and our Vidur . . . it is wonderful news."

"It must be."

She waited till he fell asleep and crept quietly to the outer bathroom. She could see Baba's open umbrella, outside, sitting at a bench. It was a good job for the old folks in their Vanaprastha aashram, watching out for everyone else. She might have to do it some day. She closed the shutters and sat down on the floor. She had hidden Abhimanyu's parcel under her sari by strapping it to her thigh. She unwrapped it and found a small black device. It was no more than a screen with headphones attached. She put them on and then pressed 'Play'.

A jangling, thumping sound of electric strings rose and engulfed her. With it, started a video, which showed headlines and news cuttings. She did not recognize the sources. The sound was muffled and unclear, as though it were emanating from behind a thick curtain.

'LAND OF EXPLOITATION AND TORTURE: DVARCA'

There were pictures of fences and Arjuns guarding them. There were graphic photos of people being beaten, water-boarded, and burnt.

It was unlike anything she had seen or heard before. The song galloped along and a gentleman breathed and cooed, as all the instruments came together. A non-*bhajan* had started and she was listening to it, in disbelief. The sound was almost atonal at times but it kept up its unsettling allure. She sat up and listened.

*'Give me one more chance and you'll be satisfied,*
*Give me two more chances, you won't be denied . . . '*

'THOUSANDS MURDERED IN STATE PURGE'

The article carried images of a cavalcade of jeeps surrounding burning buses. People ran in all directions. They all looked Dvarcan to her.

*'Well my heart is where it's always been, my head is somewhere in between*
*Give me one more chance, let me be your lover tonight*
*You're the real thing*
*Yeah the real thing*
*You're the real thing.'*

'SHASTRI'S DVARCA FIGHTS ISIS.'

Scenes from a war zone, with planes conducting air-raids on bunkers, bases, and black flag-bearing Caliphites.

*'Even better than the real thing.'*

She could not believe her eyes or ears. The headlines were from foreign newspapers, over the last many years. The gentleman singing had a cocksure, drunken, soothing voice. The words meant nothing to her—they were in an alien language—perhaps from some place in Hedonesia. They were not about God and Country though, she could tell. It did not sound like something from the Caliphate. It had little to do with the Orient. This was definitely something that came from the Far West.

'LETTERS FROM DVARCA: I REFUSED TO KILL MY OWN.'

There was a picture of Dvarcan army men who had surrendered their weapons.

*'Even better than the real thing.'*

There was a softer interlude that allowed the song to die down a bit before rising up again, stronger than ever. The whole video lasted little more than three-and-a-half minutes and the power indicator was close to fading-out. Her pulse was already somewhere in the stratosphere. She had never seen anything like it before.

"DETECTION: ELEVATION IN HEART RATES. PLEASE REPORT"

She rushed to pack away the player. It fell and suffered a crack. Before she knew it, there was a voice-call on her DDs. She answered and an elderly Vanaprasthi on the other end of the line was doing his night duty as a Watcher. Such calls were not uncommon. Cardiac irregularities in the middle of the night were indicative of deviant, or even terrorist behaviour.

"Is everything okay, Mata ji?"

"Yes, thank you. Everything is alright. I was just . . ."

"Yes?"

"I had a nightmare about pariahs in our fair city."

The Watcher understood this.

"Have no fear Mata ji, we will fight the phony phantasm with powerful prayer!" He asked her to get comfortable and started to read her the *Hanuman Chaalisa.*

*"Jai Hanuman gyan gun sagar,*
*jai Kapish tihun lok ujagar."*
Victory to thee, oh Hanuman,
ocean of wisdom and excellent qualities,
victory to thee oh monkey-god,
who illuminates all the three worlds with your glory . . .

As he read from the holy text to ward off evil and dispel all fear, a new message from XX appeared on Jyoti's DDs.

"HOPE YOU LIKED IT. AFTER MONTHS OF TRYING, WE FINALLY FOUND A WAY TO BREAK THROUGH THE FIREWALLS. WE WERE ABLE TO TOUCH THE DARK FOREIGN WEB. THE SONG YOU HEARD, ATTRIBUTED TO A 'U2', WAS THE FIRST THING WE FOUND. THE ARTICLES AND REPORTAGE FOLLOWED. THIS IS ONLY THE BEGINNING."

"Who translated the news stories? Are they true?" she messaged back.

"WE DID. THEY ARE ALL TRUE. IN OUR BID TO FIGHT THE SICKNESS OF THE CALIPHATE, WE SEEM TO HAVE LOST OUR WAY. WE BROKE OURSELVES IN A BID TO BREAK THEM. BUT THE HOPE OF A DEMOCRATIC, OPEN, AND INCLUSIVE COUNTRY IS NOT DEAD. WE NEED THE TRUTH TO BE KNOWN, TO FREE AND SAVE DVARCA."

*"Vidyavan guni ati chatur,*
*Ram kaaj karibe ko aatur."*
You are the repository of learning, virtuous and accomplished,
always keen to carry out the work of Shri Ram . . .

"This is all deeply unsettling. It is hard to believe . . ."

"I COULD NOT AGREE MORE."

"Why did you give this to me?"

"BECAUSE YOUR EYES ARE OPEN. YOU HAVE SEEN THE LIES YOURSELF."

# 24
# *ALIBAN

SS6.2 was in recovery mode. The Vishvakarmas had him under observation behind heavy security at their lab. There was no contact or follow-up from Arjun Virdi and the young scientist had given up on the prospect of a meeting. Perhaps it was for the best.

The subject, entertaining as ever, had an odd habit of walking in circles and shouting. He would do this only when he felt that he was alone. Sometimes he would dance. The scientists gave him a new set of clothes that he promptly wore inside-out and front-side back.

"Time is running out."

"I heard him singing the other day. It was actually . . . pleasant. There was a tune."

"What was the melody?"

"An old song. I wonder where he could have heard it . . ."

The Vishvakarmas pondered over the actions of the poor madman and tried to piece together his past. He had become a fascination for them both.

They tried different experiments to see what sort of stimuli might relieve him from his usual wordless paranoia. Music seemed to work. Anything without percussion pleased him. His head would swim, dip, and bob like a buoy at sea. He'd smile and look up at the ceiling with the sure gaze of a Watcher studying something intently. There was nothing up there, but he followed it with such attention, that at times the scientists were convinced that he could see things that they could not. The slightest sound of drums would cause him to convulse and hide. He'd raise his arms up to ward off an invisible hammer. He'd swat and snap and gnash his teeth, till they stopped the song.

Films too had a similar effect on him. They showed him a short clip of bombs being dropped on a town during an air-raid. He giggled and rejoiced. In his excitement he shouted his favourite phrase at them, at the top of his lungs.

"Shahtooti anjeer!"

"Yes, Shahtooti anjeer, well put."

"C-C-C-Caliban lives!"

"Do you mean Taliban?" Was he starting to make sense?

"Shahtooti anjeer, Shahtooti anjeer. Bombs away!"

He threw himself in Vishvakarma's lap. He had been reduced to just a bag of bones. His muscles atrophied and his ribs stuck out under his floppy shirt. He rolled out again and started demonstrating what he meant, by 'bombs away'. His hands were fighter-jets and they flew about in hurricane-spirals. He stood at the eye and made loud noises, pitching and yawing, like an enthusiastic child at play.

The Vaigs tried visual presentations and slideshows too. Paintings captivated him. He got up and walked towards the projection and blocked the art with his shadow. It was unclear whether he was enchanted by the bright colours, or his umbra that bounced over them. His man-shaped pall distended across the screen, rising and falling, ducking, and weaving in freewheeling sciamachy. He pushed his hand out into the light and breathed in the thick plume of dust in the air. It bounced and dangled in front of the projector. He blocked the beam and captured the entire masterpiece by Ujjayan Delakar on his crumpled kurta.

The portrait showed Goddess Durga, leading the people through the ruins of a battlefield. She waved the great flag of Dvarca as followers held up their guns and weapons. Bony, defeated Caliphites lay scattered at their feet. SS6.2 pulled off his shirt and waved it above his head, as though he were one of the victors. The slideshow ticked on, to another great work by the same painter. It was the *Entry of the Dvarcans at the gates of Lahore.* These romantic paintings were part of the State's collection and were used often as symbols of pride and achievement. They marked events in the Nation's history. Their funny friend sat down, gaping at the works with tears in his eyes.

"Do you like the work?" a nurse asked him, moved by his sudden change in disposition.

"SS6.2, hey . . . do you know this painting?" She nudged him.

He nodded his head and they all rejoiced at this admission of understanding.

"What do you know about it?"

"Narangi. Gajar. Narangi. Kaddu." His manner went from sombre to rabid in mere seconds and he bit the nurse's nose. She pushed him away and fled the room immediately, shrieking, and bleeding in distress.

They gave up on him after that. The senior Vishvakarma sent in a report that requested for the Re-appropriation of an Unwanted Non-person (RUN). They made his last few days easy by allowing him full use of the projector and access to their complete archive of mounted paintings. He sat in his room quietly, flicking through the images all day. Breaks were uncommon and usually required some sort of unavoidable bodily compulsion, like going to the bathroom, eating or sleeping. He said nothing. He made no more sounds. He just immersed himself in the classic, great paintings of Dvarca's State collection.

It was a matter of time before they would take him away for Project L.

"What do you think they will do with him?"

"No one really knows. There are a few urban legends about a Resource-Review that would determine his use for the State. He could end up spending the rest of his days in a field, getting fresh air, toiling, and earning his keep."

"Or?"

"He could be put down."

If he were to survive the Resource-Review, all his work and labour as a binaaydi would earn Bindus for others. This was because pariahs had no use for Bindus. They were forsaken to the cycle of rebirth and were likely to return as lesser creatures in the next life. Turning in a binaaydi was therefore a great thing—it contributed to the quota of unassigned Bindus in Dvarca. Slave labour benefited everyone.

Vishvakarma still checked up on his Shahtooti friend every now and then, looking in through the glass window and metal mesh of the door. He brought the man his food, instead of delegating the job to the nurses. One night, he opened the door and placed a tray of dry mealy porridge on the table inside. It had been chipped away, possibly in one of SS6.2's dance-attack frenzies. He looked up and saw the prisoner-patient sprawled on the floor, his arms and legs stretched out.

"Here 6-2, here boy . . ."

"The villainy you teach me, I will execute." A shockingly clear, scholarly invocation was heard.

Vishvakarma did not believe his ears.

"I'm sorry . . . What did you say?"

SS6.2 got up and looked him in the eye. He was a different man, sober, quiet, and thoughtful.

"Only I, shall better the instruction!"

Vishvakarma backed out of the room and locked it. His arms and legs were covered in goose-flesh. What did SS6.2 mean? He looked up again and there he was, the incoherent madman with his face stuck in the glass window, puffing rings of spit with his mouth open. His eyes screamed and he let out a blood-curdling cry, followed by his haunting catchphrase: "Shahtooti anjeer!"

There was a calming presence, a familiar face when the RUN was executed. To take the notorious biter away, none other than Arjun Virdi accompanied the policemen. He pretended not to recognize Vishvakarma and ignored him.

They watched as the subject changed hands and cuffs. At the lab, people used to push him around, sometimes in wheelchairs. With the Police he was dragged along like a monster on a leash. SS6.2 stopped. He pulled the guards back with him and stood before Arjun Virdi.

"S19 2083! What better instruction? I shall better the instruction!"

"Take him away . . . now . . ." Arjun Virdi ordered the guards.

"You came! You came to see me! The villainy you teach me . . . oh what sweet villainy!" The educator struck SS6.2 and he fell to the floor.

"Count your breaths and make them last, you traitorous shit! Get this maniac out of here. He is not long for this world."

They took him away, kicking and screaming.

# 25
# THE STING OF MOTHERHOOD

Jyoti felt cold. Anyone would, bare-bottomed with both legs up in the air. She was as helpless as a baby during a diaper change. She'd spent half an hour waiting on the benches outside, imagining the exam over and over again. She was finally in her esteemed neighbourhood Aditi's office. Nurses milled about her private parts, cleaning and wiping away like hummingbirds around pollen. The merriment was far from contagious.

"Come on now, you've done this before, cheer up!"

Jyoti tried her best to play along and be compliant.

"Even good deeds lose their sheen when they are done with a sour disposition." The calloused janitor lady with her bucket of rancid black water in the corner, flashed a toothy grin and lunged onward with her mop. Could she be high on the fumes of phenyl? It seemed as though she'd been working over the same spot for the past half hour, stepping from side to side and then forward and back. There was a meditative quality to her labour and Jyoti tried to let it distract and entrance her. Freezing paste across her skin brought her back to the moment.

"How have you been feeling these past few days?

"I've been great," she smiled.

"Have you been going to work?"

"I have had to . . ."

The nurse performed her duties with the same care and vigour one would exhibit in dusting off furniture. She continued to lift and pull, placing the braces of a C-tripod under Jyoti.

"Dr. Aditi at your cervix!" the doctor joined them finally.

The nurses burst out in peals of laughter, falling over one another oafishly around the expensive equipment. Jyoti was not amused. She'd heard, seen, and read the terrible pun before. The round-faced doctor marched in with confidence as her rosy cheeks kindled a sparkling smile between them.

"Someone's going to be a mother!" she clucked. The slender, long surgeon's fingers of her right hand clasped her left wrist and she sat down on a stool beside Jyoti.

"Would you like to see it?"

The Mata ji nodded. Doctor Aditi pulled out a polythene bag from her coat pocket. There was a pen-shaped plastic pregnancy test resting comfortably in a fold of the bag. The fold opened up and there it was, a glistening little red dot confirming the contents of Jyoti's womb. The mother of two was to be a mother of three.

"You're going to get a medal!" Aditi patted her forehead, dabbing away the beads of perspiration. They were born more out of stress than exertion.

"If all goes well that is . . ." Jyoti spoke, apprehensively.

"Oh come now, you're still young, your vitals are great and you are already a veteran. Besides, *shubh shubh bolo*." She crossed her hands, under her ears, begging forgiveness for the bad thought. '*Shubh shubh bolo*' itself was sort of a go-to phrase for medical practitioners. She'd use it to reassure her patients when they seemed perturbed or concerned.

The nurses activated the C-tripod and its thin mechanical arms rose into position.

"Right . . . for God and Country now! We're going to plant the eye on you."

"Yes, let's get this done. I only have the morning off."

The nurses set up all the clamps and fastened Jyoti into stirrups to limit her movement. Doctor Aditi, smiling reassuringly, manoeuvred the C-tripod into position. A nurse handed her a sealed plastic container. She popped it open and pulled out a tiny chip with her mint-green plastic tweezers. It was no larger than a pea. She lowered it into a receptacle on the tripod with great care and then stood behind the console.

"For God and Country, Jyoti!"

"For God and Country . . ." she barely whispered.

The doctor started up the tripod and angled and guided it into Jyoti, passed the clamps, inches inside. Jyoti shifted suddenly at first contact with the tip of the probe. It had rubbed her skin.

"Don't move! Nurse, could you please . . ." she said with a tilt of her head. The nurse immediately switched on the forty-two inch display on the ceiling. It was meant to distract and entertain troubled mothers. The video showed a lake, surrounded by thick flourishing greenery. The sweet ripples of a *santoor* accompanied gentle waves on the lake's surface as a butterfly fluttered by. A phantom wind blew blades of grass into the water and they scattered like shooting stars against a bright blue sky. Jyoti thought she saw the fin of a shark emerge from the water. She dismissed it immediately as a figment of her imagination.

One of the helpful nurses pulled up a chair and held Jyoti's head, caressing it like a prize winning melon. She tilted her face up by her chin and looked into her moist, reddened eyes. Jyoti tried to shake her head free to see what the doctor was doing. It wasn't supposed to take that long. She was supposed to feel a tiny pinch, like a staple inside her.

"I'm almost there . . ."

Jyoti would be on their radar, literally, for the rest of the pregnancy. The chip was used to monitor womb conditions, fluid rates, and foetal progress. It would raise an alert whenever an exception occurred, for the local hospital Aditis. They could respond with either a further investigation or treatment, depending on the case. It also made the Mata jis easier to find in case of emergencies. There had been some apprehensions about the safety of the technology, with some versions doing more harm than good. Through recent improvements, though, the F&E (Failure and Error) rates for the chips had dropped to under 0.25%. This was well within the Government's standards for items planted on citizens. Research and development teams were working on setting up an identification system that could be part of the human anatomy, with no wear and tear or maintenance. They saw the need to tag everyone, including the men.

"The chip was faulty last time . . . it didn't pick up my Nakul's heart rate accurately."

"This is state-of-the-art. Would we give you anything but the best available?"

The nurse holding her head tilted it back again and looked into her dilated pupils through her steamed-up DDs, and flashed a wide grin, worthy of a *navrasa* mask for *Rati*.

"Why is she doing that?"

"What?"

"Smiling at me like that . . ."

The women stopped.

"She's trying to make you feel better. Please stop distracting me, it is very important that I get this right."

"Sorry."

Jyoti tried to distract herself. The wallpaper had little baby Krishnas on it. She started to say her prayers.

"*Yaa Devi sarva bhuteshu . . . shakti roopen sansthita . . .*"

Before she could go any further, she felt a crunch inside her. It was like a bee-sting, but on the wall of her soon-to-be-award-winning uterus. The *santoor* music, the lake with the butterfly, the thuggish nurses with their programmed patience all came to a grinding halt. All she felt was a sharp pain. It was a unique sensation, incomparable with any other. There was no surface to blow and soothe, or kiss and mend. The ruptures were invisible and deep. They had sunk their teeth into her again. She tried to calm herself.

" . . . *namastastaya namastastaya namastastaya namoh namaha!*" she shouted out loud in one quick burst. The bite grew softer, as though the teeth had fallen out and now she was being held by a pair of subcutaneous clenched gums.

"All done!" Doctor Aditi exclaimed in triumph. She walked to her desk-console on the side as the nurses retracted the C-tripod and started to clean and sterilize it. Aditi registered herself through her DDs and placed the chip-box on a barcode reader in front of her. A red laser scanned the box and a number appeared on the console screens. It showed her location, along with all of Jyoti's details and vitals.

"We're all set now!"

Jyoti sat up slowly.

"We'll guide you out."

It was the administration's belief that having little jokes and 'humorous' taglines took the edge off the rather serious business of medicine. All the medical announcements, posters, and communications were thus infused with inane puns and idiotic wordplay. Despite the best efforts of the Eugenics crew, there were still some niggling ailments that crept into the lives of good people. They were welcome illnesses, kind acts of an all-seeing overseer to instil humility, and encourage introspection. It was never made clear as to whether the administration had taken to infecting certain sections of some batches with said diseases. It was certain though that they had everyone's best interest at heart.

'LET PRANAYAAM TAKE YOUR BREATH AWAY!'

'MALE OVER 40? COLON YOUR DOCTOR NOW!'

The posters were everywhere and stretched from floor to ceiling, hinge to hinge, sill to sill like frightening wallpaper. The administration used rhyming couplets, cartoons, speaking calligraphy, and even pop-up art to remind visitors about all the horrible things that could happen to them.

'BE POSITIVE. YOUR BLOOD COUNTS! DONATE TODAY FOR EXTRA PUNYA!'

'WE HAVE YOUR BEST INTEREST AT HEART. GET AN EKG TODAY.'

A half-yearly full-body scan was encouraged. For some kalaavas, it was compulsory. DDs were frequently bombarded with mails and reminders. People were encouraged not to dismiss the messages as 'spam'. There were tiny questionnaires at the foot of the mailer that required a response. A 100 per cent correct submission earned the responder 31 PBs, so people read up and replied regularly.

'DON'T BE NERVOUS ABOUT MULTIPLE SCLEROSIS!'

'CALLOUS ABOUT SKIN DISEASES? THINK AGAIN!'

'WATER YOU WAITING FOR? DRINK SEVEN GLASSES A DAY!'

The pharmacy mails, espousing the wonders of Ayurveda were much more colourful and came with a call to action, to order some useful invigorators through the DDs. The messages usually featured a faceless Aditi or Sanjeev in their traditional white lab-coat, giving a thumbs-up or three fingered okay to the viewer.

'BETTER LIVING THROUGH CHEMISTRY. TAKE THE JVK RELIGIOUSLY.'

# 26
# THE VOYAGERS

It had been a long, taxing month and she was already exhausted when she got off the bus at the Industrial Complex for the afternoon shift. Another Jyoti, her neighbour, was waiting at the stop. She was leaving.

"For God and Country, Jyoti ji, how are you?"

"I am well, and you? I see they changed your lens! How is our Vidur coming along?"

"He's fine. Everything is fine. Are you leaving for the afternoon?"

"Yes, I have been summoned . . ."

Jyoti comforted her namesake, "What happened?"

"Where do I begin, Mata ji? It's my son. He has been going for football practice every day in this forsaken weather. His uniform always comes back filthy and we have been using too much detergent and power to prepare for the next day. The local authority saw a spike in our usage and wanted to investigate. I have to go for a Disciplinary Committee Review."

"Oh my, how high was your usage?"

She pulled the mail up on her DDs and projected it on the bus-stop wall for Jyoti to see.

"Hey Ram! That is a lot—almost three times the average for our block."

"Yes, I hope there has been some mistake," she pulled the projection down pessimistically.

"Why don't you buy more uniforms?"

"He already has three sets, Jyoti. It might end up being the same amount of trouble, to get an allowance for more clothes."

"I am sorry, Jyoti. Do take care." She wanted to carry on, but sensed the onslaught of more complaining.

"*Amma* ji is very ill."

"I am really sorry to hear that . . ."

"The doctor is experienced, we are lucky to have a Santri Sanjeev. He has said there is very little hope, though. Soon she will be gone."

"That is heart-breaking . . ."

"I suppose it is best to not be too attached to anyone or anything in this world."

Jyoti looked at her. Was this just her way of coping? Or was she really this dispassionately detached?

"Yes, I suppose so."

"It is just such a harrowing procedure, you know?"

"Why?"

She searched around on her DDs for a trail of communications.

"This was the preparatory note that we got from the Centre of Veteran Affairs. You can take a look at it too. They want us to . . . to prepare for our mother's final voyage." She forwarded it.

"I must be off now. Take care, Jyoti."

"You too."

The message from the Centre of Veteran Affairs was a list of items that were required for the antim yatra pujan: A 50 ml vial of water from the Ganga, three fistfuls of rose-petals, 5 leaves of fresh green tulsi, 150 gm of *havan samagri* and a box of camphor. Jyoti felt uneasy. For some reason, she thought back to the time before the blast. She felt compelled to take a quick detour, to visit the site again.

The whole area was blocked off. Most of the rubble had been cleared and in its place was an empty crater. She had not noticed it earlier, but the lamp posts with cameras had also been dismantled and removed. She walked around and tried to remember where the building entrance had been. For the first time, she forced herself to visualize what had happened that day. It had haunted her ever since, but this time she decided to face her fears.

The sun grew stronger and she saw her dark short shadow, following her around. It made her think of the chairs in the Waiting Room on the day of the blast. They were turned away, oblique and unnatural, but they had all faced the same curious direction. Even the guard in the corridor and the lady at the reception were similarly positioned. She looked around to get her bearings. All their heads were in the north. All their feet, pushed to the south. They had been deliberately arranged in the same orientation!

The strewn rose petals, the brown chaff, husk and grains, the lamps and the north-south alignment, they were all parts of the same enigma. They were all required for an antim yatra pujan, or final voyage. Even the green clump of spit, now that she had the courage to think about it, was a chewed-up leaf of holy basil or Tulsi. She was overcome with shock and grief. The dreadful occurrence at the Admin Building was not a terrorist attack. It was a mass cremation, as per the teachings and practices of Navmarg. She could think of no reason for pariahs or Caliphites to go through the trouble of following the rituals. It had to be the work of Navmargis.

"You should not be here Mata ji!"

A patrol car had pulled up behind her and a policeman stepped out. He held up a scanner to her DDs, ignoring the look of horror behind them.

"Please move along to Shed 7. Your shift starts in 10 minutes."

She nodded.

"Are you crying?" the tall Arjun stood with her and looked out at the crater.

"Don't be upset, Mata ji. We have caught one today. Just now. Would you like to see? It will cheer you up!"

He called her along and took her to the car. Two other men sat inside. The back door was flung open and she could now see that a handcuffed, half-naked prisoner was lying with his face down in a rag. Their prized catch writhed like a fish out of water. She knew his face, even though they had met just once before. It was Faiz.

"Pranaam Mata ji!" the other policemen spoke.

"We caught him lurking around Shed 5. Have you ever seen him before?"

"No, never," she averted her gaze.

"He is a binaaydi spreading all sorts of lies and filth about Navmarg. Show Mata ji the cloth . . . his handiwork."

Like a new-found relic being revealed at a Government function, they unfurled a tattered duster with stitching on it. She could only make out the letters, 'LIES OF THE STATE'. There was a list or paragraph below it, but the policemen wrapped it up before she could read any further.

"He uses our tools, to make this hurtful and deceitful apparel . . ."

"Apparel?"

"It is the inside of a shirt, Mata ji. Some of them have actually been sent out." He hit the prostrate man with his stick.

"I thought it would please you to see him suffer. Did you lose someone in the attack?"

She did not answer the question.

"Well, this dog was responsible for it!"

The policemen tied Faiz's hand with a piece of rope. They pulled him to the rear edge of the car and stretched his arm out, holding him down.

"Jai Dvarca! You also, you also say 'Jai Dvarca'."

Everyone present at the scene said 'Jai Dvarca'. With a loud snap the rear door was slammed and they broke his fingers.

"That'll teach you to spread lies! Savage crow!"

Jyoti backed away. The half blown ruins formed a telling backdrop for the screaming man being beaten by the Police. They had forgotten all about her. She suspected that they might have even forgotten about the prisoner or what he had done. There was a peculiar relish evident in their quick and deliberate movements as they taunted and tortured their new toy.

The beast of brutality danced on their shoulders and guided their arms. It served itself.

***

*"A dangerous binaaydi was apprehended earlier today, in connection with the Industrial Complex attack four moons ago."*

Narad Vedshankar reported, as Gandharva stopped working to watch the news. They showed a man with a broken arm being pushed into a jail cell.

He had come out of the DCR, a lot poorer, but largely unscathed. Sure there was a course to be taken, but it was not the end of the world. The re-education classes had been oversubscribed and he could only get a slot six moons later.

They had installed new dangling banners all around the office:

'ASK NOT WHAT GOD AND COUNTRY CAN DO FOR YOU.'

'ASK WHAT YOU CAN DO FOR GOD AND COUNTRY.'

They seemed to speak to him personally, crafted specially for his new situation. Work had picked up, as promised by his superiors. Gandharva made headway with his reports. It was too soon to be certain about his promotion, but he felt hopeful. He had increased his efficiency and had started to do things in a smarter way. He had figured out how to automate some of the reporting work. It was generally considered taboo to create an unauthorized program, but he had managed to set up a few simple lines of code that called each other in pockets, to run through large amounts of data and score them.

This freed him up to pay attention only to anomalies or apparent irregularities in the records. Anything that didn't seem extraordinary, didn't need his review, he thought. His Peet Gandharva mentor seemed pleased with the pace of his progress and had set a meeting for later that week to officially review his standing. This was good news.

He waited impatiently for the next puzzle. He took a sip of his hot tea and clicked through a three dimensional histogram that showed the relationship between Punya earned over time and different job functions. The functions were split further into basic demographics. He was trying to find out whether the productivity of different functions changed with age. The bulletin continued in the corner of his screen.

*"The binaaydi was caught inside the Industrial Complex, where he has been posing as a worker for many months. He murdered a Kuber and stole his identity, and has been masquerading as a citizen ever since."*

They showed a helicopter shot of the Industrial Complex before cutting in for a brief discussion with the policemen that made the arrest.

"The terrorist, a Caliphite, is the leader of a band of pariahs that has plagued our great Nation for the past few years. He is an uncouth, uncultured, hateful beast who goes by the name Faiz."

*His image appeared on the screen.*

They showed him from various angles, each one more devastating than the last.

"During investigations he revealed that the reason for attacking the Industrial Complex was to end our way of life. He was arrested very near the scene of the crime and resisted our Police forces. He has no known accomplices working in the area, but the Dvarcan forces are planning to crack down on his entire network. He showed no remorse for his actions and said that he would happily do it again."

*A pie chart in two halves appeared in the broadcast.*

"In response to a poll conducted earlier today, Dvarcans have made it clear that fifty per cent of us would like to see this man executed publicly. The other half would submit him to Project L."

Gandharva wondered why he had not been polled, for some reason he never got to be a part of such inquiries. He smirked to himself, thinking he'd probably side with the red half of the pie. A public execution would be satisfying.

*The broadcast returned to a video of the Industrial Complex.*

"One hundred and eighty-six innocent and brave souls died in the attack. The Ministry of Defence and Disaster Evasion has issued a statement assuring citizens that this evil mass-murderer will be punished soon. Further, a new offensive is being planned—it will be taken right into the heart of the Caliphate, to destroy the roots of this evil."

"We would also like to warn our viewers about the possibility of an identity theft epidemic. Exercise caution. Stay vigilant. If you suspect anyone, inform your local authorities immediately."

Gandharva almost dropped his cup of Tulsi scented *chai.* He was so caught up in his righteous blood-lust that he did not realize a new test had appeared.

He fumbled for a pen and pulled his notepad closer. He had made it a habit to print every test and hide it in a neat little folder in the bottom drawer of his desk. He went about plotting the numbers on a graph-sheet. There seemed to be no pattern and he chose a figure at random, submitting it as the answer. Before he could continue with his work, another test started. There were fewer numbers this time and they appeared in a haphazard arrangement.

He was able to solve it quickly. He printed-out the two tests and placed them side-by-side. He had noticed that from day-to-day, the orientation changed and the blank or un-numbered spaces varied in shape and size. He opened his stock folder of old tests and tried to imagine where they might figure on a map of Dvarca. A successfully completed test from earlier that week, looked a lot like the helicopter view of the Industrial Complex in the report. Gandharva smiled to himself and started a new search on his DDs.

'News: Pariah arrests', the clean and resourceful Dvarcan web, yielded thousands of results.

# 27
# UNREST

The entire city was asleep, but for Jyoti. She sat on the floor in the common toilet. It had become like a sanctuary for difficult questions and subterfuge. Gandharva had finally fixed the water-closet with a new drain-clearing acid. She had harangued him for days.

She really was cattle. A piece of meat. A mother who could be easily manipulated and moved from place to place and job to job at the whims of the authorities. She feared the biggest question of all, aching to break free from every pore of her body. What if it really was, ALL a lie? What if Navmarg was just a way to control people like her? There was only one source of information. There was only one source of guidance. There was only one true way.

Maybe it was the price they paid to stay safe. To trace the history of how Dvarca came to be, was to trace the history of the fight against the Caliphate, terrorists and pariahs. She did not know if the condition they were in, was actually necessary. She did not know if it was best for her and her family. Did it make them strong? She did not know.

The grotesque stories of cruelty from the brief video haunted her as much as the faces of the people in the blast. Abhimanyu had opened her eyes. But could she trust him? Could she trust *them*? More snippets from foreign newspatras spoke of border wars and bombings all over the world. The madness was not limited to Dvarca alone. There were rival ideologies and evil demands being put forth by diseased regimes everywhere. The wars must be real, surely? But was terror and oppression the only way to fight terror and oppression? An equal and opposite insanity?

She wrestled with her place in all of this. She hated the Caliphate and blamed them for all that was wrong with the world. She thought of *My Road to Navmarg*. She remembered the page-numbers and could recite the appendices. She did not know who would be better than Shastri ji to lead the Nation.

The questions kept coming. What good was the truth when it only caused her distress? What good was information, when it only made her feel alone and vulnerable?

A message from XX popped up.

"JYOTI, WILL YOU HELP US? WE NEED YOU NOW."

# 28
# THE PRICE OF CIVILITY

SS6.2 had been gone for a long time, but the memory of him lingered and troubled the young Vishvakarma. He could not help but think of the poor binaaydi that day. They were about to test the next generation Speech Sentinel on new subjects. It should have been a happy day for him, but it remained bittersweet.

The system had come a long way. It was calibrated for 55 languages. The doctors were quite confident that they could track and alter Arabic (classic, MSA, and colloquial with five variations of dialect), Pashto, Dari, Urdu (Rekhti, Dakani), Kurdish, Balochi, and three other pidgin tongues that had been named, Pidgin 1, Pidgin 2, and Pidgin 3. All major world languages were covered. Even English made it to the selection, though very few in Dvarca spoke it.

Some of the higher-ups, including a minister, wanted a demonstration. A lot of *Punya* and effort had been sunk into the programme, and it was time to show results.

They took all their equipment and set it up at the interrogation chambers of a prison facility. Gone were the days of the enormous contraptions and unseemly cones. Everything was smaller and sleeker now. They had been given two binaaydis for testing. All they needed was for them to talk to each other.

"Do they know that they are part of the test?"

"No, Minister. We have planted our Sentinels on both the binaaydis without their knowledge. They are undetectable. *Om bhur bhuvasvaha tatsavitur varenyam, bhargo-devasya dhimahi, dhiyoyona prachodayat* . . . Jai Ganesh Deva, let's pray that our efforts deliver results!"

Two men were brought into the interrogation chamber and all that stood between the fiends and their foes was a two-way mirror. It was strictly stipulated that prisoners were to remain hairless after one of them had tried to smuggle a blade in his beard. They wore regulation orange attire. The colour irked them.

"They look just as I had imagined they would."

"We . . . must remain quiet, Sir. It is a sound-proof room, but let's not take any chances. They mustn't hear us."

The prisoners in the test-chamber were strangers to each other. One of them sat in the left corner while the other paced about, studying the walls of the room. He searched himself in the mirror and spoke.

"What do you think they want now?" He mimed fixing a puffy pompadour, after which he fussed over his air-moustache and long phantom beard.

"I am a cartoon villain, you anjeers!"

"What did you say?"

"Anjeers."

"Is that a thing? Are we calling them figs now?"

"No, I meant to say anjeer. Holy shakarkand what is happening to me?"

He stepped back from the mirror, perplexed. He slapped his ears and mouth.

"I don't understand."

"Anjeer! Not anjeer."

"Are you mad?"

"I have this, this stinging sensation in my head. Do you have it too?"

"Oh, who the anjeer cares?" They stopped and faced each other, sharing a moment of abject dread. They realized that it was happening to both of them.

"My word . . . what is this?"

"Anjeer."

"Anjeer."

"Kesar anjeer."

"*Sarson chameli.*"

"What have you done to us now?"

"I am a shopkeeper. I am not a terrorist. Please. Stop this cruel torture!"

"They are hijacking us . . . anjeer-ing Nazis."

"Nazis!"

The darkened observation room, that had till now been revelling in the success of the trial, was shaken up by this word.

"Why is there no taboo for using the word 'Nazi'?"

"I don't know, Sir, it may not have been in the list that was given to us."

"Who gave you your list? You are obviously using an older version!"

As the discussion about banned words continued, one of the men on the other side in the cell had taken to banging his head against the mirror glass. He was using the choicest local swear-words in three or four languages, but they were all being reduced to a rotten salad of fruits, herbs, and vegetables.

"It came from the Taboo and Outrage Committee's latest report."

"Did it have the N-word addendum?"

"N-word addendum, I—I do not recall, Vishvakarma, do you know about this?"

The underling was too pleased with his work to care.

"Hundred per cent success rate, Sriman. Across all languages! The sensor is censoring superbly!"

"Did you hear the word Nazi when I said it? Or did you hear something else?"

"I heard Nazi."

"When I say anjeer or any variation thereof, I hear anjeer. Do you also hear anjeer?"

"This just *badaams* my mind."

"I'm sorry, did you just say 'badaams your mind'?"

"Badaam. I will badaam you all away you kesar anjeers. You are twisting my words!"

The Varaha man smiled.

"I thought 'blow' was fine. We just don't use the phrase 'have a blast' anymore."

"Vishvakarma, this is very good. But, what if the Forbidden Words are thought? Or written?"

"Ramanathan ji, that would be an extension of the project scope. It is not in our original plan or brief . . ."

The man in the left corner was rocking back and forth, clearly disturbed and on the verge of a breakdown.

"God save us from this shakarkand."

The other man genuflected and held his palms up together.

"Mary had a little lamb, little lamb, Mary had a little lamb, and its fleece was white as snow." He fell to the ground, defeated.

"Where did that nursery rhyme come from?"

"It's a prayer Mahoday, we just censored his prayer successfully."

The Dvarcans rejoiced.

"That man in the corner, what is he doing now?"

"Praying probably. In other words, losing his religion."

"See how he is fuming? He looks like he is going to explode."

"Row, row, row your boat gently down the stream.
Merrily, merrily, merrily, merrily, life is but a dream."

"With a moo-moo here, and a moo-moo there,
Here a moo, there a moo, everywhere a moo-moo.
Old MacDonald had a farm, E-I-E-I-O."

"Instead of converting their prayers to nursery rhymes, we will convert them to our prayers, in the next phase. It would expedite reconversions and it would also make them see that we are in fact, helping them be better human beings."

"This is *Hour of Honour* material, if I might say so myself. What would mark a victory for Dvarca as clearly and emphatically as the sight of a rabid dog, learning his place, repenting, and mending his ways?"

"I agree, this has great potential. Most extraordinary." The Minister approved.

"You will pay for this!" the test subjects kept trying more words. They could no longer curse, they could no longer pray. Suddenly, one of them had a bright idea.

"I know what you want. I know what you want to hear." He stood in the middle of the room, raised his fist in the air and spoke with great purpose.

"For God and *Kakdi*-ry!"

"What was that? Did he just try to say 'For God and Country'?"

"I believe so Sir . . ."

"Kakdi-ry! Kukkudu-ku!" the pariah burst out laughing.

Vishvakarma was furious.

"You have desecrated our motto . . ." the Minister barked.

"We just . . . over-corrected Sir."

"You cannot correct our motto!"

"It is easily fixable. You see, what he said, sounds like . . ." Vishvakarma was pointing at his screen.

"I know what it sounds like. I demand that you address the situation immediately. If this is to become a publicly deployed technology, bugs like this need to be removed."

"Of course, Minister, please give us a few days and we will fix this."

The captives were repeating the mangled motto like broken records. They laughed hysterically.

"Put an end to that, would you?" The Minister asked. Soon, a platoon of guards entered the chamber and started to thrash the convicts.

"Looks like we've incensed the censors! They always were very sensitive!"

"Shut your mouth, you dirty terrorist!"

They struck them till the laughter died down. The Minister watched as their limp bodies were dragged back to their cells. Young Vishvakarma excused himself to retrieve the instruments implanted on them. He was quite shaken by the cruelty and on the way back, took a detour to the toilet, to hyperventilate in private.

"You know, it is not easy being a leader. You must think a few steps ahead of everyone, if you are to be successful."

"We are most thankful for your support and guidance, Minister," said the bitter scientist.

"Yes, I am sure you are. This show of indigenous brilliance aside, have you thought about detecting sarcasm?"

"Sarcasm? Why?"

"You see, there are many ways to dissent and provoke. Your measures, although effective, to a fault . . . only cover direct slights and curses. They will help us eradicate certain trigger words from the lexicon. However, it still worries me that some people have a way of seeming to pay you a compliment, while meaning to cut you down." He looked at the Vaig blankly.

"What I mean to ask, my dear Scion of J. C. Bose, Stalwart of Science and Theology, Master of Puppets, have you never experienced the clever use of sarcasm?"

The Minister's demeanour changed from flattering to threatening.

"People must mean what they say and say what they mean."

"I understand. I see what you need now. Where would technology be, if it did not have religious visionaries to push its buttons?"

The minister gave him a cold hard stare that made him fear for his life. He shrank behind the equipment.

"Do you really think you can reform pariahs this way?"

"We may not be able to rehabilitate them, but we can use them to show our strength."

"Yes, I suppose it is always easier to make things look like they are working, than to actually make them work. Some would say it is even better."

"Very good, Minister."

"I will see to it that your division gets the funding you need. I want the new and improved Sentinel on the *Hour of Honour* within six moons. Civility shall reign over curiosity in our Dvarca."

"That is a great vote of confidence, Minister. Thank you."

"I know just the man you will rehabilitate."

"Who?"

"The Industrial Complex bomber, Faiz."

# 29
# NIGHTMARE FROM MOSUL

"Impure residents! You have three choices. Convert; pay the religious levy; or face death. This is the official decree issued by the Caliph in all cities across the Caliphate. Come out now and take option one or two. After that, you leave us no choice but to cut off your heads!"

Armoured trucks and tanks ripped through the middle of the city. The children hid on the first floor of an abandoned building. Mira stopped a little boy from wandering off. He was too young to understand the danger. There were two other scared little girls and an elder boy in his teens. He had led them there. He whispered the same words she'd heard for the past few months, "Walk quietly, stay low." They were hiding. The city had been overrun and evil men could be heard delivering their ultimatums over a bull-horn.

"Should we surrender? Should we convert?" Mira asked.

The announcement continued: "If you want to pay the levy you must agree to abide by terms of a neo-*dhimma* contract."

"What? What does that mean?"

"They taught us in school. It is a practice under which infidels are protected in the Caliph's lands in return for a special tax known as *jiziya*. Aurangzeb the terrible had enforced it in old Bharat during his reign."

"They are still in the seventeenth century, like that wicked Mughal!"

"I repeat, you have three choices: Convert, pay, or suffer the sword," the announcer declared.

"Jiziya must be paid in gold. Thereafter, in accordance with the contract, you must curb displays of your faith. You can remain whatever degenerate religion you are, but you must live, breathe, walk, and talk like a good Caliphite. Any deviant will be beheaded."

The children watched as tank after tank rolled past the unrecognizable city square. Was this really her Dvarca? How did they come this far? Were they always lurking and waiting for an opportunity like Mahmud of Ghazni?

"What are you doing?" She asked the elder boy who was now gathering little shards of glass.

"Shhh! I am trying to protect us."

"Where are my parents?"

"Dead, probably. Look out on both sides of the street. I will be right back."

Mira watched him go down the staircase. She prayed that all would be well. She prayed that Nakul would descend from the sky in a helicopter and rescue them. He'd unleash a wave of *kalaripayattu* and destroy the enemy. She pulled all the children close to her. She could see only the tops of their heads as they huddled together, stranded, and fatigued. She tried to comfort them.

"Catch him!" a loud, shrill voice pierced through the afternoon air.

"Come out! Son of a bitch! What are you doing here?"

They had found him. Mira quickly pushed the little children aside and asked them to huddle in the corner.

"Face the other way."

They did not.

"Look the other way, please. Everything will be alright."

She could see what was going on in the square. A crowd had gathered and they were pushing the boy around. A big man dragged him to the centre of the square and struck him.

"Are you a Dvarcan?"

He did not answer.

"Are you a mute?"

The crowd laughed and rejoiced.

"Did you hear the announcement? Become one of us. Pay in gold. Or die here by my sword. You have complete freedom to choose."

They were all armed and most of them wore black cloths over their faces. The big man picked the boy up and placed him on top of a razed pedestal. It was the stump of a fallen statue.

"What will it be, infidel? Your chain? Or your head?"

The boy was wearing his amulet. His dented DDs were hanging off the side of his face. The big man lifted his sword and its blade gleamed under the merciless sun. He waved it about to display his prowess.

"I am Mahmud of Ghazni. I am Aurangzeb. I am a Caliphite and you are an ant in my way!"

"What will you give up? Your chain, or your head?"

"Look away! I told you to look away!" Mira ordered the little children. They buried their faces in her side.

"Let's say a prayer."

"Is Lord Krishna going to stop their swords?"

"He is all we have."

"In the name of Allah! Cut it off! Cut it off! Spray his blood across the land!"

"In the name of the Caliph!"

The cheers grew louder. The helpless boy was pushed to his knees and a swarm of bloodthirsty jackals stood around him. They watched in relish as the big man with the sword adjusted his *keffiyeh* and prepared for the execution. Dust rose around him as the boy mustered enough strength to say a few words.

"You do not scare me. Your Caliphate is doomed. You are all doomed." He smiled.

The crowd charged at him, striking and swiping with sticks. The swordsman saw this as an encroachment on his moment and pushed them all back.

"Go back! Let me do this! Give me some room, please, Jabir come on brother, what is left? What is left for me? You go . . . go back to the line. You, what are you doing? Go and wait there. I am the instrument of justice. I am the man with the sword. What is the point? Hey!"

They were all so enraged by the boy's words that they bit, lunged, and snatched at him, any which way they could.

"I don't want to decapitate a corpse! Okay, done. Done? Are you done? Go back there. Step away from the infidel! He is mine! Mine!"

Finally they gave the executioner some space.

"That's better. We have a system. We need to follow the rules. He has to die by my sword and once his head rolls across the square, we will leave it there. For all to see. Someone sit him up straight, please."

"Why must the infidel sit up straight?"

"How am I supposed to chop off his head if he is lying on the ground?"

"Just lower your sword, like this, see?"

"Yeah just do that, Abbas."

They were all showing him the direction of the sword with their forearms. A single, sweeping motion from top to bottom was all that was required.

"What kind of executioner are you?" they laughed.

"It makes a big difference if he is sitting up. He will be up to here, see?" Abbas marked the height of the boy in the air. He then waved his sword in a swift motion to show how he would cut the head off in a lateral motion.

"This, you see? This is much better, there is a chance I might get some lift on it and the head might fly up."

He sliced through the air again and again to show them how he would do it, and accidentally nicked Rasul who cried bloody murder.

"What! It is your fault. If you would all just stand back and let me do my work . . ."

"This is a bad gash, Abbas, you've sliced open his stomach."

"I can't help it, I am a good swordsman. He was in the way."

"He is bleeding, Abbas."

"Yes I can see he is bleeding, please, take him to the doctor and have him stitched up, it is no big deal. Happens all the time. It's a small sacrifice! Am I right guys?"

The response to this question was lukewarm humming and grunting. They carried a shocked and howling Rasul off and put him in the back of a truck.

"Where were we? What do you say? This is your last chance. Do you want to join the Caliphate and be a loyal servant like me?"

The boy pushed himself up and presented his neck. "I'd rather die than join you, or bow to you."

Abbas's face lit up with glee. "The boy dies! The stupid infidel dies!"

"Quick, strike him before he slumps again."

Abbas got into position and raised his giant sword. He waved it about in an infinity shape to show what he was about to do. The crowd backed away slowly and gave him more room.

"Death to the infidel! Death to Dvarca!"

He raised the sword far back above his head and looked down at the shrunken form of the boy he was about to kill. The crowd cheered. Mira watched from her perch.

Blood oozed out and the sword was marked red with a wide spatter. Abbas fell to the ground, his eyes rolled up to the back of his head in shock. The crowd turned on itself to find safety. They started to drop one by one, as shots were fired. The boy sat in the middle of the square, on the stump of an old statue, smiling as the enemy was gunned down. Two Dvarcan army DEM4 helicopters descended on the square and shot almost every last one of the Caliphites. Mira ducked down behind the wall of the second storey hideout. Her prayers had been answered. God had sent the army. "Thank you Lord Krishna. Thank you Dvarca." She moved her lips in deep gratitude.

It was her very first time at the V-lab. She woke up before they could come for her. It had been an incomparably unpleasant experience. Mira sat at the centre of the room rocking back and forth as a nurse and a technician came to her aid.

"You did very well, little girl! That was beautiful."

She turned to them, horrified: "It was a nightmare!"

"Take the pills please!" They thrust the little grey capsules into her mouth and offered her a drink of cool, refreshing water.

"It reveals what is deep inside of you. Sometimes it shows worlds of wonder, sometimes it reveals dark fears and malice."

"Why is there so much violence inside me?"

"It is a mark of our times, Mira. You overcame it. You saw how your prayers were answered, didn't you?"

"I saw the Dvarcan army kill the Caliphites, yes."

"Yes!"

"C-can I dream up things that I know nothing about?" she whimpered.

"That is the purpose of the V-lab. Your *aatma* has access to worlds that our earthly senses cannot perceive. Visions reveal the unknown and connect us to our spiritual roots. God has spoken to you."

"Did he survive? The boy in my Vision?"

"What do you mean?"

"They beat him and tortured him. Grown men spared no strength when they attacked him. Did he survive?"

"This is not something that happened, Mira. This is something that you envisioned."

"What does that mean?"

"If you believe he survived, he survived—it is not unimaginable."

"He did have a smile on his face when the DEM4s descended."

"It is quite clear. Today, you saw the brutality and viciousness of our enemies. You also saw how to overcome them. You saw your compassionate, kind, giving self, come to the forefront when you cared for the children with you. Your maternal nature shone through this period of adversity and your prayers rescued the boy in danger."

"Come now, I think that's enough for your very first experience. Let's get you some more water and review the peaks and troughs of your soul's adventure."

# 30
# KNOW YOUR PARIAHS

*"Anhonee ko honee kar dein, honee ko anhonee*
*Ek jagah jab jama hon teenon, Brahma, Vishnu, Pashupati."*

Gandharva stepped into the drawing room, in time to see the last slide of the classic film. He had not told anyone that he was being forced to take a refresher class in Pariah Identification. He was too ashamed.

"Well, children I will see you tomorrow morning," his goodbyes were cut short by an important announcement on the television. The screen showed a frail calf tilting her head to one side, looking directly into the camera.

"*The simple story of an innocent being, raised in a foreign land . . .*"

The gentle bovine blinked, her kind eyes twinkled.

"*. . . for slaughter! For the ravenous appetites of those who care nothing for Mother Earth and her beautiful creations. Shastri ji's latest literary gift to the Nation, 'The Mooer's Last Sigh'.*"

"Get me one!"

"Me too!"

"What a sweet baby cow, how could they kill her?" Nakul asked.

"They do not show mercy to children, what hope does a cow have?" Mira spoke in a low, knowing tone. Her attention turned to her father and she asked him bluntly: "Where are you going?"

"I have an offsite meeting for a couple of days. Need to do a few field visits."

"Where? What field work could a Gandharva have?" Nakul mocked.

"Behave yourself! Papa is an important man and has important work. Isn't that right Gandharva?" Jyoti came to her husband's defence. It would have been more convincing, had her tone been less patronizing.

"He is an accountant. He plays with numbers."

"Nakul!"

"Let it be, Jyoti. I will see you all tomorrow."

He left without further ceremony. The bus was on time and he boarded it for the Centre. None of his fellow passengers appeared to be course-bound. They were all too relaxed, enjoying the sound of the radio. It was an update from the world of Vigyaan.

*"The Government of Dvarca, under the leadership of the Honourable Pdt. Shri Dr. Shastri is contemplating whether or not to share our technology for ocean-based energy extraction with Hedonesia. Gone are the days of the brain-drain when some of our best minds made a bee-line for the once functional West. Today the Hedonesians are in shambles, especially when it comes to technology. Dvarcan Scientists at the OMNI subsidiary, Halibutron, have devised a method for the extraction of oil from ocean fish. Western negligence caused a vast number of oil spills off our scenic coasts. It has fallen to us, to clean up the mess created by the self-serving Cowboys of Hedonesia. They have invited us for a knowledge exchange, the first of its kind in almost forty years."*

There was no question that Dvarcan scientists, *Vaigyaniks* or Vaigs as they were affectionately known, had delivered a solution that was both simple and cost-effective. Gandharva knew that Hedonesia, with its rampant drug-abuse and loose morals was not to be trusted with these gifts. It would be like playing a snake-charmer's flute to enchant an ox. He got off at the Centre for Re-alignment. An alert appeared on his DDs, just as he entered the building.

"AASMANI GANDHARVA SECTOR 17, BLOCK 8A, THE CENTRE FOR RE-ALIGNMENT WELCOMES YOU FOR YOUR PRESCRIBED COURSE: IDENTIFYING PARIAHS K01. WE LOOK FORWARD TO REFRESHING YOUR CONCEPTS AND RE-ACQUAINTING YOU WITH ESSENTIAL DOCTRINE OVER THE NEXT THREE DAYS.

YOUR FAMILY HAS BEEN NOTIFIED OF YOUR ABSENCE WITH THIS MESSAGE. MAY YOU LEARN QUICKLY AND EFFECTIVELY.

*THIS EMAIL WAS GENERATED BY A LOCATION SERVICES ROBOT, PLEASE DO NOT REPLY."

Jyoti was copied on the note. She was in the drawing room with the children when it came through. They were busy with their assignments.

"What's wrong, Mother?"

"Nothing Nakul. Finish your work quickly, it is getting late."

She read the message again. What had he done to be sentenced to a re-education course? Identifying Pariahs was quite a touchy subject, onc that they had been taught and re-taught.

"Ma, may I have some *makhanas*? I am feeling hungry."

Jyoti went to the kitchen to fetch the snack. She poured a handful of puffy white *makhanas* into a bowl and salted them lightly. The kids preferred to have them toasted, but she was in no mood to oblige.

"Are you toasting them, Ma?" there were giggles from the dining table.

"You concentrate on your work. Stop thinking about toasting or roasting."

She started the stove and dropped the little puffs into a pan. She turned up the heat and watched them go from wafting bulbs of snow to pinkish-gold clumps.

"Here you go."

They were gone before she sat down. Nakul inhaled most of them.

"Sorry!" he grinned impishly.

"You can have more with dinner. Are you done?"

"Almost, I have a few more chapters left."

"Don't come crying to me after your test tomorrow."

"I don't cry, Mother. You should know that."

Mira was not impressed by his bravado. She tugged at her mother's sari and whined.

"Does this sound good to you? The principles of cloning and gene replication can be traced back to the time of Raktabeej. A new demon was born whenever a drop of his blood touched the ground. The only way to stop him from cloning himself was to contain the blood in a vessel, held, and controlled by Goddess Durga herself."

"Yes that sounds correct."

"The homework question asks for two examples. Should I talk about how Divya Drishti originated in the *Mahabharata*?"

"Yes, that is a good example. Sanjaya was able to watch a live telecast of the battle and describe it for the blind king, Dhritrashtra. Incidentally, this was also the first time someone had given a running commentary of any event." She scribbled away with renewed gusto. Jyoti wished she could use some Divya Drishti at that point to see what her errant husband was doing.

Her first ever class about pariahs was a revelation.

*How frequently must something happen, before one can form a legitimate, statistically significant hypothesis that may lead to a stereotype?*

Six instances are numerically adequate to formulate a proposition. This is the double-hat-trick rule.

*Under what conditions, are the traits being considered for a stereotype valid?*

The traits being considered for stereotypes must be repeated by different members of the same group in independent and unrelated scenarios. The exhibitors of the behaviour-in-question must not be known to one another and must not be aware of the observation itself.

*How are members of a group defined? Who forms a unique group?*

A unique group comprises of people who are one thing, before they are others. They may have well-known but not necessarily publicly declared common beliefs, predilections, characteristics or desires. The group may, or may not be aware of its existence. The group may, or may not be dangerous.

*How big should a group be, for a stereotype to exist about it?*

A group about which stereotypes are being formulated, can be as small as two distinct individuals.

She had so many pre-fed ideas that lingered in her mind too, as stereotypes. They had found their way into everything, like termites. She asked her own question:

*Did it matter that the stereotype was positive or negative?*

No! Any preconceived notion about a person because of his or her perceived relation to a group, was an act of violence. It was a reduction of the being to a few traits.

"Ma?"

"Yes, Mira?"

"Do zebras think that someday they will lose their stripes and become normal horses?"

Jyoti smiled.

"What about horses wishing to look more fashionable, like zebras?"

Mira, sufficiently amused, dived back into her books. Jyoti had to pull her head back slightly.

***

"You should already know! Look at it!"

Gandharva was struggling. He was in the first row and inches away from the hologram. The teacher moved around him like a threatening wasp. He had just recovered from a bout of hiccups and was making full use of his uninterrupted cadence.

"Are you having a migraine? Would you like to take a little nap?" he barked like a drill sergeant on the brink of battle, trying to rouse his delinquent troops.

"No, Sriman, just give me a minute to study the question, please."

"A minute? Hear that, class? This wide-arsed-ne'er-do-well Gandharva would like a whole minute to assess a threat!"

The teacher swung his body around to stick his finger in Gandharva's face like a venomous stinger.

"Look at the hologram and tell me. Is that a pariah or not?"

"He . . . he is . . ."

"And how do you know? You worthless low kalaava toad?"

Even though the teacher had been berating him for most of the session, Gandharva felt a sense of warmth and gratitude towards him. He was finally the centre of attention for something. Someone cared enough about his development and understanding to get so bent out of shape over it. This was oddly satisfying and in an uncontrolled moment of glee, a hint of a smile found its way to the corner of his hairless mouth.

"What the hell are you grinning about? You pervert! You overpaid, underqualified *munshi*!"

"I am not a munshi, I am a bureaucrat . . . Sriman. I work at the Ministry of Finance and Salvation."

The teacher straightened up and a cold new menace descended upon his visage.

"Not for long! If you do not answer correctly and quickly, you are as good as gone. Do you realize that this re-certification costs the Nation? Do you know that you could be dismissed and banished from Dvarca?"

Gandharva nodded enthusiastically, but still could not answer. He flipped through the study materials furiously.

The teacher slowed down and split his words, to appeal to what he now considered a weaker intellect. Each deliberately spoken chunk of words hung in the air like a tossed grenade in slow-motion.

"Why. Do-You-Think. That-This. Is-a-bleeding-pariah?"

"The acronym."

"Which acronym?"

"BEAST."

"BEAST. Yes. Now expand and explain."

"B stands for bow-shaped bones—this is because pariahs avoid sunlight—they end up with diseases that change the shape of their limbs, E is for ears and eyes—the eyes are sunken—while the ears . . ."

"Have you forgotten what the ears of a pariah look like?"

He felt his own ears and rubbed his left lobe, trying to remember.

"Sharper! Pointy! Yes, the ears are supposed to be pointy for a pariah."

"Continue—"

"A is antlers, they have antlers or horns in the worst cases, which they often hide under caps and headgear. S is saliva which they cannot control. S is also smell, they reek of foul and abnormal odours because of their disgusting diets. Lastly, T is for tails, which are hidden."

There were no acknowledgments, celebrations, or congratulations as the teacher moved on to the next question.

***

Jyoti hummed sardonically at the thought that her foolish, cowardly husband was being re-indoctrinated in the art of judging from afar. She turned to her children, who sat there with their textbooks, diligently learning what she was trying desperately to unlearn. She had one foot on the shore and the other in a boat.

XX: "I RESENT HAVING TO ANSWER FOR A GROUP I DID NOT CHOOSE TO JOIN, FOR TRAITS I DO NOT RECOGNIZE, LET ALONE ESPOUSE."

# 31
# TWO TESTS

The little boys put their heads down and scribbled away. It was their last paper-exam. For higher grades of study, all students worked off ChaturPads. Nakul could not wait to get his hands on one of them. The things he would do! The only thing standing in his way, was this one last paper: Strategy. It was an interesting subject that required the study of history, logic, and the application of theory. He had always been exceptional at applying what he had learnt. He had fashioned weapons from sticks and stones that looked like those from the epic paintings of Maharana Pratap.

Though he was named for Nakul, he felt an affinity for the great Maharana and sometimes thought that he was a reincarnation of the great man. He had taken to calling one of the fairer fat boys from the Kuber section, 'Chetak'. He rode him around during recess, whipping him with a thin stick. He'd offer him the only currency the children had, pods of tamarind, in return for his 'loyal service'. Chetak was not amused, but he took the delicious *imli* anyway. They used to collect it from a tree in the school compound.

*"The Caliphate has attacked our country, intending to subjugate us. They will not stop their carnage at any cost, and have sworn to fight us to the last man."* Below the question was a map, showing the battlefront and the lines of approach adopted by the invaders.

*"Devise a course of action to thwart this attack."*

He thought about the question and looked around at the other Nakuls working away. No one ever seemed to think as hard as he did. They just wrote rote answers and submitted them, as though there were a reward for finishing before time. He weighed the different tactics they had learnt and came up with a combination that he thought would win. He defined the parameters of the attack and decided that no Dvarcan life would be sacrificed. As it took shape, it started to please him and he wrote a long extension of the answer. He visualized the battle sequence and drew some of its scenes with the precision of a gifted soothsayer.

An enemy tank blew open like a Venus fly-trap, its metal bowels covered in squishy sinew and blood. It did not stop rolling as one of the operators had fallen dead, right across the panel, forcing the hunk of steaming junk forward. Another missile was dropped just in time by a second pass of the Dvarcan Air Force, neutralizing the rolling waste, along with a host of other targets. The infantry was positioned at a favourable elevation, and managed to shred through the fleeing Caliphites. He pictured himself sitting atop a 40-mt tower, setting his sights straight and reloading. He fired away with surgical finesse till the loud rat-a-tat-tat ceased. He reloaded again.

The Air Force was making its third pass, and this time they released drones. They were X360s and they packed a punch. He scribbled the OMNI logo on the back of his floating angels of death as he sketched them descending upon the war zone to scour it for signs of life. They would find two enemy combatants and arrest them as prisoners of war. He pictured himself, now walking amongst the ruin, gun in hand, stepping over corpses. It gave him great pleasure and he drew another panel in his little graphic strip about Caliphite annihilation. He decided to show the victorious Dvarcan army haloed by a rising Sun. It was quite realistic, because the enemy did have a penchant for sneak attacks in the middle of the night.

He examined the faces of the fallen soldiers and saw that one of them was in need of medical attention. His left side had been burnt severely and he lay on the ground, waving his right hand for help. He walked closer to the stricken man to bring him in for questioning. As he sketched and illustrated the features of the half-blown man, Nakul shocked himself. It was Gandharva! This made him stop his fantasy of carnage. He wrote that they would squeeze the prisoners of war and do whatever it takes, through enhanced interrogation, to find out more about the opposition's offensive.

He mentioned that capturing at least two enemy fighters was imperative. You would need one to confirm the stories spilt by the other. He went on to make side-notes in support of this claim, by providing gory details of past misinformation that had cost Dvarcan lives.

It was unshakeable though, the thought that he saw his father as a defeated enemy combatant. It disturbed him and he looked up at the clock at the centre of the room, behind the invigilator. There were about five minutes left. He decided to quickly revise his answers.

***

*Hindutwaah* was one of Mira's favourite subjects and she felt over-prepared.

1) *Which popular game did our thirteenth century poet Gyandev invent? Describe it.*

*Mokshapat.* It's a game with ladders and serpents. The ladders in the game represent virtues and the snakes, vices. In ancient Dvarca, or Bharat, the game was played with cowrie shells and dice. With time, the game underwent several modifications, but its meaning remained the same. Good deeds take people to *Moksha* or salvation and evil to a cycle of rebirths. It was stolen and converted into a game of chance by western imperialists. It now masquerades as a mere trifle of a pastime for their misinformed youth.

2) *Who was the first person to discover the duration of the Earth's orbit? Was it:*

   *a) Bhaskaracharya*

   *b) William Smart*

   *c) Copernicus*

   *d) Ptolemy*

   She ticked Bhaskaracharya with pride.

3) *Who wrote the book, 'Milestones of Ancient Dvarca'?*

   *a) Pandit Shri Dr. Nirmal Shastri*

   *b) Govardhan Patwardhan*

   *c) John Woxley*

   *d) Denis Bergkamp*

   *e) Fashoosh Mashoosh*

   That was an easy one too and she marked option a).

4) *Which of the following medical procedures and treatments did Charaka Samhita by Charaka, written 2,500 years ago, include?*

   *a) Plastic surgery*

   *b) Embryology*

   *c) Brain surgery*

*d) Anaesthesia*

*e) All of the above*

She ticked e).

It was crucial to establish one's supremacy through the repeated itemization of one's achievements. For a person to do this about him or herself would seem boastful, petty, and obnoxious. To do it for an entire culture though, was noble. Lists were at the heart of a lot of pride, associated with the great Nation of Dvarca. They seemed to lionize Dvarcan culture to a point of euphoria, where one could not help, but be swept up in the joy of being for God and Country.

Question 5 was a doozy.

*5) What is Hindutwaah and why is it essential?*

Hindutwaah is a Dvarcan national movement that marked the revival of ancient knowledge and texts. Noted Vaigs and Vidurs worked hard to connect the present with the past using ubiquitous clues and signs. Hindutwaah has two main facets. It is first and foremost, a response to the vile and revolting march of destruction led by the apostles of the Caliphate. It provides a strong, unifying voice against the advancing threat of global jihad as a just and necessary response to extremism.

Secondly, it celebrates the greatness of a superior civilization, once marred and held back by jealous marauding invaders and selfish occupying bigots. It owes its roots to Navmarg and like the father philosophy, is essential to all Dvarcans.

# 32
# BENEVOLENCE

Swarms of children gathered for the common recess. Games of football and cricket broke out on the field. On an ordinary day, he would have joined them. He'd become quite popular, thanks to his sporting prowess. But Nakul sat under a tree, sketching away furiously.

"What are you doing?"

He looked up from his work to see who had dared to interrupt him. It was a porcine Samyukta sitting a few feet away, cross-legged in the grass. She stole glances of him while thoughtfully picking blades of green.

"Working."

"Why? You should be playing."

"*You* should be playing."

"They won't let me."

Her braids fell on either side of her face concealing most of it. She pouted and looked at the clumps she had removed from the ground, throwing them over her shoulder. He recognized her. She was one of the few overweight children, who often became the butt of a joke.

"You could use the exercise."

She turned away from him.

"You're so good at football. They could use you in the game. The seniors are beating them."

He'd been so lost in his art that he did not realize that a proper game was underway. He'd ignored their calls earlier.

"You should not waste your gift," she spoke sheepishly.

"And what is your gift?"

She did not answer.

"Can I see what you are painting?"

"I'm not painting, I'm sketching."

"Isn't that unusual? For a Nakul?" She turned to him. He glared at her angrily.

"Can I see it, please?"

"Beat it, fatty. Leave me alone."

She got up and walked towards him, blocking out the sun. She was much bigger than he, wider, with thick legs resembling the stumps of a Peepal.

"How did you get so big? Did you eat your family? Daughter of Ghatotkach!"

"Why are you saying this?"

"You deserve it. Go help out in the canteen or something. They might throw you a scrap. You can help clean up the leftovers."

She pursed her lips and contorted her mouth to one side. She could hold it no longer. Huge tears streamed down her pudgy cheeks and she left quietly. Her efforts to befriend and impress the school hero had failed. He did not think twice about her and went back to his artwork. He darkened some lines and erased others; he shaded with fervour and scrubbed the white sheet of card paper till the disparate lines blended into a seamless portrait. It was almost done.

He took it back to the classroom to leave it in his desk.

"*Beta* Nakul!"

He recognized the voice and assumed that the call was for him. It was Virdi Sir and he was carrying some papers, huffing his way up the stairs.

"Yes, Guru ji?"

"I have to tell you. Your Strategy answer sheet is one of the best I have ever seen."

"Thank you, Guru ji."

"The detail, the thinking, I believe you are—I shouldn't say it—but I must . . . I believe you are ready for actual combat training. This is exceptional work. Just astounding how you have dissected the scenario and imagined all possible outcomes, included all risks and provided a step-by-step approach to neutralize the enemy. Good work."

"Thank you, Guru ji."

"Keep it up!"

"Thank you, Guru ji."

"I will show this to everyone, every teacher will know."

"Know what?"

"That—that you are doing so well! They might push you harder but it will be for your own good. We all need that extra push to make us achieve our full potential, no matter how good we already are, yes?"

"Yes, very true Guru ji."

"What is that you are carrying?"

"Nothing, just some other work."

"May I see it?"

"It's nothing, a personal project."

"There is nothing personal in Dvarca. We are all a big family. Show me!"

He hesitated a great deal before pulling the sketchbook out in front of Virdi Sir. He looked away bashfully and prayed that this little inspection would not last long.

"Oh my! *Om namah Shivaya.* This . . . did you draw this?"

"I did."

"Why?"

"I—I was still thinking about the Strategy paper. I felt that I had left some details out, from my submission. This is just a . . . a continuation."

"It is remarkably detailed. Are you sure you made this?"

"Yes!"

"I have never known a Nakul to possess such skills. Why this image though, specifically? Is he, is he one of ours? Are you commemorating the brave soldiers of Dvarca that might have lost their lives?"

"No Sir, in my strategy, no Dvarcan dies. This is an enemy combatant."

"He's blown to pieces. His whole side is missing. But his face, it is calm and quiet. Is he dead?"

"I don't know."

"He looks as though he might speak any minute. 'Death to Dvarca!' Or some such blasphemy." He bit his tongue. Excitement was getting the better of him.

"He really looks like a real person! Who is your inspiration? Even the sketches in your paper, they were very realistic."

"I saw it all, well, I imagined it and pieced it together on paper."

"May I keep this?"

He did everything to convey his reluctance non-verbally but how could one refuse a Guru?

"It is for you. Be my guest."

"Good boy. Good boy. Come by and see me tomorrow at recess. Okay?"

"Yes, Guru ji."

Virdi ripped the sketch out of the book carefully. He ran up the stairs, still looking at the page and shaking his head in amazement. Nakul did not know what to make of it. He went back to his classroom, and sat down in a new-found torpor. He laid his head on his desk, sleepily. There was some movement behind. He picked up his wooden scale and flung it in the direction of the noise.

"Ouch!"

It was the large little lady from the playground. She was huddled under a desk at the back of the class with her fingers in a small tiffin bowl.

"What is that? What are you doing here?"

She got up and started to run away. He sprang out of his seat and cut her off at the exit. It was like a grape blocking a watermelon.

"I am a tiger, you elephant. You cannot escape me. Stand back. What is that in your hand?"

"It's nothing."

"Show it to me!"

She revealed a half-eaten bowl of *halwa.*

"Where did you get that? No wonder you are like this. You are supposed to only eat your quota! Thick numb-skull!"

"I was hungry."

"We are all hungry. We are all always hungry. Do you see me eating someone else's food?"

"I am sorry. Please don't tell anyone."

"You do not belong in this classroom. You do not even belong in this wing!"

"The boys get badaam halwa, we only get *suji* halwa. I wanted a change. I am so sorry. Let me go now, please."

A game of restless shifting ensued, where she lumbered from side-to-side and he blocked her path.

"Finally you are getting some exercise. What is your name?"

She did not answer and was getting visibly upset. She wiped the halwa off her hands onto her salwar and focussed on getting the little boy out of the big doorway.

"You are a Mira, right? You must be."

"I am a Samyukta."

He lifted a scale from someone's desk and started poking her back with it. She was afraid of getting hurt and retreated. He goaded and taunted her like a pompous fencer. He smacked her swiftly at the back of her hand much like a teacher chastising a student. She fell back and hurt her head on the big table at the head of the class. It was the teacher's desk. She was in pain and tried to rub the hurt spot. She looked up at Nakul angrily, but he did not notice the change in her disposition. She'd been pushed too far. Even so, Samyuktas, like Miras, were conditioned to be kind, nurturing, and protective. They were forbidden from hurting others. Nakuls were trained not to fight women. Yet, there they were. She got up and dusted herself.

"Look at that, you're crying again."

She charged at him with all her might, hoping to land her fist on his face and knock him out flat. He was too quick for her and bent to the side. He tripped her with his feet and she fell again, with a thump on the dusty floor of the classroom. Chagrin marked her face and she spat up a cloud of dust.

"Am I bleeding?"

"No you aren't, you baby hippo."

Just then a pack of boys returned from recess. The bell had rung but Nakul and Samyukta had not heard it.

"What's going on here?"

"She was stealing food!" he declared loudly.

She still lay on the floor. He walked up to her side and placed his foot on her back.

"Take a picture, I caught a big one."

They had a big laugh. She pushed him away and rose up to leave. A teacher arrived and all the boys quickly ran to take their seats. Except Nakul.

"What happened to you?"

She just walked up to him and hugged him, crying profusely. He pushed her away slowly and asked her to go to her class.

"Do you need to go to the dispensary?"

She shook her head to say 'no'.

"What are you doing in my classroom?"

All the boys spoke in unison: "Stealing food!"

"I stopped her." Nakul claimed the spotlight.

"Well done, young man! And you—you are a big girl! This is appalling. You will be severely reprimanded and I will have a word with your teachers about this. Maybe even your parents." He scanned her identification on his DDs and submitted a record of her misbehaviour to the school's administration. It would now appear on her permanent record that she was a food-stealing, class-skipping, troubled child.

"Please Sir, it won't happen again."

"Looks like it has been happening for a while! Just look at your record!"

He was reading her file, finding patterns in past dalliances and making a note of her recidivism.

"You are habitually away from class. Don't you like to study? Is school a joke to you?"

"No Sir." She raised both her hands and pressed her palms together, begging forgiveness.

"What big hooves you have!" Some wise jester remarked from the back of the class.

"Please go back to where you belong. You are late and you have also delayed us."

"Yes Sir. Sorry Sir." She went out and disappeared. Nakul sat down triumphantly and the lesson began. It was Moral Science.

"Let's open to Chapter Five, '*The Benevolence of Maharishi Dadheechi*'."

The girl ran as fast as she could. The entire wing was for Arjuns, Nakuls, and a young new batch of Sahdevs. She hid and bawled in a broom closet under a staircase. The dusters started moving and knocked against her feet, as though they too, were coaxing her to return to the world. She liked it in there, it was dark and quiet, but for the whirring and bopping of some cleaning machines. Her DDs fogged up but she didn't care to clean them. Like clockwork, a disciplinary email notification arrived. She was now officially on probation. Her parents knew too. She cursed her luck and blamed herself for being stupid.

"What the hell are you doing here? For God and Country, this is my room!"

The Janitorial Superintendent walked in. She hopped to her feet.

"Why are you crying, little one?"

"Is that supposed to be funny?"

He deactivated the cleaning robots with a simple voice command. He was still blocking the door.

"What happened, sweet girl? Why do you cry?"

"I don't have to talk to you."

"You are right, you don't. You are a brave little girl. You just have tears in your eyes."

"I hate this place and everyone in it. I can't bear it anymore."

He offered her a handkerchief to wipe her face and DDs. It was thick and made of *khaadi*. She snatched it from his hands and left the room.

"Take care! For God and Country."

She soaked up all her tears in the cloth and dried her face too.

They were about to issue a search party for her, and to stop it, she would have to reach her class within the next minute. She barely made it. There were more admonitions and complaints. More chuckles from her peers. Lessons on restraint were prescribed for her to learn that 'COMPLIANCE IS ITS OWN REWARD'. She sat with her nose buried in her tablet.

She realized that the Superintendent's handkerchief was still in her hand, clasped and bunched like a little brown bud. She opened it up and saw that there was some writing on it, stitched in a language that she did not understand. She scanned it into her DDs and naively searched for its meaning on the glorious Dvarcan web. The teacher stopped in the middle of her sentence and looked at her.

"What—what are you doing?"

"Nothing Ma'am."

She cancelled the web search and hid the cloth away. The lesson resumed.

The bullying did not end at school. Her parents were deeply disappointed in her and served up a scathing attack at the customary family dinner. Samyukta had finished her food and was eyeing her brother's plate. She played with her braids to distract herself.

"Why am I the only one who is cursed with a brainless behemoth? Samyukta. Look here."

"Sorry, Father."

"I don't know where you get your appetite. Thirteen-year-old girl and she eats like a gorilla. I don't want any more complaints from school!"

They had a small home and the bathroom, drawing-dining room, and bedroom were within a few feet of each other. Her father was a struggling Kuber with a taxing job. She had apologized repeatedly, but he could not let go. Her unacceptable behaviour reflected poorly on him as a parent and ate away at his monthly score. Her mother was upset too, but she was distracted, trying to feed her defiant, skinny brother. He preferred eating directly from the styrofoam boxes and had mashed everything into a yellow gruel. Only the peas had survived and retained some of their character.

"Vidur, *babu*, please, eat your peas."

He refused and dodged the spoon. The mother lost her patience and forced it into his mouth. The boy turned away from his plate and threatened to spit the morsel out. He tried to make it look like he was choking. It was an old trick and it did not work anymore.

"Enough! I have had it. I am calling the Varaha to take you away!"

Just then, the front door burst open and a squad of armed guards marched in.

The father got up from the table to receive them. "G-Good-good-evening Mahoday, what seems to be the problem?" They needed no invitations and pretended that he was not there. Little Vidur raised his hands up in surrender and chomped with a passion reserved usually for his favourite *barfis*. Mother backed away to the wall.

They searched the apartment and turned everything upside down. They opened the father's mouth and looked inside with a torch. They took the mother to the back room to make sure she was not hiding any illicit substances.

"Where is it? Where the hell is it?"

They slapped the little boy on his back and a half-chewed pea flew out on the floor.

"Pick that up, son." One of them ordered. He reached for it and held it in his hand.

"We don't waste food in Dvarca."

He put the pea in his mouth and swallowed it. It was cold and he pushed it past his throat with an uneasy squelch. The mother returned, violated and upset.

"Pack up the container! You are not supposed to eat out of it."

She took her son's plastic cutlery and the styrofoam food-boxes to the kitchen. The guards had searched everywhere. There was a small trophy on the table in their drawing room. It was brass and shiny, showing a man diving down into a well of some sort. All the edges were smooth.

"Oh wow, an award! Very nice! 'WORK WILL SET US FREE'." The guard read the inscription.

All this while, Samyukta had stayed put at the table, sitting quietly as they went about their destructive upheaval of her home.

"Your daughter is up to no good, Kubera."

"She ate more than her share. It is most upsetting and heinous but does it really warrant an inspection of this nature?"

"We are not here about the stolen halwa," he sneered and sat down at the table with Samyukta.

"Where did you get it?"

"What?"

"The cloth, this cloth, you scanned it into your DDs today. At school, no less!"

He showed them a distorted print-out of a photo of the brown *khaadi* handkerchief with the strange text on it. There were thick black lines through the words.

"What is this now?" the parents exclaimed.

"We've been dealing with a bunch of insurgents and Caliphate sympathizers. Nasty anti-nationalist, anti-growth, liberal-farts have been trying to poison the hearts and minds of our impressionable children. Especially young, disturbed children like your obese daughter."

"Samyukta? Is this true?"

"Do you know what it says?"

"No, of course I do not, Sriman."

"Who gave this to you? Where?"

"I found it lying around at school. I thought it was litter and picked it up . . ."

The armed men were not impressed.

"They do these things. They leave these little thought-bombs lying around for children to find. Sometimes they give out sweets. Just last week, there was a young boy who found a laddoo with a wrapper that said 'Death to Shastri'. Do you understand what we are dealing with here? Do you not see the danger of letting these poisonous elements into our holy air?" He banged the table to make his point.

"What is so holy about our air?" Samyukta asked. This blasphemy was not tolerated and he slapped her across the face. Her parents, in a show of solidarity and correctness, smacked her too.

"Shameful. Repugnant! You need a boot-camp! Maybe they will be able to extricate the flab from between your ears. I am going to personally recommend it."

"Take her off our hands, by all means. She has been nothing but a menace," the Kuber added.

"What did it say?" Samyukta sobbed.

"What?"

"The cloth, what did it say? Have you even read this thing that you are raging against?"

The guard did not want to seem ignorant and leaned in across the table.

"It says Shastri is a dog. It says Navmarg is a lie. It pledges support for our enemies and condemns Dvarca." He scrabbled.

She smiled, letting him know that she saw through his forced fabrication.

"Keep smiling, keep smiling. They will come for you little girl, they will come for you, and you will become the citizen you need to be. Just you wait. Just you wait and watch."

He lodged a verbal report so that everyone in the room knew what was happening.

"I hereby recommend this lost, bitter, dangerous little girl for boot-camp in Sector 4, to learn her place in our fair society. She has been uncooperative, deceptive, and wilfully offensive."

The guards stormed out, just as briskly as they had arrived. Samyukta ran to hide in her room. Her fate was sealed.

# 33
# BAM

"Here it is. I knew it. You are a very lucky woman, Jyoti! There is a very productive period on the horizon. You and a handful of other people stand to benefit from a *Punya* multiplier that is likely to make you very rich very quickly, spiritually speaking of course," the munshi sounded excited.

*Shani* was in transmigration and *Rahu* was in regression. This combination of planetary movements would prove to be devastating for some people and beneficial for others. Munshis at the Bureau of Astrological Mensuration (BAM) used mathematics and prayers to determine the impact on their flock. It was their job to warn or encourage them about the future.

"It is a lucrative time for you. Just work harder than usual. Try to exceed your targets and give no one a chance to say that you could do better."

They were supposed to meet every six months, only this time, she had an ulterior motive. It was impossible for pariahs and binaaydis to enter the Bureau. It meant death. Even she had been checked, quizzed, and patted down before being allowed to come through. Abhimanyu and Dhruv had given her an inconspicuous gadget that they had only ever referred to as 'the Filter'. It was a small black cylinder with wires and pincers. Taped to its side was a small blade. It all fit comfortably in her palm and she rolled it around anxiously. They had assured her that it was not a bomb or explosive of any kind and for some reason that now eluded her, she had trusted them.

"That is great news Munshi ji, but will it be enough? My medical costs have increased after the accident and my pregnancy. Not to mention my DD lens. I must make up for this sudden *vipada*."

"Stop being so dramatic, Mata ji. Everything will be alright. The lens cost was nothing . . ."

She had worked her entire life for OMNI and the Ministry of Industry and Innovation. She was an expert and her output had improved hundredfold since the day she started work. She was a model worker and a recipient of many medals, yet she struggled. It was simple mathematics that drove them every year. If you completed a thousand units in one week, the next week's target was eleven hundred. Outputs were, therefore, never good enough. She was sick of the design. It had never changed and the emblem was part of her, stamped in her memory like the scar of a lash, reopened every day, every hour, and every working minute.

Take a patch from the spotted bucket carefully, place a new shirt under the needle promptly, hook the needle and thread swiftly around the third and second bobbin, place the emblem two inches from the centre button neatly, measure the distance from the armpit precisely, calibrate till you are in position and focus the needle at the starting point of the emblem's top right edge, start pedalling. Pedal hard. Harder!

Move the shirt to ensure that fifteen stitches land along the border of the emblem every ten seconds. Complete the border and ensure that the two pieces are now one. Slide the shirt into the green striped bucket on the right hand side. Take a patch from the spotted bucket. Repeat.

The women were encouraged to say prayers in time with their actions. It was a great way to keep the mind from wandering. She favoured Om namah Shivaya over all other prayers and muttered it to herself unknowingly, all the time. Karmacharis and sentries kept a watch and reported damage at the earliest possible indication, to limit the time spent on a spoilt product. She had never seen anyone wearing a shirt that she had made, but that was a different matter. It must have been shipped to other parts of Dvarca, just as most of the products that were allotted to them, came from distant quarters and specialist factories.

"I can set aside more shifts for you. You can earn more on the weekends."

"I have two children Mahoday, and a third is on the way . . ."

"That does complicate matters. What about your husband, could he help out?"

"Why would he not?"

She looked around the messy room. She had been told that the adapters, routers, and circuitry were above the ceiling boards. She looked at the squares above her and found the odd one. She felt the spokes of the black toy in her hand. How was she going to stand on top of his desk and plug it into the network?

"There are a few options . . . they need volunteers at the hospital in your Sector, they need temple cleaners, that's one of the highest paying, and then there are the *pundits* and their *rasoi*. What do you think he would prefer?"

"I will speak to him. How much for the temple cleaner's work?" She wiped beads of perspiration from her upper lip. She felt parched.

"It is 151 PBs an hour for men, 101 PBs for women. I can allot three hours for the next few weekends."

"That is most kind of you, Munshi ji." She started to feel unwell and the room started to spin.

"Don't thank me, these opportunities keep coming up. Your work KDR has also been generally impressive." He typed away with great speed on his giant computer.

"What about my baby-bonus?"

"Yes, that is subject to approval. Which phase are you in?"

"It's been four months since the UET."

"Oh then you are still far from your first pay-out. I would not count on that alleviating any pressure any time soon. Are you alright?"

She nodded uncomfortably. The munshi could see that she was sweating profusely.

"You have a balance of about 19,840 PBs."

Jyoti held her head and leaned to one side as pressure built up behind her eyes. She took a deep breath; it turned into many.

"Your target for moksha in this life is 5,59,301 PBs. That means that a lot more needs to be done, and I have not even counted the amount required for the antim yatra pujan ceremonies. Mata ji, are you feeling well? You look pale . . . can I get you something?"

"No, I am alright. I understand."

"We did not ask for our heavenly debts, but it is important that we do our best to repay them."

"I know . . . fate is fair." The nausea was unbearable.

She held up her hand, "I—I need help—"

The frightened munshi looked at her. The palpitations might as well have been contagious. He got up from his chair and shouted.

"There is a pregnant woman who is unwell! Call an ambulance!"

"I need my Aditi . . . I need my Aditi now . . ."

"Stay here Mata ji, I will go and get someone!"

He ran out of the consultation room yelling for assistance. She took the opportunity and climbed on top of his table. She pushed the square in the ceiling. It did not budge.

"Call an ambulance!" someone shouted. She could hear footsteps and commotion outside. She punched the square and slid it to the side. There it was. The circuitry looked different from the one they had trained her on, and she panicked even more. She used the blade to shave the wire and connected the two loose pincers from the filter. The lights on the filter stayed dim. It was the wrong orientation. She fumbled and rotated the device, nearly dropping it. She could barely breathe. She reconnected the pincers. Light. Magnificent light! Dhruv had to get into the network. His first order of business was to tweak the surveillance footage in the room. She waited to hear from them. Seconds felt like hours as the commotion outside grew louder.

XX: "IT IS DONE. WE ARE IN. LOOPED REPLACEMENT FOOTAGE IS QUEUED. WELL DONE."

She pulled the ceiling square back into place. She had a moment of relief before she dismounted, stumbled about, and collapsed at the door.

***

"She has been through a lot lately."

The Aditi spoke to Gandharva.

"You should be doing more to make her feel comfortable. Her vitals have been quite erratic. Especially her blood pressure. This is not normal. She is exhausted and very tense."

"Is the baby okay?"

"The baby is fine. But your wife seems to have a strange nervous condition."

"What condition?"

"Would you say she is anxious, easily perturbed?"

"No, I have not noticed this."

"Talk to her. It is bad for the baby."

Jyoti lay in a hospital bed. She was praying when he pulled the curtains and entered. He sat down beside her.

"How are you feeling?"

"I am well."

"Praise Krishna!"

"Praise Krishna." She fiddled with the hospital rosary.

"You don't need to worry so much about Punya. I am doing well and I will do better. For you. For us. The munshi told me you were asking for extra work."

She looked away, sheepishly.

"I know how brave you are. Don't think I don't see it. Don't think for one second that I don't see how much you do for us."

He held her palm and pressed it in his hands.

"We will make everything better. Look . . ."

He pulled out a projector from his satchel.

"What are you doing?"

"I just want to show you something."

"Where did you get that?"

"Borrowed it from the office. I've been doing some work on my own—it's not important. I want you to see this . . . look."

The projector beamed up a hologram that began as fluffy pillows, and finally took the form and definition of walls. A couch, a television, a rug, and an altar appeared. It was their apartment. Gandharva proceeded to pick away and point at different objects, sizing them up, and shaking his head.

"This is what we have."

He keyed in some details on the controls and a second three dimensional holographic image appeared.

"There we go, a telling juxtaposition. You see that? This is how we should live. For our age, gene-tag, and job functions, this is how the ninetieth percentile lives. Do you see that big TV? The carpeting from Bengal? The couch, Indore's finest! And now look at us—our house has none of these things. Why is that?"

She was not expecting this from him. It felt like a kalaava review.

"We don't talk about this. But we should. We should share our goals. We should work towards them together. I want you to have that carpeting from Bengal. I want us to work so hard, that they give us an award for being the best Dvarcan family of the year."

"I don't know what to say."

"I want us to have all this. You will not need to work extra shifts."

"I want to earn my own Punya."

"That you will. That you do. I just don't want you to put more pressure on yourself, especially when you are with child. Our child."

She searched his face to see if there was more to what he was saying. It was all about transactions and acquisitions. She smiled at his folly and he took it as understanding. He held her hand and said a prayer, with the apartment-holograms still whirling above them like castles and *khayali pulao* in the sky.

# 34
# THE GIFT

Arjun Virdi had put it up on the wall in his room after making a few additions to the sketch. Most notable was the text he had stencilled-in at the bottom, in bright letters alternately in black and red, 'DIE CALIPHITE SCUM!' He beamed as he greeted his star pupil. Nakul was shocked, flattered, and disturbed in that order. It was his father on the wall, defeated and half-dead.

"Have a seat, Nakul."

"Thank you, Guru ji."

"I am very happy today. Very happy."

The teacher shut the door. For some reason it made everything in there sound louder. The creaky fan sped along to its own beat and there was a strange whirring noise from one of the concealed risers to their right.

"Thank you for putting up my sketch. It is an honour, Guru ji."

"The honour is mine. I am pleased to inform you that you have topped your cohort once again. That's five years in a row, son!"

There was a brief moment of silence as the doting Arjun fawned over young Nakul.

"How do you do it?"

"I guess I have my teachers to thank."

"Do you see that you excel at things they are still learning?"

"My peers?"

"Everyone, all of them. You have surpassed even some of your seniors."

"I don't know."

"Your physical development, intelligence, strategic thinking, and application of knowledge, these are all exceptional. Do you know why?"

"Why Sir?"

"You are the first of your kind, Nakul."

"I don't understand."

"You are a new Nakul. The Ministry of Community Development and Animal Husbandry has named you Parshuram."

"Parshuram?"

"Yes. A special new gene-tag of warrior-administrator-leaders. We were supposed to keep this from you till you were more mature, in years. I made the case that you are already much more advanced than boys twice your age."

Nakul's head grew 10 sizes and his heart sped along like an unfettered cheetah in the wild.

"Can I tell everyone about this?"

"Ah, no. You must keep this to yourself. Only the Ministry, you, and I can know. Even your parents do not know that you are part of a test. They think you are ordinary."

"They think I am less than ordinary," he looked up at his sketch again.

"I doubt that, son. You know every now and then, the Vaigs get it right. Science rarely manages to keep up with human ambition, but when it does, it gives us people like you."

"Thank you Guru ji. This is incredible."

"Feels good to know that your skills and abilities came from on-high, doesn't it? You were born with a gift. Excellence is in your nature."

"It is humbling, Guru ji, truly. Though I do owe my deep interest in matters of war, administration, and leadership to people like you, my teachers. I thank you for giving me direction. Tell me, how am I different from other Nakuls, genetically speaking? Do I have special powers?"

Virdi laughed.

"I am surprised you have to ask me that. You are clearly better in every conceivable way, from intellectual acumen to stamina and endurance."

Nakul nodded in agreement. He disregarded the few times he had been defeated in a race and the odd B-grade in studies.

"At the next Annual Day function, you will receive almost a dozen prizes. I thought we could give you a small reward earlier."

"What's that, Guru ji?"

He reached into his drawer and pulled out a bag. With great care, he removed a book from it and held it up for Nakul.

"My personal copy of Shastri ji's great book. It was distributed at a convention 15 years ago. It's an early reprint. You can tell, as they moved some of the chapters around, after this version." He opened it to flaunt the date on the copy.

"I want you to have it."

"I couldn't possibly take this from you."

"I insist, it is part of your curriculum next year. Have you already read it?"

"I have heard bits and pieces, over the years. But no, I have never read it from start to finish."

"It's yours. Take it. Cherish it. You are already a valiant Navmargi. This will show you how the great man thought."

Nakul held it in his hand and caressed the simple orange and purple cover. It was sparse in design and had the words '*My Road to Navmarg*' in a small, bold font at the centre. The supreme leader's name followed, in a slightly larger font below.

"Thank you, I have no words."

"I would also like to introduce you to the 'Art of Shooting'. I have booked us a time at the range next week. Don't worry about the age limit, I will take you in."

"I get to fire a weapon?"

"Many weapons! You get to start your training early." Nakul left Arjun Virdi's office. He ran to the playground and found a secluded spot under a tree. He could not wait to open his prize to the first page . . .

# MY ROAD TO NAVMARG

# NIRMAL SHASTRI

Her suffering was my suffering. Her desires and aspirations were my desires and aspirations. Her trials and tribulations turned out to be profoundly, deeply, personally my own. She cradled me in Her arms and She shaped my world. Today I can say with pride, that I look after Her. She is mine. She is ours. She is Mother Dvarca.

In this book, I would like to share my vision and story with you, to shed light on who I am and who I want to be, in the hope that you may benefit from it. I cannot claim perfection, but I can state with no qualms, that my life has been a relentless pursuit of this ideal.

May these stories change you, the way they have changed me. May you too find your way through Navmarg.

For God and Country

Pdt. Shri Dr. Nirmal Shastri

*'Few men can claim to have their lives so deeply intertwined with the life of our Nation. Shastri ji is a unique stalwart in this regard. He has spent his entire life working for us all. We owe him a great debt.'*

—Lal Narad Vedshankar

Hon. Minister of Media Control and Communication

*'I hope this book will be an inspiration, an education, and a guide for the youth of our Nation as they find their feet and march with us to a new tomorrow.'*

—Lal Gandharva Gupte

Hon. Minister of Finance and Salvation

I.

In this business where saying is doing, I must admit that I am a lonely stranger. Lonely, because there is no one else around who seems to be saying the things I wish so desperately to hear. I suppose it has become my lot in life to present these truths to you, myself. I am a stranger to this business because I am no wordsmith and I have no shame in admitting that. I do not know how this will end and I cannot promise that it will be pretty. I am just a man of action, compelled by circumstance to open his mouth and speak to you, my slumbering friend, my dear friend, my pacifist, my believing non-believer, my placid platoon, my army in waiting, my gentle giant, my fellow infidel.

At this time I am in prison. They have accused me of murder. I did not kill Dhansukh Paramhansa. He was my closest friend and these charges are preposterous. It is all part of a conspiracy to malign and discredit our movement. Anyone who knows me, would attest to the fact that I am incapable of hurting a fly, let alone my dearest comrade—may he find peace.

This book is divided into five parts. This first part speaks of my vision for Dvarca—how I want our country to be. The other four chapters recall incidents from my life that have made me the man I am today. *They* fear me today because I dare to speak the truth. They have tried in many ways to destroy the *Shakha* because they are threatened by our national popularity. In these dark times, when we needed to unite against a common enemy, they have chosen to bicker and condemn me, to settle old scores. Their ruse is so plain.

Poor Dhansukh's body was never found. In my recorded testimony I told them where to look for him. He gave his life for the cause. He died in my arms, in that cave in Mahajageshwar. To prevent further investigation and to keep us from uncovering the truth, *they* destroyed the entire cave. I can never go back to the point of my rebirth and we can never revisit that shrine inside the mountain. Because of a few meddling, petty fiends, Mahajageshwar is lost.

The country is in a bad way. We are on the cusp of a great war and our people need me more than ever at this time. That is why I have written this book. I seek a new Nation. I seek not a weak Bharat of selfish, cowardly, and corrupt politicians. I seek Dvarca, my ideal.

**In my vision, Dvarca will be:**

- A Nation based on the sacred principles of Navmarg (the guiding light for humanity).
- Ruthless towards the promulgators of the evil Caliphate (and all who challenge Navmarg).
- Immune to the failed experiment of multiculturalism (a homogenous, peaceful society).
- A bastion of safety for cows (they are kind, generous, and holy).
- Never wanting (a land of plenty, where people take only what they need).

What does it mean to be a Navmargi? We decide. What does it mean to be a Dvarcan? We decide. Life is a battle for meaning. Politics is a war of nouns. If our definitions survive and thrive, we have won. I invite everyone to join me in making this Nation great again. Let us band together, vilified infidels, targets of beasts, and victims of the past! Let us all come together for the defence of our Nation and our ideals. In it, lies our salvation.

### Our guiding principles

We must never suffer the pariahs. We must insist that they pledge allegiance to our flag. The *Dharmic* man must forever be vigilant, watching over his shoulder for signs of terror. Evil manifests itself in many ways, most commonly as pariahs. They are everywhere and they are out to harm us. It is, therefore, the duty of every able-bodied man and woman to be on high alert at all times and look out for signs of these demons.

Here are my thoughts on what we need to change, to become a great Nation again.

**Values**

The distribution of wealth and rewards is inequitable and must change. In the new economy, in days to come, we will install a system that recognizes the contribution of an individual, weighs, and values it in a new way. We must impose radical new benchmarks for the measurement of remuneration and the determination of what is important to us all. A man's work and worth will be measured by the extent to which he improves the lives of others. My eyes have been opened by the great revelation in Mahajageshwar. I have learnt how to reinstate our traditions and at the same time, drive our population towards progress.

We will shoulder development and foster benevolence. This does not mean a complete annihilation of the profit motive, most certainly not. It means that there must be an equitable distribution of those profits, a sharing in taking. This can only be guaranteed if we all agree on what is good and holy. Only when we realize that we have a common end in sight, can we begin to check and balance the means.

The other problem I see is that certain types of behaviour seem to forge success. Certain occupations and industries have brought us to the quagmire we see ourselves in, today. They encourage selfishness and profit. Those who share in the profits are far too few. Successful people live in bubbles and protect themselves from the grotesque realities of our towns and cities. They spend day after day, going through a series of impervious conduits of private comfort, without once caring for the people that make it all possible for them. There are a significant number of poor people in this country living out squalid lives at the feet of their masters. This can only change when we base rewards on values. We must ask ourselves, "***What is the good that we have done?***"

**Family**

Upon being asked whom they would save, at any cost, most people answer: their families. What is this bond? Where does it come from? It is from fathers and mothers to their children. It is a connection of blood. I would like to expand this definition of family to cover the whole of society.

We are connected to one another. We are connected through ***our stomachs***, born, and bred on the same food, the same crops and supplies. Brothers and sisters have their mother's cooking in common. Every mother makes her daal a bit differently. Every mother makes kaddu a certain way. These nuances, when recalled, are bound to put a collective smile on the faces of her children. Long after she is dead and gone, the memory of her *achaar* lives on. This is power. This is the most basic and easy to understand adhesive for a group.

Similarly, ***our hearts*** ought to be connected by our heritage. Sadly today, this is not the case. We should share a reverence for the same great religious, historical, architectural, musical, literary, and scientific monuments. We do not respect our national symbols the way we respect and protect our temples. We must all learn and celebrate our past to re-establish our superiority in every field.

***Our minds*** are not one today, either. We quarrel and debate endlessly. There are as many ways to do something as there are people thinking on it. This is undesirable and counter-productive. For progress to occur, one voice must lead the way. All others must fall in line and think of ways to serve the grand plan. If they do not, they might as well be terrorists, blowing up bridges and houses, instead of strengthening them. We have a lot of original thinkers today, but their ingenuity is restricted to serving themselves. If this genius were given a new road to walk on, what could it not achieve?

I envision a society wherein we all share ***the same stomachs, hearts, and minds.*** Where we all have the same father, obey him and accept his wisdom. We will continue to live in smaller family units, within which, the larger bond will be learnt and demonstrated.

**Defence**

While diplomatic solutions, discussions, and sweet exchanges catch up with ground realities, it is necessary for the defenders of the Nation to take a stand. Teaching others the language of words takes time. Until then, we must use our fists.

What is your ideal State, where do you think it will end? The last terrorist turns in his weapons? The end of animosity? The end of conflicting ideologies? What would it take for this special mix of circumstance, opportunism, and hate to never repeat itself? What do we need? Are you going to tell someone that their child died in vain? What good could come from such a discussion?

The country has not been able to live up to the sacrifice made by our martyrs. We have failed them and we do not do justice to the lives they have allowed us to lead. We owe them a great debt. But who are they? Are they not from us? Are they not our brothers, sisters, fathers, uncles, neighbours? They are us. We owe it to ourselves. Liberties paid for in blood, must not be squandered. Liberties saved through sacrifice, must not be taken for granted. Military losses are a measure of how much a Nation values certain principles, borders, and causes. It shows how far we have gone, how far we can go, and how far we want to go, in defence of what matters to us.

It would be just and necessary to demand, from hereon, that every transgression from our enemy be met with a retaliation that is at least three times as destructive. Only then, will they learn that their actions have serious repercussions.

## Language

There are very few opportunities for the masses to lift themselves out of their morass. Education is segregated and only the rich have access to the best forms of schooling. They learn and equip themselves to be the most employable. They preserve their privilege by furthering this divide. It is all linked to language. The playing field is uneven. Sadly today, English has become the norm. To be hired, one must speak it, to be taken seriously, one must read it. This must change. We are living in a slave mindset.

We have been crippled by years of British rule. Our expression remains colonized. As a citizen and a Navmargi, I resent this. There needs to be a single, strong alternative. The notion that regional languages must grow and flourish, is also misguided. It takes us back centuries, to a time of small kingdoms with their egotistical petty differences, their pride. We are not those people any more. We have a common language, just as we have a common heritage. This language, one of our greatest gifts to this world, is Sanskrit. It is the language of our scriptures. It is the mother of all thought and expression.

I propose a resurgence of Sanskrit as a solution to India's problem of language. Those who oppose it are against our heritage. Those who oppose it are against our Nation. They want us to remain disunited, fighting like babbling children trying to get our way. We must acknowledge and accept that Sanskrit is the glue that can hold us together. It will facilitate mobility, create opportunities through easier collaboration and it will put an end to the unearned, undeserved hegemony of the West. They will themselves one day, line up to learn Sanskrit!

***

The bell rang and Nakul had to return to class. He had only made a small dent in the Great Leader's book. He hoped to have it autographed someday.

# 35
# POWER TO THE PEOPLE

Abhimanyu and Dhruv sat together, huddled over their make-shift computer, in the sewer below the Bureau of Astrological Mensuration.

"We are not terrorists."

"We are patriots."

"Doesn't that sound a bit too much like them?"

"No, we sound different."

"We do not believe in the killing of innocents."

"The Caliphate though . . ."

"The Caliphate makes a living off it."

"We must let our people know that we do not espouse any ideology other than the charter of the League of Moderates."

"I was thinking about that name—we may need something a bit more aggressive."

"You want the League of Moderates to have an aggressive name?"

"Something that says, 'come to us'. As opposed to something that allows people to dismiss us easily."

"Peace Patrol?"

"Sort of an oxymoron."

"But we are vigilantes. We want to take things into our own hands and restart dialogue in a fractured world."

"Voice of Reason?"

"Too adolescent. Too young, wide-eyed, and self-righteous."

"How many coordinates have we got?"

"1,35,886 and counting." The ticker on his screen kept score.

"We have friends on the other side, who want to engage us."

"There has been nothing from them for days. Maybe we scared them."

"I don't think it us that they fear. They might be in trouble too."

"They might be dead."

"You might hate me for asking you this. What'll we achieve?"

"By telling the truth? We'll be able to take back the story."

"Yes, but stories only affect those who are open to them. Most people are too far gone."

"I wish this was all over. I wish Faiz was free."

"People must learn that he is innocent. How many on the counter now?"

"1,38,652 . . . I hope it doesn't overheat."

The Filter had a limited radius and its bandwidth had never really been tested. They were using it to pull DD numbers and coordinates of Dvarcan citizens, from the otherwise secure network. They had to make the most of the extraction, before the batteries died.

***

Jyoti was feeling unwell that morning and decided to stay home. Baba was still asleep and she had little to do other than watch television. She had finished with her prayers and had a big breakfast. Her appetite had returned and the giddiness had started to dissipate too. The sensors lit up and acknowledged her presence in the bathroom. She felt her belly and looked at it in the mirror. For all practical purposes, her sari was red. All other colours were just pigments of her imagination. She tried to sneak a glance from under her DDs and spotted a sliver of 'grey' cloth.

The doorbell rang and Jyoti took her time to waddle over to the entrance and answer it. The local Vanaprasthis had brought her a tonic. They had started visiting her every week, to help around the house and care for her while she was expecting.

"You didn't have to, Mata ji."

"Of course we did. We are all having a Vidur. How could we leave you alone when you are feeling sick today?"

"I am a lot better."

She took the *kullar* from them. Three sweet, petite women stood in front of her.

"We want to watch you drink it, do you mind?" This was not an unusual request and it seemed to give them great satisfaction. The old ladies waited as she lifted the *kullar* of cool milk and herbs to her lips and finished it in a few sips.

"Does it help you?"

"I think so."

"You must believe that it will help you. That is the most important thing."

"Yes, Mata ji."

"How is your boy doing? I hear he is already some kind of a hero?"

"He is alright, he works hard but he is a bit naughty if you ask me."

"Naughty children make for serious adults. We need men like him."

"For God and Country."

"For God and Country. This was very nice of you."

"Just invite us for an *uchchaaran* when your Vidur starts interpreting the great texts."

"I will, Mata ji."

The old ladies entered the house.

"We are not done. Have you met Neel Mira? She lives across the street."

A beautiful young woman was with them. She came forward with a respectful nod of the head. She was expecting too.

"We thought we could all help you do your Requisitions this month."

Two of them went to the kitchen and one of them sat down in front of the TV. They were feisty old ladies with a healthy sense of pluck. They were bent with age, but brimming with energy.

"How many months till you pop?"

The Mira pulled off the *pallu* of her saree and stood proudly, displaying her stomach. The two mothers shared a knowing smirk.

"About two—"

"You definitely are about to. Please go and rest!" Jyoti urged her to leave, but her suggestion was not accepted. The women started pottering around and Baba, disturbed by the noise, came out from his room to see what was going on.

"Please go back to bed Baba, you have had a long night."

He shut the door, grumbling to himself.

"He is quite a grumpy old coot," one of the ladies piped up, they all shared a laugh.

Mira sat down with Jyoti on their couch and caressed her hand softly.

"Are you going to start scaling back your shifts at work?"

"Yes, I think I should. This is my third child and I can't believe how much harder it is."

"She is my first," the Mira said coyly. She looked over to see the Vanaprasthi Ammas busily going through tins of supplies in the kitchen and counting bars of soap in the store.

"Did you have an annunciation?" She whispered.

"I did for my first child. I have a Mira who is 12."

"Was that easier? I would have liked to know that they were coming for me."

"I don't know. I don't question their decisions."

"You know, I actually heard that some girls tried to run away when they heard about the IMP visitation—tried to disappear! Can you imagine?"

"They walked out on their dharma?"

"Oh no—they were caught. Caught and impregnated."

"Jyoti, *beti*, you are running low on almost everything . . . this order is going to be a big one," one of the Ammas shouted from the kitchen.

There had been many unexpected expenses lately. The weekly *pujas* had become more costly and the contribution to the pundits' *dharamshala* had also been increased. They said it was in lieu of Gandharva's promotion. It had been on the cards for quite some time. The Requisition was a list of items that every household ticked from a list. Supplies were delivered accordingly, usually within one half-moon cycle from the time of submission.

"You are lucky we came over today."

"Yes, thank you, Mata ji. I really do appreciate it."

"*Lok-Shakti* is about to start. Could we watch it with you, please?"

They turned the television on. The opening music for *Lok-Shakti* had just concluded. It was a show in which people would send in photographs, sound-recordings, and video captures of fellow citizens committing infractions or crimes. The show had no host and it was just a stream of snippets broadcasting the good work of citizen spies.

The first criminal that day was an Annapurna agent who had been caught digging his nose while making a food delivery. The amazing, interactive element of the television show was that viewers could react to what they saw on the screen. A barrage of comments appeared as a ticker. All sorts of animal names and eviscerating, biting curses were lobbed at the portly, unsuspecting nostril spelunker.

"Fire the fat pig. Make him a pariah!"

"He has no business working in the Annapurna division. He is disgusting."

"I am frightened and appalled!"

Next on the people's name-and-shame list was a four-year-old who was wearing slippers inside a temple complex. The commenting participants went absolutely berserk, blaming him, his parents, their sector, and even his school.

"How could that boy not know that he should remove his slippers?" Mira wondered.

For long, Jyoti had suspected that the incidents on the show were doctored or manufactured to drive outrage. They were usually very obvious, indisputable infractions that everyone could pile-on against. Mob justice was special. Every bombardier reinforced his comrade's righteousness and convictions. Each outraged voice kept trying to out-screech the ones before it. In the midst of all the madness, these words flew across Jyoti's DDs.

"NAVMARG IS A LIE."

She could not believe her eyes.

"THE GOVERNMENT OF DVARCA IS RESPONSIBLE FOR THE MURDER OF INNOCENTS." The blasphemy continued.

"M-Mira, do you see what I see?"

"See what, Jyoti?" The Mira was oblivious.

Two of the Ammas received the same messages. Baba too, came out in his underpants, shouting about the barbaric words bouncing about on his Divya Drishtikon.

"What is happening?"

"YOU HAVE BEEN FED NOTHING BUT LIES, TO CONTROL YOU. CLICK HERE, FOR THE TRUTH."

"Who is sending these messages?" Baba called the Terrorism Helpline, but the line was busy.

"I am being attacked with inflammatory messages! They are not leaving my screen!" He shouted anyway.

Jyoti recognized the font. One of the Ammas lay on the kitchen floor. She had clicked the link embedded in the message. There was a song and video playing on her DDs. It was even better than the real thing.

***

A SWAT helicopter descended upon the Bureau of Astrology and Mensuration. The DDs broadcasting unauthorized messages to Dvarcans belonged to a deceased junior staff who used to work there. According to their triangulations, he was inside the building compound. Fifteen Varaha men jumped out of the helicopters, while a dozen others dismounted from speeding trucks that had barely come to a halt. They stormed the bureau office.

"WE DENOUNCE THE CALIPHATE. WE DENOUNCE DVARCA. WE DENOUNCE ANYONE WHO PREACHES HATE."

They kicked down doors and pushed the confused staff and munshis to the side. Some of them were receiving the messages too. You could tell whether a person's mind had been blown by how far their jaw was from the floor.

"WE CAN NO LONGER STAND BY, WHILE LIARS AND CHARLATANS DIVIDE THE WORLD FOR THEIR GAIN. MODERATE VOICES MUST PREVAIL. REASON MUST RULE. CLICK HERE FOR THE TRUTH."

"It is spam . . . no one will pay attention to it . . ." one of the senior munshis made the mistake of speaking to the Varaha. He was elbowed in the nose and they walked over him as he squirmed in pain on the floor.

"FAIZ HAS BEEN FRAMED. WE HAVE BEEN FRAMED AND PUSHED OUT OF OUR OWN COUNTRY."

*Clicking for the truth revealed a grainy, scratchy 30-second video of Varaha officers inside the Industrial Complex, setting up explosives and re-arranging people in chairs. They destroyed the surveillance cameras and evacuated the area. In a jump-cut, the complex was shown from afar, devastated by the explosion. All the footage was taken from a hidden camera.*

The SWAT team searched the entire office and came to an abandoned supply shed behind the buidling. Their tracker showed that the sender of the messages was nearby. The door was unlocked and they pushed it open. There was nothing there. One of them climbed on top of the shed and looked around. Just outside the Bureau compound, along the outer wall, lay an unwieldy and wiry shell of a computer, a pair of bloody DDs, and a connection apparatus.

"WE ARE NOT CALIPHITES OR NAVMARGIS. WE ARE THE VOICE YOU HAVE LEARNT TO IGNORE."

They shot the DDs and broke the computer. The messages stopped. Approximately 3,50,000 Dvarcans had received the strange, incendiary messages straight to their DDs that day.

# 36
# NAKUL'S TRAINING

Nakul Parshuram stood at the edge of the yellow line and raised his R9, pointing it at the target in front of him. It was a bearded man with a grenade in his hand who grinned maniacally as he charged forward.

"What do you think you should do? In one shot, how would you take care of this advancing Caliphite?"

"Is he a Caliphite?"

"Does he not look like a terrorist to you? You must kill this man. How will you do it?"

Virdi adjusted the training software and this made the advancing militant run faster. He shouted some curses and Nakul tried to keep him in his sights. He took a deep breath and fired. The simulation showed that he had struck the grenade in the attacker's hand. It blew him to smithereens. The shot had not been fired soon enough though. It would have also hurt the good sons of Dvarca.

"Faster! You must act faster! Again!"

The simulator restarted and the same crazy-eyed images of a charging, screaming, enemy trooper flickered in front of them. Nakul followed his movement and shot the terrorist in his hand, this time forcing the grenade to fall at his feet. The terrorist just stopped and looked at his bleeding hand. The grenade rolled away, undetonated. The desperate marauder reached for it. Nakul shot him in the other hand and he backed away in surrender. His blood looked bluish-green. It glowed in the simulation. Arjun Virdi watched as Nakul unloaded two more shots into the terrorist's shins, rendering him limbless. There was no sound, just the reflection of the strange alien liquid in Nakul's goggles. He smiled.

"Why—why not finish him off, son?"

"He should live. They should take him back. It will strike fear in the hearts of his compatriots and co-conspirators."

"Have you looked at it the other way, though? What if it strengthens their resolve?"

"How could it?"

"We are inspired by the blood of our martyrs. What is to stop them from being moved by this man's suffering?

"But he is evil. He is not a martyr."

"They do not know that. They think we are evil. To them, we are scum."

"Would it be better if I killed him?"

"It usually is. You are empowering him by leaving him in this state."

"If I kill him, won't his name become a rallying cry?"

The fallen Caliphite was flat on his back, waving his arms and legs around in small circles, like a helpless Hawksbill turtle. Nakul took aim and shot him between the eyes. He died and the simulation ended. Report statistics showed that he had failed the training. This was because of the number of shots fired and the duration before the threat was quelled. Nakul lowered his gun, disappointed.

"We could have taken him in for questioning."

"Yes, but that was not the objective of your mission. You must follow the mission directives closely."

"Tell me. Did it upset you when we heard reports from the front, about the beasts that urinated on the corpses of our boys?"

"It did. It hurt me. I don't understand why they did that."

"It was a final insult. They added grave insult to fatal injury. It was inhuman."

"But killing our people was inhuman too, Guru ji!"

"There are rules in battle too, son."

"There should be no rules when you are fighting demons. These are *rakshasas*, Guru ji."

Virdi had no answer to that.

"I would consider it my duty to despatch them to the netherworld with the most pain. Their end should be as horrific as the lives they led."

"Would you like to look at some of our weapons in development?"

"Of course, Guru ji! Please!"

Virdi was a Santri with orange access. They went through several chambers and numerous ID verifications, before they found themselves in a sleek, modern, bare room with curved walls.

"This is the demo centre. All our new defence technology is showcased in this room for ministers, generals, and other important people."

"I am honoured!" Nakul walked around the room.

"This is a very interesting keyboard."

"It is not just a keyboard, it is a command console. One of the Vishvakarmas will be along shortly. Ah! Here he comes."

A harrowed looking man with a clumsily shaved moustache barged into the room.

"For God and Country! I wish you had sent word *Acharya.* I would have set things up in advance."

"Not a problem, Vaig. Please show us something interesting—this young man is very curious about our latest breakthroughs in the field of applied sciences."

"What clearance does he have Sir, you are an esteemed Santri, but our young friend, how do I—you know, what can I . . . should we . . . I must first be—wait let's see."

He waffled and squirreled an argument with himself and came to the conclusion that a stock presentation might do the trick.

"Sit back—I mean stand back, stay where you are, okay?"

Virdi turned to Nakul with a look of disdain for the twitchy scientist. The white walls of the room came alive with the oblong contour of a silver screen. Their fidgety guide moved his hands about in a violent frenzy like a butterfly-collector chasing after a special breed. He wore a simple blue plastic ring that connected with the display and allowed him to move great stacks of information intuitively. He rummaged through the virtual files, lifting and sifting. Every now and then, he turned to Virdi Sir and mumbled some form of an apology.

"I am, you know, embarrassed . . . sorry sorry . . . just one more—"

"Do you want us to return at another time? How long will this search take?"

"Not long—t minus . . . a few seconds . . . one minute hold on . . . how is it that? Oh I see!"

He had found what he was looking for, and he stepped back, victorious. He raised his hands to the sky in a grand gesture, as though he were about to unveil the greatest show on earth.

"Here—now—it is ready. Please listen. Enjoy. Young . . . Sir . . . what is your name?"

"Parshuram," Nakul said.

The presentation began.

"FOR GOD AND COUNTRY—HOLY PROPERTY OF THE CITIZENS OF DVARCA."

The rest of the presentation had a voice-over in a language that Virdi and Nakul did not understand.

"What is this? It sounds foreign!"

The technician leaped off the ground and waved his hands about like a desperate pedestrian trying to warn a bus of his existence. The visuals were crystal clear and it was evident that they were about to tell an important story about some new machine. But the language was strange and musical. Alien words with inscrutable meaning rattled out of the speakers in rising and falling tones, like an army of '*Huas*', '*Kshs*' and '*Chaws*'.

"What have you done, you talking-ulcer?! I have had just about enough of your incompetence. I demand that you take this seriously. Go—get out of my sight immediately and send someone who knows what he is doing. I will take this up with your supervisor," Virdi reprimanded him.

"Sorry, I . . . different versions . . . it is—I will—"

"Do I have to throw you out?"

"One more, one more chance, right one—this is—throw if not . . . Please Sir, sorry sorry—watch now—"

The theatricality of his hand gestures was less ostentatious this time, and he backed away slowly. He slid to the ground and held his hand over his mouth, his eyes open wide.

"What is wrong with you?" Nakul asked him.

"All . . . God . . . nothing . . . Country . . . please . . . watch now . . . watch watch."

This time the sound was different but the visuals were the same. It was reassuring, familiar, heart-warming Sanskrit.

"FOR GOD AND COUNTRY—HOLY PROPERTY OF THE CITIZENS OF DVARCA."

An old-timey map of the world appeared on the screen. It changed slowly to different scenes of battle as the honey soaked voice-over tied everything together.

*For centuries, man has fought man. On land, at sea, and in the air. He has used everything, from sticks and stones to guns, ammunition, and nuclear technology. He has developed and enhanced the ability to fight and kill.*

*OMNI, Dvarca's leading manufacturer of weapons, is at the forefront of this innovation today. There are a number of grand projects, sanctioned and blessed by the Great Leader himself.*

*In this short video demonstration, we will showcase some of the innovative, new Dvarcan defence breakthroughs that will win the wars of the future.*

*The* **Sandehitron Six Thousand** *is an Embedded Proximity Device (EPD) that can make advancing armies paranoid, forcing them to doubt each other and themselves. Early testing has shown great signs of success, resulting in the formation of dangerous rifts, even amongst friends.*

*Continuing in the field of psychological warfare, is the introduction of the* **t-EMP**. *Not to be confused with traditional electromagnetic pulses designed to destabilize and destroy electronic equipment, the modern t-EMP stands for Trauma Empathy Magnification Pulsar.*

*It evokes feelings of grave physical discomfort in enemy combatants, inducing symptoms that resemble post-traumatic stress. Upon exposure, enemy combatants will experience the trauma of losing limbs, loved ones, and suffering cruel torture.*

*Armies need rest, just like anyone else. The* **Insombinator** *makes the latter impossible by converting normal human beings into sleepless drones. They are forced to remain awake using subliminal audio waves. They lose their alertness and experience extreme fatigue, making them easy targets.*

**Agnistambh Seven** *is in development and takes after its ancestor* *missiles of the Agni series. Equipped with new mapping technology, the A7 determines the breadth and extent of the enemy force before impact. It can split into 50 sub-missiles. The combinations are endless and chosen in the air, as it assesses the target. It distributes the weight and form of its impact, to cause maximum destruction within a radius of 20 kilometres.*

*For interpersonal combat, the* **R9** *has undergone major improvements with new sights and seekers. A target chosen in advance can be marked with a standard t-Node to attract bullets fired from the mother gun. It is ideal for difficult assassinations and executions.*

*We hope you have enjoyed this peek into the next generation of OMNI weaponry. When you think defence, think OMNI.*

The presentation came to an end with a beautiful graphic that morphed different weapons into the OMNI logo and their tagline. Nakul could not suppress his awe. He had walked closer to the screen without realizing it. He placed his hand up on the blank silver oblong and turned around.

"May I see it again, please?"

"Which did you like the best?"

"They are all incredible. I don't know what to say," there was a touch of sadness in his voice.

"What's wrong?"

"It just appears that we will need fewer warriors in the future."

"We will always need strategic thinkers. We will always need courageous leaders. Do you fear that we will be replaced?"

"The machines appear to do things so much better."

"Yes but who is making them? Who is firing, triggering, and guiding them? Without essential human involvement, these bombs and missiles are as good as scrap. What do you say, my flustered Vaig?"

"I'm just a Vaig, Sir, my opinion does not count."

"Are you trying to replace us?" Nakul asked him earnestly. The scientist rose to his feet and moved about in an indecisive manner. Just as his words seemed to take his sentences in different directions at once, he seemed to be torn.

"Answer the boy."

"Maximize their losses, minimize ours—kill their boys—not . . . our boys . . . our boys are young and good—theirs are—"

"That's the first sensible thing you've said all evening. Minimize our losses, maximize theirs. The fewer we send out into battle, the fewer we will lose."

"But I want to be out there." The young boy blurted out his demand in the typical whiney tone of a petulant pre-teen.

"Why? God—oh—this one."

"Quiet, Vishvakarma. From now on, you only speak when you are spoken to."

"Not speaking to me now? You . . . oh well."

Virdi Sir placed his hand on Nakul's shoulder.

"I can see that you want to serve your Nation."

"More than anything else, Sir. I want to be a martyr. If I were a pilot, I would pump the Caliphites full of bullets and missiles till all my ammunition were finished. If they were not wiped out, I would fly my plane into their base and burn it. So what if it is my blood. So what if it is my life. I will make sure that my dharma is fulfilled. My karma must match it."

The Vishvakarma slid to the exit and excused himself with another slew of disconnected apologies. Nakul and Arjun Virdi watched him slither out.

"Don't worry about him. I am proud of you, my son. We will find a way to realize your dreams. I have nominated you to be our Pupil of the Year."

# 37
# THE SLOW EPIPHANY

Gandharva had received the trick messages on his DDs. He knew they were ridiculous and refused to click-through to the unregulated pages. It was waste, spam, trash. There would only be deceptions there. It was an invitation to a wild-goose-chase and the starter's gun was pointed at his beliefs. He could not be lured.

There were reports of arrests almost every other day. Demerits and infractions piled up. He looked over his metrics and was pleased to see that the revenue from retraining had quadrupled in just a week. He wanted to make sure that Punya was being allocated correctly and searched for anomalous demerits or reductions.

He sorted the results and saw that there was a surge in the number of people with enormous reductions of 10,00,000 PBs through single transactions. Code 302—it was the largest penalty possible. The drop of so many PBs was a special demerit inflicted on people who went from being Dvarcan citizens to binaaydis. Perhaps more people were exhibiting questionable or unpatriotic behaviour. He pitied them. His sense of curiosity and balance forced him to pound out another query on his keyboard. He searched for the largest quantum of Punya earned and sorted the results. An unfamiliar amount revealed itself.

Some people had been awarded 3,00,000 PBs. These earnings were also through single transactions and happened on the same day for groups of people. The charter had no mention of this credit amount! It was also strange that all these cases had no fiscal activity after the enormous PB credit. He did not understand this and tried querying the personal details of the people who had earned the heavy payload. His system froze and an alarm started. He looked around to see that two guards were trotting towards his desk. He tasted copper and his heart was in his mouth.

"Aasmani Gandharva, Sector 17, Block 8A. Come with us."

"What for?"

The guards smacked him across his face.

"Ask no questions. Come with us."

They dragged him out of his chair as the entire office watched. They took him to a meeting room and threw him in. He waited there for what felt like an eternity. It was 10 minutes. What had he done to incur their wrath? That promotion was completely out of the question now. Maybe his entire career was over. Maybe even his life. He tried to call Jyoti, but his DDs had been blocked. He walked in circles in the meeting room. The door opened and his Peet Gandharva walked in. There was a Peet Arjun of the Varaha with him. The two of them sat down as guards shut the door and left them to talk. There was no escape.

"We are worried about you, Gandharva."

"Why are you searching for specific, individual account details? You know you cannot cross-query, it is beyond your kalaava."

"I know. I apologize. I just—I came across an unknown quantity and wanted to know more about it."

"What quantity?"

"Credit transactions worth 3,00,000 PBs. I can't find them on the charter."

The Peet Gandharva looked concerned. "Who else knows about this?"

"No one, I just noticed it. After that pariah email—there have been a lot of demerits and maximum penalties. I was assessing the accounts for my stock and saw this huge credit, for a group—"

"He does not seem to be lying. The Prevarication Indices are within acceptable limits."

"Good . . . what do you think Arjun ji?"

"He is consistent and quite thorough with his curiosity. It might kill him some day, but it is in line with his past dalliances."

"Dalliances?" Gandharva was unsure if the Peet Arjun was paying him a compliment.

"We will get to the matter of the 3,00,000 PBs in a minute. Did you know that we have been watching you?"

"W-Why?"

"Where have you been going every day at lunch?"

"D-Different places—" Gandharva was petrified.

"Each of your *different* places was the site of an arrest. Yes? You've been visiting spots where pariahs have been arrested. You even searched for a list of these locations on the great Dvarcan Web."

"I did—it's all very silly really, I was just trying to see if my hypothesis was correct."

"What hypothesis?" The Arjun spoke.

The Peet Gandharva smiled and decided to offer an explanation.

"Arjun ji, to keep our low-level Gandharvas alert, we test them regularly."

The Arjun braced himself for what seemed to be the beginning of a long story.

"We test them through random numerical puzzles that pop up in the middle of their work. This Gandharva has been taking snapshots of these tests or puzzles and printing them out. Storing them for posterity." He tossed Gandharva's folders on the table. The Varaha man picked them up and flipped through the print-outs.

"The games ask a very specific question: which is the odd figure in a random set of numbers? Tell us Gandharva, why did you record these tests?"

He hesitated to answer at first, but then realized that telling the truth was his only option. Lying would be of little use as he felt that he was doomed anyway. His holographic dream apartment melted away in his mind.

"The number scatters are like aerial views of . . . certain places in Dvarca. They looked like buildings and roads to me. Like maps—"

"Maps of what specifically?"

"Places where pariahs were caught. It is always in the news. I just happened to—"

"Connect the dots?"

"I am not quite sure what the connection was. I dread to think that in any way I might have—"

"What?"

"I don't know ji—"

The Peet Gandharva spoke with great pride and authority.

"We are currently perfecting a new crowd-scan program. It is still in the testing phase, but it maps the movements of all Dvarcans. It represents and scores them mathematically. If you are an ordinary God-fearing, Country-loving Dvarcan, your behaviour in public spaces is not likely to be suspicious or irregular. Your path is easy to understand and eventually predict."

"Predict?" Gandharva was impressed.

"Eventually, someday. For now, we are just trying to pick out binaaydis based on their different movement patterns."

"How is this movement tracked?" The Arjun inquired.

"We compile this information from many sources. All DD positions are constantly tracked, which is no surprise. Citizens often also simply tell us where they are, and at other times, we triangulate their position from transactions or interactions with people, sentries, polling robots, and other machines. Add all of that together and you end up with a lot of information. We use these data-points to construct a Motion Locus Score or path-measure for every subject. The loci become numbers on maps, and we get our Gandharvas to study and compare them—to find out who does not fit in with the crowd."

"Can that not be automated? The comparison?"

"Not yet. The system has to be trained and taught. There are an infinite number of Motion-Loci with corresponding, complicated formulae and transforms. We are helping out with the programming in a manner of speaking. It is an extremely complicated neural network with a very large number of inputs and weights. For the machine to sieve out the dregs, it has to learn how. We are teaching the machine how to think, if you will."

"I see—and it works? They track them down?"

"This man right here, throughout the course of his career, has contributed to the correct identification of 21 different suspects. He does not even know it. His quantitative ability, otherwise best used for tracking and reporting Punya metrics, has also been a valuable defence asset!"

"How many did I get wrong?"

"Oh, that is not important, Gandharva. At such an early stage, success-rates do not matter. Successes do."

"Why don't we set up an entire department to just track the pariahs? Why these games?" The Arjun was still sceptical about the whole thing.

"There used to be a team of quants who did this all the time. They were grossly underutilized and were becoming increasingly inefficient. We thought it would be best to use our top mathematicians and accountants for the job. This way we get to also split the problem into many small manageable parts without having to explain it to our people. Besides, you'd be surprised how productive Gandharvas can be, when they don't feel that they are working."

"Except him, he figured out that he was working. Isn't that right?"

"I did not know the full story . . ."

"But you still investigated. That is not your dharma at all."

"I am really sorry. I am ashamed of my behaviour—"

He wanted to jump out the window. The two Peets were messaging each other on their DDs. Gandharva realized that there was more.

"You cannot mention this to anyone. Secrecy is one of the key tenets of your dharma."

"I understand—absolutely."

The two seniors kept messaging each other in silence. They studied his facial expressions. The Arjun spoke: "The question now is, what should we do with this fellow?"

"Project L?"

"No Sir . . . please . . . not that. I have two children and a third who will be born any day now."

They both moved their heads slowly, in the affirmative.

"Do you want me to step outside, so that you may talk to each other?"

They both moved their heads slowly, in the negative. A few minutes passed by without anyone saying a single word.

"There are few occasions, in our time of service, where we might do something truly extraordinary, something that sets us apart. Wouldn't you agree, Gandharva?"

"I suppose so, yes. I am very sorry about all this. I know it is not my dharma."

"How would you like it to be your dharma? There is a delegation leaving for Hedonesia. We would like you to be a part of it."

"A delegation?"

"We need someone with your unique skills to be a part of the mission."

"What is the purpose of the mission?"

"Very good, very good question. We have been invited for a conference. It is a knowledge exchange, led by OMNI's Halibutron division."

"Oh, I had no idea that was actually happening."

"It is. The West would like to know how they can work with us on new energy and to fight the growing influence of the Caliphate in their lands."

"We want you to be our Junior Assessor. You will accompany me, on behalf of the Ministry of Finance and Salvation. Do you accept, Gandharva?"

"Remember that a true Dvarcan serves his country, in whichever way is asked of him. If you decline or hesitate, you will be incarcerated under Project L."

"If you think I am good enough for this assignment, I will not question your judgement."

"You are curious like a Vidur, methodical like a Gandharva and somewhat brave, like an Arjun. We have a shortage of generalists in Dvarca. You should do well."

"I will do my best."

"Very good. Mention this assignment to no one. Not even your wife. Your kalaava will be upgraded to a Hara."

"I am going to be a Hara Gandharva?" he could not believe his ears.

"That's right. Your family will be looked after, while you are away."

"When do we leave?"

"Soon, Gandharva. Very soon."

"Thank you!" He touched both their feet and started to leave.

"About the 3,00,000 PB transactions. Do you still want to know?"

"I am unsure, Mahoday. Should I want to know?"

"You will need to visit the Mahakali temple in Sector 2."

"A pilgrimage?"

"I will arrange a time and let you know. They will expect you."

# 38
# PARALLEL

After being chosen to be Pupil of the Year, Nakul Parshuram had learnt that his life-long dream of meeting Shastri ji would come true. The Great Leader would himself, give young Parshuram the award. He had not finished reading *My Road to Navmarg* and had been hiding it from his jealous elder sister. He resolved to read as much of the book as he could, before the ceremony the next day, in the hope that it would give him more to say to the great man. Surely as a winner, he would be entitled to an autograph?

He opened the book to the first chapter about the leader's life and started to read under the cover of his sheet, with a small torch. It was a tale from Shastri ji's early childhood, in his own words.

***

II.

I must have been nine years old. We were testing out the old air-gun that we'd recently unearthed from one of the many trunks in the store. We were rummaging for toys and other knick-knacks. Our hunt ended when we found the gun. It lay there amidst raggedy curtains and dirty sheets. My cousin and I wiped the dust off, greased its hinges, and cleaned its nozzle. It was readied after years of disuse and we carried it out into the park a few blocks away from our house. We shot twigs and stones, taking turns, rationing our pellets. *Ma* had given us enough to buy only one box. She had also told us to be careful, which we were. Well, I was careful. My cousin had to play a movie bandit for a while, jeering and asking for all the young women of the village (Rampur, for some reason) to be delivered to him peacefully. I asked him what they were for and he sniggered for a moment before announcing this to the world: "Laundry! They will wash all the clothes."

I laughed louder than him and he did not appreciate it. To assert his supremacy, he took to shooting little pellets around my feet, forcing me to shut up and stay put. It was clear that he was Gabbar and I was to be a mute Kalia. We searched the park for worthy prey and came to the conclusion that something life like or living, would be a true challenge.

He found a little doll lying in the mud. He picked her up and flung her under a tree. We hid behind a small mound in the park. It had always been an impediment to budding footballers and third-man fielders running backwards with their eyes fixed on the prize in the air—it had tripped and hurt many. That day, the wretched mound served as a bunker for us. We hid behind it like combatants in the field, waiting for the enemy to make a move. They had to reveal themselves to us before we could pounce on the opportunity. We were ready to fire. We were ready to protect 'our border' at the 34th parallel! That's correct; the scene had shifted from the impenetrable ravines of Rampur to the treacherous peaks, troughs, and valleys of the border in Kashmir.

The doll was our stand-in for the savage Pakistani army General, looking dapper in his pink frock and platinum-white tasselled hair; on his way to order his troops to break the cease-fire (again) and charge down the cricket pitch towards the main road that led back home, before he went back to Karachi and led a coup (again). My cousin was sweating as he now sat with his back to the mound, whispering short mispronounced prayers in enthusiasm. He turned to me and asked me how I could be so calm. I shrugged. He held me by my collar and pulled me closer to him.

"If we don't stop those bastards, they will run us over. They will take everything, your parents, your toys—everything. They will move into your house. Do you want that?"

"Sir, no Sir!"

"Then take this gun and shoot that General between the eyes!"

"Why between the eyes?"

"That's where his strength lies!"

"I thought it would be in his navel."

"This is not the *Ramayana.* We need to shoot that guy between his eyes."

"You do it," I pushed the weapon back into his hands.

"Are you afraid?"

"I am not afraid, brother."

"Then shoot the General!"

I took the gun from him, placed it quietly on top of the mound, and positioned myself behind it, looking at the doll, trying desperately to set the sight between the evil General's eyes. How still he looked, scuffed, brown, and hunched up. My cousin continued with his taunts and challenges, now leaning into my ear, whispering about how I needed to be more like Arjun and less like our little sister.

"Take the shot! He's running away!"

"Damn it!"

I pulled the trigger. In less than a second, we saw the doll rock back, slightly. We were both disappointed by the tame result of our attack.

"Did we hit it?"

"I think so—"

"What do you mean you think so?! What kind of ineffective, incompetent, stupid soldier are you?"

"I am a General, not a soldier."

"I am the General. Let's go see what you've done."

We walked over towards the doll and stood over its motionless corpse. The shot was good and it had found its mark. The sights on the gun were a bit off and I had ended up shooting her in the eye. The gun was quite old and weak, and the pellet was stuck there, partially hanging out, partially coiled, like a half-open harmonium. My cousin froze and held my hand suddenly. He whispered.

"There are spies everywhere, brother, look—"

He pointed up at the lone crow minding its business on the branch above us.

"How do you know he's a spy?"

"See how unmoved he is by our actions?" The bird was rather nonchalant.

"Yes, he doesn't care, really—"

"Wrong. I hate crows and I know them well. This guy is a spy. I am telling you. What do you think he's doing there?"

"What do you mean? There are crows everywhere. They come to the house too. Ma feeds them bread every day."

"How do you know you can trust him? He's seen us kill his General and now he'll tell the others. Do you want them to attack your mother at breakfast tomorrow? They have no soul you know!"

"Crows don't have souls?"

"Crows are loyal only to crows. They don't care for us. Why should we care for them?"

The game was getting out of hand and I could see where my brother's instincts were taking him. He wasn't satisfied by a mere dent in a toy doll. Something more significant would have to give. He wanted to kill the bird.

"Give me the gun—"

"Just scare him away okay? Please, promise me you'll just scare him—"

"He is a pest. He spreads diseases and builds nests where he shouldn't."

He grabbed the gun from me and pushed me back. He took three steps and loaded the gun with another pellet.

"He's a sneaky little bastard too. If he gets away, he'll come back for us. I have to make this count."

"What about other crows? Won't they see that you have killed their kin and come looking for you?"

That gave him pause.

I continued: "If someone did something horrible to you, it would be as good as doing something horrible to me."

"Spare me, weakling, you will think long and hard before avenging me. You'll think of reasons to let them go."

"That's not fair! I am really getting tired of these games."

"Shut up—"

"Leave the crow alone . . . please . . ."

"You know who ruined the Tulsi plant in Grandma's garden?"

"Who?"

"A crow you idiot, it was a crow!"

"Well then let's go look for that particular crow and—"

"And what?"

"And teach him a lesson."

"By what? Stopping his free breakfast? Scolding him? Back off! Enough!"

He pushed me and before I could do anything to scare the bird away, he shot it. He couldn't have missed at that distance. The pellet struck the bird in his chest and he crowed his last, falling from the tree, a big black mass of wings and blood. He fell close to the doll and my cousin looked down at them both triumphantly.

"You killed him—you killed the poor thing—"

"No, come look, he's still flapping about, fluttering in the mud. Now he won't bother anyone, ever."

Was there a lesson to be learnt from what my brother had done? Are there crows in our midst, who disrespect and use us? It was a glimpse into the future. It is only the wisdom of years that opens one's mind to the truths we learnt as children. I have started to think like my brother, a lot, these days. There are some things in this world that can no longer be tolerated.

***

Young Nakul fell asleep with the book in his hands, dreaming of killing crows, and strangling dolls.

# 39
# A SHOW TO END ALL SHOWS

Waves of disturbance filtered through the microphone as a helicopter hovered above the open-air auditorium. It was marked with the symbol of the office of the Great Leader. He had arrived. It hung above the stage, flipping the decorative, and ornamental drapes up and about in a frenzy.

Nakul's heart pounded with anticipation as he looked for Shastri ji. Cries of 'Jai Dvarca' rang out throughout the grounds. Gandharva and Jyoti huddled together, watching their son. It was a moment of great pride. They had never attended the *Hour of Honour*, live. No one from the family had ever been on the show before. It was a big day for them.

Mira was unimpressed. She leaned back in her chair. Her vision was obscured by the people in front. She felt no need to stand on her chair and cheer like everyone else. She wasn't sure if she felt envy. All her life, he had been everyone's darling. He could do no wrong and this was sort of expected. She hated herself for seeing her failure in his success. It rattled her and she tried to suppress her petty malnoia by occupying her mind with something else.

She turned to her mother and started calculating when Vidur was due. The little bump had grown into a glorious orb. She wondered if he too would emerge one day from the womb and steal her thunder. Of course he would, the clever little reptile. He was probably already smarter than she could ever hope to be. It could not be more than a few days, she wondered. Jyoti saw her staring at her stomach and held her by the chin, asking her to smile.

"This is your little brother's big day. Please don't be so morose."

"I'm not morose, Ma. Do you think I am?"

Jyoti pulled her close. It was too loud for a meaningful heart-to-heart conversation. Shastri ji's personal security force rumbled onto the stage from all directions. They formed a wall of guns and muscle. They were all from the Varaha brigade. At any given time, they were armed in 16 different ways. They wore special DDs that permitted them to tap into the view of any other DD in a 1-km radius. They also had a direct down-link from the Control Centre and could request access to any State camera in Dvarca. X360s descended upon the crowd and started their customary waltz of vigilance. The crowd followed them as they swept the area in a sort of welcome wave.

"Does Shastri ji not feel safe, Ma?" Mira asked. No one heard her.

People punched the air in a manner that would make one think they were all about to be given an award. The stage was finally set for Shastri ji. All his vehicles came with an extendable mechanical jaw. It was like a private elevator that lowered or lifted him to safety. In this case, the bright beams of shiny steel protracted downwards, stretching like a pair of radio antennae carrying a bubble.

There he was, in the flesh, the Great Leader himself. He was let off on the stage and he marched out, without breaking his stride. He raised his hands to acknowledge the support and admiration from the electrified auditorium.

A drum sounded out loudly and everyone stood up for the anthem.

"Dvarca, Dvarca, Dvarca . . ."

Nakul was beside himself with happiness. He could barely sing the words. The moment was so overwhelming. In many ways, this event would not have taken place, if it were not for him. He stood in the wings, waiting his turn and looked out at the mass of cheering citizens. He could only see the back of Shastri ji's head. He would follow it anywhere. Into a pit of cobras, into a lagoon of sharks, into the mouth of the Caliphate, he would do anything for that man and his people. He clutched the book tightly in his hands.

After the anthem, everyone was asked to sit down. The Varaha security moved to the sides of the stage. Shastri ji climbed up to his roost, 15 metres above, to sit in his trademark white-and-gold chair. Many songs had been written about it. The people had demanded that it be made of the finest materials. It kept changing shape and growing over time. It wasn't just a seat from which the leader would preside and conduct the work of the people. It was a veritable hieroglyphic of all of Dvarca's achievements. Every time there was a milestone for the Nation, it found a place on the chair, in the form of a protruding sculpture or new carving. In one glance at the throne, the history of Dvarca's many achievements could be learnt, not that Dvarcans believed in resting on their laurels. Shastri ji stroked the pyramids on the right arm of the throne. They represented the Temple Uprising of 2058.

"Are you devout without a doubt?'

"YES!!!"

"That's lovely to hear. Ladies and gentlemen, today's programme is a very special one. It is about re-education and excellence in education. In the first part of today's show, we will show you the latest Dvarcan technology that has been developed, to re-educate those who hate us!"

Vishvakarma and his underling walked out on stage. Even from the way they walked and the distance they kept from each other, one could easily see that they were master and apprentice.

"Come on out you geniuses! Don't be shy!"

The master was given the microphone.

"All deviousness is first an idea. For this idea to become truly dangerous, it must be spoken or written. Our research and development programme aims to stop this. We can now censor words, as they are spoken. In a few moments, we will be able to show you how it works. Could we bring out the Caliphite scum please?"

A man in chains was pushed out onto the stage. He fell to the floor with a loud jangle. The younger Vishvakarma guided him to the front. The crowd jeered and booed at the sight of him. They had forced him to grow out his beard. It is easier to hate people who look like the people you are meant to hate. The producers of the *Hour of Honour* knew their audience well.

"This man is Fashoosh Mashoosh." He paused for laughter. It was a made-up name. Fashoosh Mashoosh found himself in all sorts of scrapes in Dvarcan jokes.

"He was captured on the border with a van full of explosives that he and his compatriots were planning to use in a school. Can you believe the inhumanity?"

At this moment the show's emcee stepped forward and interrupted the flow of the presentation. The Peet Vishvakarma was confused.

"Do you just want to listen? Or do you want to get involved?"

The crowd shouted out loud. Gandharva was jumping off his seat.

"I can't hear you, do you want to get involved?!"

"YES!!!" was the resounding response.

The emcee pulled the vexed Vishvakarmas off to the side of stage as the Caliphite stood haplessly in the middle.

"Let him have it!"

A barrage of oranges, tomatoes, and shoes were flung at the man on stage. Some of them were direct-hits and hurt him on his face and stomach. He turned around and cowered to protect himself.

"This was not part of the plan. Why are we doing this?" Vishvakarma whispered to the emcee.

"Please! Every time we get one of them on the show, we let the people teach them a lesson. It is cathartic." He handed he scientist a squishy tomato and asked him to join in.

"They will damage my equipment . . . can you stop them please?"

Without thinking, Vishvakarma ran out onto the stage. He was met first with a derisive chant and then with an overripe orange on his chin. He raised his hands up and implored the people to stop. The guards took to the stage like a curtain and drew the scientist back. The crowd stopped throwing produce.

"This shower of rotten fruits and tomatoes is harmful to the delicate instruments attached to this man—I mean, this prisoner."

"What instruments? I don't see anything." The emcee was feeling left out.

Vishvakarma approached the sore Caliphite. He reached behind his ears and plucked something, as inconspicuous as a strand of hair. He held it up.

"This, this is the thing that we are here to talk about. Our invention, in service of our Motherland, this is the device that will make this Caliphite a civilized human being."

"Fuck you and your country!" The man in chains exclaimed. "I am not a terrorist, I am just a mason. I was abducted by—"

He was struck across the face with the butt of a gun. He passed out immediately and fell at Vishvakarma's feet. The pompous showrunner shook his head and walked to the edge of the stage, stepping over the body of the unconscious convict.

"There are many ways to censor and silence the enemies of Dvarca. We were meant to see one way, but we have seen another. The gun is mightier than the . . . er . . . Vishvakarma ji, what do you call your device?"

"Speech Sentinel 8-2."

"The gun today has proved mightier than the Sentinel. Would the scientist care to try again?"

"Yes of course. May I request the fearless guards to bring the next dreadful prisoner out?"

"Yes, please proceed."

Fashoosh Mashoosh's limp and powerless body was dragged off the stage. He was quickly replaced by an identical-looking man, who resisted being pushed out to face the mob. It was Faiz. His right arm was still in a bandage.

"This prisoner . . . well! You all know this prisoner! He is Faiz, the Industrial Complex bomber. He too, has our Sentinel on him."

The mob was ecstatic again. Vishvakarma could not see any faces. They were just a mass of dark outlines screaming, shouting, and baying for blood and righteous entertainment. Faiz trembled and tried to speak to Vishvakarma. He pleaded, searching for some semblance of sense in Vishvakarma's eyes, just as the scientist sought reason in the mob's unbridled joy.

"Come Vishvakarma, show us what your Fashooshi monkey has learnt," the emcee winked.

"Faiz, please insult our God and Country."

The crowd gasped at the heinous request. Someone threw an orange at the Vishvakarma.

"No, no, it's okay. Let him try. Please!"

The prisoner said nothing.

"You have to attempt to blaspheme, for us to show you the path of piety."

The guards goaded him with a gun from behind, striking him in the back of his ribs.

"Curse! Do it. At least say a prayer then. Start us out nice and easy."

*"Yaa kundendu-tushaara-haara-dhavalaa*
*Yaa shubhra-vastra-avrtaa,*
*Yaa veena-vara-danda-mandita-karaa*
*Yaa shveta-padma-asanaa,*
*Yaa Brahma-Achyuta-Shankara-prabhrtibhir-Devah sadaa poojita*
*Sa maam paatu Saraswati Bhagavati nihshesha-yaaddya-apahaa."*

His voice rang out across the speakers in the auditorium. The congregation had never seen a Caliphite speak such pure Sanskrit. They clapped and Vishvakarma heaved a sigh of relief. It was working. Shastri ji pumped the air and laughed out loud.

"Thank you, Faiz. Now, please do us a favour and insult our Motherland. Insult the Nation. The people . . . anything."

He refused again.

"There must be something you want to say. All that pent up hate and anger."

"I want . . . to thank Dvarca. I want to thank the gentle guards for breaking my spine and every bone in my hand. I am grateful for the just treatment meted out to me and my kind. Some people are not worthy of equality. This hour, this show, is an embodiment of virtue and it is what makes Dvarca great. Even those of us who have never meant anyone any harm, we must be blamed for the work of our so-called brothers. Paint anyone who disagrees with you in the same colours. It is just and necessary."

This tirade was followed by a moment of silence.

"He is reformed! He sees the light!" The horde erupted in hurrahs.

Faiz continued: "There is only one way to be a Dvarcan. And that is Navmarg. I am a rotten pea in a pristine pod. I must be thrown out, trampled, crushed like an ant. I am so thankful for the boot on my neck. I lick it in gratitude. Hurt me more, I say. Kill all pariahs. Kill all binaaydis."

"We have broken through to him! He realizes the folly of his ways."

"I deserve to be broken," he spoke with great difficulty, started to spasm and then dropped to the ground.

"What happened?" the host turned to the only person in the room who was not celebrating. Vishvakarma checked Faiz's pulse. The prisoner was laughing, coughing up blood. His ears were oozing crimson too.

"What did you do? What the hell did you do?"

"There is no God but Krishna, and I am his humble servant." With those auspicious last words, Faiz died on the stage.

The new and improved sentinel was meant to detect the wicked tones associated with sarcasm. It was designed to shock the speaker, as a warning. Under normal circumstances, the speaker would abort the mordant utterances and adopt a more direct approach. If the speaker continued in his insulting tone, the shocks would intensify and amplify. In this case, Faiz ignored the impulses that were slowly frying his insides and continued with his double-meaning diatribe. He died of a cardiac arrest. The emcee cued the drummers. They brought everyone to frenzy again. Only Vishvakarma sat beside the corpse, in shock.

"At least he had the chance to beg forgiveness before passing into the next life. He atoned for his sins, if only verbally. Maybe the Maker will be kinder to him next time. Maybe he won't be reborn as a rodent. He may even come back as a dog, or a bird."

Vishvakarma looked into the stony eyes of the deceased man. He had nothing to say. He had just murdered someone.

"You should feel proud of yourself Vishvakarma. You helped to rehabilitate and redeem him. Your technology has much scope for the future."

Shastri ji felicitated him from above and the entire assembly applauded his feat. He tried hard to smile for the cameras. He felt a very real pain, an ache in his heart. This was not the work he had set out to do.

There was a brief intermission during which ads for OMNI were broadcast all over Dvarca. The crowd calmed down, and whispers of approval and celebration filled the auditorium. Nakul braced himself for his big moment.

The darkened stage lit up again, with a spotlight on the host.

"Now, for part two of our special *Hour of Honour* programme. Please join me in welcoming two very important stalwarts of education in Dvarca. Tonight we honour them. He is the eldest teacher in the Manned Air Vehicle programme. He is our foremost Drone-Acharya. Today we recognize him for his years of service, and for producing five out of five of our top pilots in this year's APSG exams. It is my great privilege to invite Honourable Shastri ji to gift our Drone-Acharya of the Year, Santri Vidur Aryabhatta Valmiki, with this commemorative trophy."

Shastri ji sprang to his feet and raced down to the stage. He seemed ageless! A member of his inner circle handed him a silver statue of Goddess Saraswati. He raised it to show the crowd and stole a bit of applause, before giving the prize to the Santri Aryabhatta. The old teacher smiled a toothless grin and folded his palms in modest genuflection.

"This next son of Dvarca has completed arms training, advanced strategy training, and venom production at the tender age of 11. His passion for his country is both fierce and infectious. He is our National Pupil of the Year, Nakul, son of Gandharva and Jyoti of Sector 17, Block 8A."

The boy touched Shastri ji's feet and stood up slowly. He bowed and raised his palms, pressed together in a salute, *My Road to Navmarg* tucked under his arm. Shastri ji was impressed. He stood back, watching the young man's flamboyant display of humility. Nakul turned to the crowd and shouted.

"Jai Dvarca! Dvarca ki jai!"

They loved him for it and shouted the slogan back. They clapped as he walked towards Shastri ji to collect his statue of Goddess Saraswati. He took the statue and looked up at the Great Leader. His moustache was perfect, not a hair out of place. It was as though the ubiquitous posters and images he had seen forever, had come to life. He stepped closer to the leader and the alert guards raised their guns. The leader asked them to stand back. He understood that all that the boy wanted was an innocuous hug.

He stretched his arms out and welcomed Nakul. It was sheer bliss for the young man, who before he knew it, was locked in a warm, somewhat sweaty, soft envelop of *khadi* and cotton. He smelt sandalwood and roses. Nakul tightened his grip around Shastri ji's waist and pressed hard. He knew this would probably never happen to him again, and decided to milk it with unabashed enthusiasm. He felt a bit uneasy. Shastri ji too felt that there was something amiss, a strange protrusion was stabbing him in his thigh. He pulled the boy away and there it was for all to see, a small bulge in Nakul's pyjamas. He did not know what was happening, or why it was happening.

"How?! How dare you!" Shastri ji shouted.

The emcee jumped up between them.

"HE HAS A GUN!"

"No . . . no I don't."

A Varaha soldier held an R9 to Nakul's head. "Put it down son. Put the gun down."

"I don't have a gun."

"We'll see about that!"

He pulled off Nakul's white kurta and threw it into the crowd. It fell on the ground as people climbed on top of each other to avoid being touched by his profane belongings. The protuberance was still there. It was under his pyjamas.

"What . . . what is that?" the Varaha man was perplexed.

"I am sorry, it's not in my control. Stop, please, make it stop."

The cameras zoomed in on him and numerous flashes went off in quick succession.

"Check him!" A Varaha commander shouted.

"It could be a bomb."

That was when the chaos started. The first 12 rows emptied out in a matter of seconds.

"I don't have a bomb . . . please . . . listen to me—look!"

Nakul pulled the drawstring of his pyjamas and dropped them to the ground. There was no bomb. There were no weapons. Just a taut skinny twig and two berries.

"What are you doing? Cover your shame!" The guard turned him around and he now faced Shastri ji, whose famously calm demeanour was quickly giving way to outrage. He covered his face.

"Arrest this horrible boy!"

The Varaha men and Police from the crowd moved towards him.

"Pervert! He is a pervert!"

"Spy! This cannot be!"

"Caliphite!"

The emcee urged people to stay in their seats and not throw produce. He reminded them not to risk hurting the Great Leader, who was quickly whisked away by his security.

Nakul, confused, frightened, and angry pulled up his pyjamas and pressed the knob down. He tried to push it between his legs but it just sprang up. His worried parents were on their feet. They could only see that the crowd had turned on their son, suddenly hating him. His prize and his book lay abandoned on the stage, forgotten in the bedlam. He reached for the book.

Guards leapt and lunged at Nakul. He dodged them and started to run. He bolted for a side exit. The common people avoided him as though he were an untouchable. They were convinced he had a disease or that he was still carrying some sort of concealed weapon.

"What happened in there, little boy? Is the Great Leader okay?"

"Everything's a mess, please go in and help."

The man started to run towards the ruckus when he stopped abruptly. They must have broadcast Nakul's likeness. He turned around and chased after the boy.

"Rascala! Rakshasa!"

Nakul eluded him as he turned a corner. Dusk had given way to night and street lamps lit up the roads like floodlights at a stadium. People were milling about outside and they turned to see him in the middle of the street. He was the shirtless offender, the disgusting little boy who had done the unthinkable on stage. He took a few swift steps towards a narrow side alley as they watched him. He could not tell if they were frightened of him or if they were just surprised to see him.

Then, with a loud cry of '*Har Har Mahadev*' guards, policemen, and the Varaha burst through the gathering and ran towards him. He ran into an alley. His DDs were being tracked and constant messages ordered him to stop. He was nearing a crossing and was certain that they would be waiting for him there. He scaled a wall to jump into a compound. He cut his hand on some glass. It was a small nick, but it bled profusely. He kept going. It was a provision centre that was shut for the night. The windows were blocked by huge metal grills. The footsteps of the pursuing wolves grew louder.

# 40
# BREAKING THE BOY

"YOU HAVE SHAMED YOUR COUNTRY AND YOURSELF."

"TURN YOURSELF IN. SURRENDER."

"What is wrong with me? What is this?" All his efforts to push it down were in vain.

"Why is this happening?"

It was still there, between his legs. The source of all his embarrassment and national ignominy stood brazenly at attention. He stuck the Great Leader's book in his pyjamas and started his way on a pipe that ran up the side of the building. He pulled himself up to the second floor, close to an open window. It was a few inches beyond his reach. The distracting text continued to be beamed straight to his DDs, with blinding frequency.

"THERE IS NO ESCAPE."

"STOP. STOP. STOP."

He pulled off his slipper and used it to pull the window open. He flung himself onto it and hung on for dear life. His wounded hand burnt with pain. Shots were fired and they landed inches from his head, smashing the window pane into thousands of shards. Some of the pieces struck him. He could hear dogs barking below. Torch-lights lit up behind him, and as he hung onto the window frame, he could see his shadow on the side of the building.

"NAKUL! Stop! This is futile." It was Virdi on a bullhorn.

"I need you to get down from there and come with us."

He could feel his arms weakening and his grip loosening. They would make a great example of him, he would be the next Faiz. Another shot was fired and this one landed on his head's shadow. He hauled himself into the building through the smashed window. He put his slipper back on and negotiated the glass-filled room quickly. The guards were banging down the front door. He limped along and tried to remove his DDs. They were hooked up to his chain. All the blessings of all the gods were delivered to children at the age of five, along with their first set of DDs. He remembered his ceremony, where they registered him as a citizen. Today, he felt that God was plotting against him and his Country loathed him.

"Where will you go? What is your plan, Nakul?" Virdi continued. He had always known that his teacher was affiliated to the Varaha. It was still heart-breaking to be hunted by your mentor.

He pulled himself together and realized that it was absolutely necessary for him to remove his DDs. It would trigger a Category Five alarm, but they were already after him. There were vicious canines and horned pig-men on his tail. Pig-men. He'd never thought of them as that. He hobbled through a corridor as the metal shutters opened downstairs. The barking dogs were in the building. They were getting louder.

"THIS IS YOUR FINAL WARNING. STOP. SURRENDER."

"COMPLIANCE IS ITS OWN REWARD."

He had no choice. On the edge of a door, he banged his head repeatedly, trying to fracture the bridge of his DDs. He hurt himself and possibly broke his nose in the process. There was a small crack that he struck a few times, before pulling his glasses off with all his might. Blood covered his hands as his nose gushed. His forehead hurt and he was stunned. The DDs came apart and he now held two monocles, one in each hand.

His head swayed with the impact and his eyes smarted. The unchecked new light and colours disoriented him. Nothing looked the same without the red lenses. He rubbed his eyes and felt around for support. A siren blared and the bright lights of search helicopters plunged in through the windows of the building. He snapped the arms of his DDs, breaking off the lens rims. He crushed them with his feet, before collecting the scraps and throwing them into a cupboard. Only small fragments dangled off the metal bands of his neck-chain.

"Nakul, son of Gandharva, if you want to stay alive, surrender now."

He ran to the end of a corridor and came to a thick glass window. Beams of light blurred and bent through the pellucid wall and formed odd shapes of diffused blue-and-yellow on the walls inside. He'd never seen those colours before. He could not help being captivated by them even as he searched for a hiding place. He'd been trained by the best, but he was still a little boy. There was no way he could fight his way out of there. A single step in the wrong direction now, would put him in the line of fire. He was surprised that they expected him to 'surrender'. Did they not know that it was anathema for a Nakul?

He jogged up another floor, treading lightly. Suddenly a burst of gunfire broke out downstairs. They must have zeroed in on his location by tracking the DDs. He did not hear a warning, or a final threat. They had just opened fire. He reached the top of the complex and came out through a roof door. Lights swarmed about like giant fireflies. Two helicopters covered opposite angles and swept the sky like hawks. He crawled into a chimney and held his breath.

It smelt of day-old food. There was a sack at his feet. He pulled it up and wore it over his head. The entire Varaha brigade emerged on the rooftop. It was a mess of shiny white kurtas, thick vermillion bands with shimmering gold insignias, black helmets, and guns with torches. Nakul could hear them move in unison. He stayed huddled in a ball under the brown net of the ratty sack. The men looked everywhere. They even lifted the water tank lids to peek inside. They were quiet, swift, and disciplined in their approach.

A beam of light lit the top of Nakul's chimney. It grew like the end of an eclipse and he could now feel its heat in a circle on his back. If he so much as trembled, he would be caught and shot. He had never been so conscious of the sounds his body made. A rumble in the tummy, his heartbeat, what could they pick up? Were they not using night-vision goggles? He closed his eyes and prayed. The light shrank away just as smoothly as it had appeared. He heard them shuffle about and leave. He stayed there until even the choppers above moved away.

He felt abandoned and alone without his DDs. Without the constant news, updates, and directives from the centre, he did not know what to do. He did not even know the time. It was a few hours before he mustered up enough courage to climb out. It was still dark. He leaned out over the side of the roof wall to see that there were still guards around the building. There was no way he was walking out of there. Were they still inside the building too? He had every reason to assume so.

He picked up a chipped loose brick from the roof floor and threw it across the street. It flew and fell with a crash. This was followed by a swarm of activity in the street. Guards and soldiers moved towards the other building. He watched as they mounted their offensive on the wrong side. He quickly wore the tattered gunny sack over his head and made his way down the stairs. He knew it was ridiculous to think that it could protect him, but it made him feel safe. Given its successful track record as camouflage, he was inclined to make it his lucky charm.

He slid past the top two floors and made his way to the ground level. He did not know the colours he was seeing. He knew black, at least he thought he did. He looked around the ground floor and realized that he was actually alone. He found a basin and makeshift kitchen. Metal pots and pans suddenly caught the bright lights from outside as the choppers returned. There was an open wrapper on the counter-top and an army of ants crawled in and out of it. He was hungry and looked inside to find a few musty *shakkar-paare*. He picked one up daintily, blowing off the ants and bit it, keeping an eye on the Varaha men patrolling the area outside.

He continued his inspection of the desolate premises and came to a back room. There was an exit that led into another alley but it was suicide to attempt an escape that soon. He sat down and finished what was left of the soggy sweets. Light had started to enter the room as dawn approached. The runaway turned to the only thing he had left over from his past. He opened the book and looked at the blank space that he had meant to fill with the Great Leader's autograph. It was not to be. He swallowed heavily and turned to the page where he had stopped reading Shastri ji's story.

***

III.

I remember everything about that day. I even remember the dream I had that morning. My father and I were guarding our gate. The house was surrounded by hundreds of dogs from the neighbourhood. They had all congregated and were snarling and barking at us. I remember feeling disbelief in my dream, as those dogs were usually quite friendly to us. We gave them water and the occasional *roti.* But they had turned on us, growling and threatening like hyenas through their rabid, salivating fangs. One of them lunged at me and I raised my arm to block him.

That was when my father woke me. I was so glad to see him. More pepper than salt, his bright eyes alert and searching. He looked worried.

"It might get worse. We should all be under the same roof."

Four days ago, a fire broke out in Sakin market. It was the handiwork of a few boys avenging the death of their sister. They had decided to burn down the shop of a man who had been accused of raping and murdering her a few months ago. The police had not found any evidence to link him to the case and had released him after a few weeks of interrogation. The word on the street was that he had done it. Justice had been delayed, and to some it seemed it had been denied. They had taken matters into their own hands and burnt his shop, in the heart of a densely populated colony, known for its narrow lanes, small flats, and poor infrastructure. The flames engulfed the entire market and had taken many lives. Hospitals were overwhelmed by the tragedy.

The brothers who had carried out the attack were rounded up and put behind bars. They were now at the centre of a different kind of storm. Their actions were being seen as communally motivated. It had been fanned further by an interview that had been playing all over the news channels.

One of them spoke through tears of anguish, his eyes red with manic rage: "There is no place for our own people in this country. There are different laws and different courts. There are different police. There are different governments for our people. You would not have rested—you would not have answered us with callousness, if you saw her as your own . . ."

Tensions had mounted and tempers flared on both sides. The poor brave girl who had lost her life was long forgotten and it had now become an ugly fight between communities. There were demonstrations, shows of strength, big words from small men hiding in offices and towers. The city was on high alert.

"Go get your aunt."

"I'd rather be here with you all."

"I will stay here. You must go and bring your *Bua*, she is not safe." He told me.

I got out of bed and left quickly. It was a long drive. I was on my way to a godforsaken shadow town at the edge of Delhi, named Khadera. Visits from my aunt were frequent, but we rarely went to her. I don't know why she had to go so far away from us. We used to live on the same block. Perhaps after my uncle died she felt the need for a change. I was away when she moved. I used to travel a lot back then and went wherever work took me. It is funny how things that were once incomparably important, become inconsequential with time.

We are greedy, impatient beings, doing what serves us in the moment, only to realize that it was unnecessary the next. I missed many occasions and obligations. I wasted years away from home, in an attempt to find my place elsewhere. I often thought about how I had been a useless son to my parents. It was a constant nagging feeling. Every time I visited them, something would have changed. I would only appear at these brief rest-stops, blissfully unaware of the trials of the journey past. They never really told me everything that transpired. Who could? I was left to piece it all together with my imagination.

I stopped at a traffic light. I had never seen my city like this before: an abandoned ghost town. Not a soul on the streets, not a single car other than mine. There was a strange mumbling noise that I did not recognize. I looked in the rear-view mirror and saw that I was the one speaking. I was saying my prayers. I did not even know that I remembered them, but they just came out like an involuntary submission, as natural as my beating heart. I heard a loud thump on the back of my car. I floored my accelerator and sped off. There was an injured man in the middle of the street. He was waving and cursing. Maybe he just wanted help.

Things started to look worse as I got closer and closer to Khadera. I saw an upturned police van, smashed to smithereens. What would they have used to cause that kind of damage? I wondered. A door had been reduced to a cone. Where were these rioters now? Were they taking a break like regular folk? Did they decide in the midst of their plundering last night that they would adjourn for some much-needed rest to have tea and recuperate? Were they that organized? What did rioting get them? Was it an expression of anger? Was it opportunism? Was it a long festering hate that suddenly found expression in the form of this spiteful outburst of thoughtless destruction?

I realized that the best thing to do would be to turn on the radio and listen for announcements that might help me navigate through the burning mess that was the Nation's capital. It was the local channel pre-set. They used to play film music and make intentionally stupid jokes in crazy voices. Today there was no fanfare or mirth. A straight-laced speaker delivered bulletins in hushed tones.

"We are in trouble, but we cannot forget that the people we are harming are our neighbours. They are our friends and family.

We must forgive, forget transgressions of the recent past and start out on the road to rehabilitation. The sooner we do this, the better it will be."

"You self-righteous shit! Stop trying to be a messiah!"

Someone had broken into their station.

"Who let you in? You can't be in here!"

The radio crackled and went silent. I kept driving. More people threw rocks at the car and this time one flew in from the back window, with a crashing sound. They rejoiced as I charged forward, my dashboard covered in window-glass from the impact. The errant stone lay just beside the gear box.

"Where are the police?"

My father called and I put it on speaker.

"Where have you reached?"

"I'm . . . about 10 minutes away. The place has fallen apart, Papa."

"I know. Sharma Uncle called and it looks like they are calling for the Special Forces."

"What does that mean?"

"It means you have to hurry."

"Did you speak to Bua?"

"I can't reach her on the phone."

That statement made me lose hope and I feared the worst for her. Still, I meandered through the small streets and by-lanes of Khadera in search of her house. It was relatively quiet in this part of town. There were no gangs of stone-throwers, no burning cars and the shops, though shuttered, were unharmed. I parked the car and walked up to her block. There was an old man smoking a cigarette, sitting alone in his balcony on the second floor. He saw me approaching and called out.

"Who are you?"

"My name is Nirmal. I am looking for my Bua ji. She lives here."

"What's her name?"

It took me a moment to recall her surname, I am not sure why.

"Jha, Mrs. Jha"

"Oh! Jha Madam? She is not at home."

"Where is she? I have to find her."

"At the end of this street, there is a left turn. Keep walking down that way."

"Is it far?"

"Not very far—"

I made my way down the narrow lane with an open drain. Dust collected on the buildings baking in the summer heat. I turned at the corner and stood before a heap of cycles. They were not parked, as much as they had been thrown together. I looked up beyond the sagging electricity lines and encroaching street-lamp poles to see a temple. It gleamed and a solitary red flag fluttered at the top. A family of monkeys bounced about, intrigued by the action below. A large crowd had gathered.

"*Jai Ho*!"

My phone rang, but I did not answer it. I snaked my way through the clammy congregation and started to hear the voice that was addressing them.

I noticed that they were all wearing kalaavas. Most of them had *tikas* across their foreheads. This was strangely reassuring to me. At the head of the crowd, standing at the steps of the temple, I could see an orator. It was my Bua. She spoke passionately.

"Our ruling deity is Lord Krishna and I know that he expects us to stand up for ourselves. One must never forget one's duty. What is your duty?"

"To fight evil!"

"Yes! Do you know how old this temple is?"

The crowd ventured a few guesses. She nodded and continued.

"This temple is centuries old. It is one of the last remaining strongholds of a tradition that your ancestors followed. It is from a beautiful time, when man lived by the Vedic way. We had science, power, and wealth, but it lies diluted and torn today, torn apart by our lack of will and our apathy."

"Tell us what we must do!"

"There was once a Golden City named Dvarca. It was home to Lord Krishna and it was the first great city in the Earth's lifetime. Today it is lost. I have faith in our people to resurrect the greatness of the past. We must create a new Nation, a new beginning for the holy land."

"Jai Shri Krishna!"

"Har Har Mahadev!"

"Will you stand by and watch as they turn the entire world into a desert?"

"No!" "Never!" The youngest ones were the loudest. No cars or scooters could pass through. The strange thing was that no one was complaining. There were no interruptions, not even Delhi's famous 'honk first ask questions later' adage seemed to apply in this peaceful paradise. Everyone was on their best behaviour. They were in the palm of her hand and answered every question with appropriate enthusiasm. Every pause was a break for applause.

"I say, let them come. Let them come and let them see our might. We are not afraid."

"We are not afraid! We shall overcome!"

"It is not only here, friends. This is a global problem. The battle has come to our doorstep. It is here. They have hurt us time and again. They hurt the world. Them. The Others. The screaming mass of violent clerics and holy warriors has burnt our homes, our people, and our country. But we are still, just watching. How many poems can you read to a man, who stands with an axe raised above your head? How many songs of brotherhood can you compose?"

"How many times must you mangle and bend history to show that yes, there was once a time, when hate was 'resentment'. Resentment was 'distaste'. Distaste was 'difference' and difference merely 'new'. The moderates and the liberals are blind to glaring, prominent, stark reminders of divisions. They would say we all belong to the same Nation, but the enemy does not agree. They would say everyone is a Hindu if he or she believes in a God, but the enemy laughs at this notion! I too, beg to differ. We are not all Hindus! We are not all the same. There are many kinds of Hinduism, with many beliefs. But there are common truths that we all understand and observe."

"Our extremist opponents have made me search for the monolith in our temple of plurality. We respect the forces that make, shape, and guide us. We know that they take many forms, but we also know that they are in essence the same energy, the same engine of creation, protection, and destruction. We have to show the other side that we were not a quivering, queasy bundle of 29 disconnected regions. We must stand together."

Hoots, whistles, clapping. People almost fell off their balconies with excitement.

"Wait a moment, wait! Who is this? Who is this I see before me?"

She was looking directly at me.

"Nirmal, beta, what are you doing here?"

"I came to take you."

"Take me? Where . . . where will you take me?"

I was embarrassed to answer. I was suddenly in the spotlight with her, hundreds of eyes studying and weighing my worth. I felt pressure as I opened my mouth again. She saved me the trouble and cut me off.

"Friends, this is my nephew, Nirmal. Greet the people, Nirmal."

I didn't know what that meant and I raised my hand in an awkward gesture to say 'Hello . . . hello.' My aunt placed a hand on my shoulder and shook her head.

"He is a good boy, but he has been misled. He has spent a large part of his adult life away from his mother, so his tongue has become alien. What was that you said? 'Hello'? Might as well have been '*As-Salaam Alaykum*'. You see, this is not a big thing, but it is a sign. Our children greet us with words like 'Hello'. Come, son of my own brother, come let me show you how we greet our elders in India."

There were gasps of laughter in the crowd. She called me towards her.

"I must take you home, Bua. Papa has asked that you join us at home." I tried to whisper in her ear.

"This is my home." She whispered back before holding me by the arm. Her skinny, bony fingers had a lot of strength in them and she pierced my skin with her thumbnail.

"Listen carefully, Nirmal. You are about to learn something. I know your mother. She has tried to teach you this before. She is a good mother, you have just forgotten her teachings. Come, see."

She raised both her hands above her head and joined her palms.

"This is a *namaskar* for your elders."

The crowd applauded. They copied her actions, as though in acknowledgment of the simple greeting. A little boy and his sister charged towards her. They fell flat, stretching the entire length of their tiny bodies, at her feet. She bent down to pick them up. She patted them gently on their heads and kissed them both. She was visibly moved.

"That is how it is done."

I looked at her and smiled. I too, bent down to touch her feet. The crowd applauded and a few others also came forward to touch her feet.

"Mata ji ki . . . jai! Mata ji ki . . . jai!"

She blessed them as they entered the temple and went up the stairs to pray. As they passed her, she had only one refrain.

"Remember who you are, be proud of yourself."

"Remember who you are, be proud of your heritage."

We had a chance to speak privately after the crowd dispersed.

"Why did he send you here?"

"My father wants us all to be together."

"Then ask him to come here. This is where his people are."

"Bua, please, just come with me. Do you really feel safe in your tiny flat?"

"It is not the size of the flat that makes one safe. It is the people that one chooses to live with, to have near and call one's own—these are the things that make one safe."

We had walked to the end of the lane and stood beside the bicycle heap.

"How did this happen?"

"What?"

"How did you get to speak for so many people?"

"I just speak from my heart. Everyone in this neighbourhood knows who I am. They feel the same way. Nothing will happen to me here. You should all move too."

I raised my hands above my head and joined my palms in a namaskar. I touched her feet and she hugged me.

"These are dark times, child. These are times when men are made."

I walked back to my car alone. I saw her standing on the corner in her white sari. Parents and parent-figures have a way of looking at you and knocking you back to your childhood, a warm sense of hope washed over me. I drove towards the South.

I used to be a scared child, growing up. I had a tendency to visualize all sorts of undesirable situations. They always played out in vivid detail and the only way I could convince myself of their implausibility, was through some sort of prayer. I'd cut deals with the almighty to have things go my way. He rarely disappointed me. As I neared my home it became apparent that there had been trouble. At the outskirts of the colony, a group of policemen were erecting their yellow barricades, stopping all vehicles from going through.

"I live here, please let me pass."

"What are you doing out at this hour? There is a curfew, have you not heard?"

"I left to pick up my aunt from across town. My Bua ji…I left very early."

They saw that my car was empty.

"Where is she, then?"

"She did not want to come."

"Where does she stay?"

"Khadera."

"She is better off."

"May I please pass?"

"You cannot take your car. Leave it here and walk. They are burning cars and attacking anything that moves."

"Who?"

"The mob"

"Who will stop the mob?"

"There are other police engaging them right now. Please stop trying to tell us what to do and listen. Where is your house?"

"F . . . F block."

He grimaced before he raised his hand to direct me to the narrow service lane. It was his way of saying the conversation was over. I left the car there. I started to walk towards my home and called my father. There was no answer. I could see smoke billowing up in the distance. Had there been a fire? The landline went unanswered too. I started to run.

The smoke grew thicker as I got closer to F block. I don't have much recollection of things on the ground as my eyes were fixed on the smoke in the sky. There were some people running in the opposite direction. There was no sign of fire-engines or sirens or police. I tried calling them. All the lines were either dead or hopelessly engaged. One would never have expected something of this sort to happen in a beautiful, gated, protected part of town. How could this happen here? Carnage is mindless and it knows no reason.

It was our home for generations. My grandparents had built it. I had played in the park nearby. It was up in flames. The gate had been pulled apart, the defunct guardhouse smashed and ripped to shreds. It was like a field of corn after a swarm of locusts had done their worst. Waves of heat and ashes rose and pushed me back as I tried to enter. No one answered my calls or cries. Where were they? I charged in through the crack in the gate and landed in the driveway. Our little garden glowed, wrapped in flames.

The bush where a hummingbird had made her nest was burnt to the ground. The glass charred and the paint peeled off. I reached the front door and kicked my way through. I could hear sirens outside. Someone had come to help us. Someone was going to save us all. That was the last thought I had before a chunk of the staircase banister fell on me from the second floor. It crushed me and I struggled to breathe. There was some rustling behind me and muffled voices strung together a course of action to free me from the rubble. They carried me outside. I was coughing uncontrollably. Smoke had filled my lungs.

Every house on our block, the entire row was on fire. The streets were crawling with servicemen and women, heroic policemen and fire department workers. “My family . . . my family is in there.” I tugged at the legs of the man who had pulled me out.

“They are looking . . . they are going in. You must leave it to us now. We will find them.”

“What are their chances?”

“Do you think they might have left the house?”

I lost them all that day. Through the smoke and fire they pulled out the charred, unrecognizable bodies of my parents, sister, and brother-in-law. My entire family died in a fire caused by a rioting mob that actually lived less than a kilometre from us. Across the park and beyond the small forested area there was an enclave. It was an illegal establishment that had grown in size and strength for years. It was a hotbed of anti-national teachings. It took them very little time to cross the short distance and wreak their havoc. The reports later said that even crude explosives and Molotov cocktails were used. Where do prowling crowds of spontaneously passionate, enraged people get their hands on explosives? It was unfathomable.

My family is always with me. I wept for them and mourn them to this day. I stood in front of the house, refusing to believe my fate. An officer from the police spoke to me. I do not remember a word that she said. There were two more explosions down the street that showered us in remnants of an uprooted building. Mr. Chopra used to live there with his two dogs. The hungry flames had found their way into the kitchen and the gas cylinders had given them a second life. I did not flinch and I remember wishing for a stray chunk to bury itself in my skull, taking me too.

I took a long, last look at my home and swore to never let anyone suffer my fate again. It was an indiscriminate act of violence, random to them but very specific to me. I could have died, just as easily, had I reached home any sooner. I too would have been nothing but a memory, in the minds of a few scarred survivors. I walked back to my car.

The barricades were still up and the policemen watched me as I went past them. No one asked me any questions. No one stopped me for identification. I put the key in the ignition and looked in the rear-view mirror. I saw the dog from our street, the one we fed and cared for, the one who had attacked me in my dream. He just stood in the middle of the lane and our eyes met. I backed out, past him as he panted and wagged his tail. I left for Khadera.

# 41
# OUT OF SIGHT

Nakul wept. He felt Shastri ji's pain and anger. He felt his sense of loss. Would he ever see his parents again? He pulled himself up to a window. The hounds and pig-men seemed to have spread themselves across the area. He was able to see a way out. He opened a back window and climbed out. A surveillance drone flew out above him. Fortunately, it was too fast to have seen him. He walked quietly, along a long wall with closed shutters of shops and workhouses, to sneak into a warehouse. It was damp and smelt like produce.

Polling robots scanned the premises as workers loaded crates into trucks. He hid behind a wooden container. When he looked inside and saw heaps of kaddus, he guessed they must be shipping them to the Annapurna division. He threw some of them out and climbed inside the crate. It was a tight squeeze, but he managed to curl up and cover himself with packing straw. Soon, a few men came and covered it shut, hammering nails to keep the lid in place. They loaded the container onto a truck.

For some reason he thought of his mother. Poor Jyoti. What must she have been going through? They started moving. They were in the midst of traffic on the main roads. There were many containers around him and they had all sorts of fruits and vegetables. He was still hungry and felt stupid for not grabbing a few before hiding. The truck entered a shaded garage and stopped.

"Three are for you." the driver shouted instructions.

Nakul could hear the sound of children playing. He was inside a school. The crates were pulled off. There was no light and he could barely see anything through the small gaps between the wooden planks of his box. He could smell rice and dust. He waited until it was all quiet and tried to push the lid off. There wasn't enough room for him to kick it open. He shook and pushed as hard as he could. He heard a crack on the side. Someone had stuck a hammer through the gap and was pulling the lid off.

He prepared himself for a fight. The lid smashed open and there she stood, holding a hammer in her hands, wide-eyed and angry, Samyukta.

"You?!"

Their eyes met and she looked at him with a hateful stare that sent an electric eel up his spine.

"Please . . . please don't!"

She threw the hammer at him. He cowered and wriggled out of the crate. She slapped him across his face.

"Please don't turn me in."

Her mouth was bunched up in lines like a melon and tears rolled down her cheeks. There was a lot that she wanted to say.

"Is it still standing?"

"What?"

"Your thing, is it still standing?"

He looked away sheepishly.

"I need to get to safety. They will kill me."

"Wouldn't that be nice? You pervert!"

"Where are we?"

She didn't believe his innocent act. "At school. I hope they catch you and kill you."

"Please help me—I beg you."

"Why should I help you?"

"I am sorry for what I did to you. You were in the wrong—I had to do what I did."

"What should I do now? I have been sentenced to a boot-camp because of you. You know what that means?"

He did not know how to answer her. He felt horrible.

"I will live apart from my family. I will practically be a pariah for the rest of my life because of this mark on my record."

She was filling a bag with food.

"I have no choice. I am not going to the boot-camp. I am running away."

Nakul Parshuram studied the tragedy that marked her face. Something changed inside him and he felt a sense of shame.

"Turn me in. Clear your record. I am a wanted fugitive. Where will I go anyway? If you bring me in, you will be a hero."

She searched his eyes for deception.

"You'd sacrifice yourself for me?"

"It's the right thing to do, Samyukta. I have no clue what happened to me. Maybe it's a medical problem and our Sanjeevs will be able to help me . . . I just think you should not run away. It is hopeless."

She handed her bag of fruits to him.

"Take as much as you can."

"What are you talking about?"

"We can run away together. Just promise to keep your thing away from me."

"It is away. I'll keep it that way."

The two of them inspected apples and potatoes in silence, like expert farmers.

"My mother said that there has not been such a—such a ghastly act in Dvarca for decades. Did you know that?"

"Someone must have drugged me or tricked me. Someone must have cursed me to make it . . . do that."

"Yes, it is always someone else's fault, a conspiracy to make you a human wind-vane in front of the Great Leader. Yes?"

They filled their bags. She started walking towards the exit.

"Where will we go, do you have a plan?"

She did not answer and he followed her. "They will start looking for me very soon. We should hurry. Get in."

They stood over a wheelbarrow and she helped him into it. She covered him with husk and fruits. He could not believe that she would do that for him. He still had the sack from the provision centre that had saved his life. He used it to cover his face.

"The look suits you."

"This is to stop people from seeing my face."

"Won't they know you by the bulge in your pyjamas?"

"Please stop it—"

"You are free to wander off and take your chances with the Varaha."

She was relishing every moment of his humiliation.

"I must give it to you though, you are quite funny, you know? For a girl."

"That's a high compliment, coming from a mangled banana boy."

He thought it best to keep quiet. She pushed the wheelbarrow along and walked in silence cutting past the sports field. Assembly was about to start and all the children had gone to the central hall. They climbed the fence and ran out on the street towards Grand Park. It was a pleasant day, but for the subterfuge and skulduggery.

"This is very close to where I live."

The smell of chandan-bel filled the air like a warm blanket.

"There are bound to be other people here."

"No, it is still early. Everyone works. Everyone has a place to be."

She stopped walking.

"What? What are we doing now?"

"We're here."

"We're where?"

She knelt down and pulled off a manhole cover. It was heavy and he helped her.

"Get in."

"In the sewer?"

"Yes, inside the sewer."

"What's down there?"

She pushed him aside and squeezed in. There was a rusty, dirty ladder.

"Samyukta?"

"Aren't Nakuls supposed to be brave? Come down here, if you want to stay safe."

With the name of the Lord on his lips, he climbed down into the hole.

"Pull the cover back." He followed her instructions.

The two of them were now in darkness, under the park, under the city.

# 42
# QUITTING TIME

*In the event of a biochemical attack, take the JVK vial. Activate your DDs to emergency mode and locate an open area to facilitate pick-up by our MedEvac drones. Say your prayers and be patient.*

Jyoti watched the public service announcement, waiting for the *Hour of Honour* to begin. She looked out the window at the pink sky, for signs of missiles, warplanes, and Caliphite scum. It seemed peaceful, but for the bustle of traffic and the occasional buzzing of her DDs. Gandharva was going to be working late that day. Baba was home and he sat down beside her.

"Is everything alright?"

"Why do you ask?"

"You are not in your favourite seat."

The old man mumbled to himself as he moved his walker out of the way.

"Jyoti beta, I have lived a—a full life. I worked hard at the plant as a youngster and rose up in the ranks. I have amassed enough Punya to see me through to a decent next life." She knew all this, but he seemed to be building up to something new.

"More than decent, Baba, I imagine your next life will be a lot easier."

"Yes. Maybe I will be able to earn more Punya in my next life."

He was finding it hard to put his sentences together. He was jittery.

"I—I think I should submit myself to the State. I want to start again."

She did not know what to say.

"Why? Are you not happy here? We need you. Your son, your grandchildren—"

"That's the thing. I fear for Nakul. I miss him deeply."

"I miss him too."

"I don't know where we went wrong. He has let us down. I want to thrash him sometimes. At others, I want to forgive him. I am torn. This conundrum will cost me, you see?"

"You have a conundrum?"

"Maybe that is a strong word. I don't think it is black and white. Was he wrong to attack the Great Leader with his private parts? Yes. He was. But was it in his control, completely? I am not sure. No grandson of mine would do this. He was dedicated to the Country and to God. It baffles me."

"It baffles me too. I am his mother. I have always had great hopes for him."

"Has he contacted you?"

"Baba! Of course not. What kind of a question is that?"

"I am just asking you. I have sent him numerous messages to get him to come back. To face the world and plead his case."

"They will never let him plead his case. They will kill him and drag his body out for everyone to see."

"I don't want this *sankat* to detract from the good work of my life. I don't want the Punya to be taken away. It has been cultivated with great care."

"It has."

"I don't know what I might do if he were to come back. If he were to show up some day, would I save him? My son's son? Or would I shun and punish him, as the national shame he has become?"

"Is it not clear to you?"

"It most certainly is not. I just don't want to be wrong."

The television repeated the biochemical attack announcement and they watched it. The thought of instant annihilation provided a moment of respite from their conversation about duties and quitting. The old man pulled out a piece of paper.

"I have filled out my forms. Could you take me to the CC tomorrow? These have to be hand-delivered. There will be a final interview."

"I see, you have made up your mind."

"You and Gandharva also have to sign a form saying that my—my work here is done. You must consent to it, before I can be one with the Ganga."

"Yes." She wept and hugged him.

"Oh, you women. You cry for everything."

The program began and Mira came into the room. She helped Baba back into his favourite chair. Jyoti hid her tears from her daughter.

"Good girl. Thank you!"

She snuggled up to her mother who now stoically watched the telecast.

"Have they mentioned him again?"

"Not for the last 20 minutes."

There were regular updates and news programmes that spoke about the villainy and debauchery of young Nakul. They had produced interviews with his schoolmates and friends who said that he was always 'different' and perhaps better off as a pariah. Some said that he thought too much of himself and maybe that was the root of his perversion. Virdi was also questioned. He said he had championed the boy's cause early on. He claimed to have been fooled and used by a young man who had obviously lost his way. "I should have known . . ." he spoke with great regret.

Nakul was now an enemy of Dvarca. Jyoti had heard and seen all the remarks about her boy.

Even Gandharva's tearful interview was broadcast regularly.

"I cannot believe it. I want to catch him myself, so that I can teach him a lesson. This is Dvarca, not godforsaken Hedonesia. I want to know if he was on drugs. I want to know if he was working for vicious foreign masters. I renounce him. He is no son of mine. We must all renounce him for what he has done."

The parents never had a great relationship. Now they hardly spoke to each other. Apart from banal requests like 'pass me the chilli', there was nothing between them. Gandharva said that he would have to work longer hours to prove his dedication to God and Country, but she knew it was to avoid coming home to her. Surely it must pain him too. Surely it must take a toll to have your son be the most hated person in Dvarca. He never showed it though. He just collapsed deeper and deeper into himself. Compliance had gotten the better of him.

***

There was much jostling behind him, but SS6.2 did not care. He had never seen the ocean before. The hypnotic ebbs and flows of the violent waves held him. For all their unrest, all their toil, the undulant body of water seemed to go nowhere. That which lay deep below, remained unchanged and unbroken, stirring in unseen currents of its own.

The collar was gone and in some ways he felt like a free man. They couldn't completely rid him of the cranial connections and left them in – a thin metal triangle to remind him of who he was. He didn't mind the few nicks and scrapes left by the procedure. He certainly didn't mind that they had to shave him clean. The spray of salty water washed his face, rising in spurts through the bars and mesh. The other prisoners wanted a chance to stand up and look out the window too. They pulled his legs and dragged him down. They would have climbed over him if they could. Twenty-nine other condemned pariahs filled their cramped compartment. They were all being taken to the islands. It was a dubious privilege to know that the "L" in Project L, meant Lakshadweep. It meant you were in a whole new world of trouble. Their fate would be assigned to them there. SS6.2 slid to the side and watched the informal human pyramid fall and reassemble. Men would do anything for a shot at hope. Men would do anything to feel free. He rubbed the rash on his neck again and smiled at his own stupidity. He marvelled at his capacity for living with despair without letting it crush him. What was it all for? They hadn't killed him yet, perhaps there was more to his life after all.

The smell of sea-rot and good old gasoline filled his lungs as their craft bumped and bobbed its way through the rising waves. A big one found its way into the overcrowded cabin. The pyramid fell apart again and like children the captives laughed at their clumsiness. SS6.2 had lost the ability to speak completely, and only communicated through gestures and animated facial expressions. It was probably for the best as he didn't know what he'd say to them. He saw no familiar faces, yet he felt like he knew them all.

# 43
# MAHAKALI

It was a day before he would be promoted to a Hara. It was the fourteenth. He waited at the Mahakali temple to meet with the Peet Gandharva's representative. He had condemned the terrible actions of his son and proved himself to be a loyal citizen. He went out of his way to assist the investigative authorities, the fearsome Varaha men, in their search for the fugitive boy. He gave long interviews and shared all access to Nakul's belongings with them. He had become a symbol for impartial, unflinching belief in justice.

"Good-evening Aasmani Gandharva. You are right on time." A priest in yellow drapes welcomed him. He was in a rush and assumed that the bureaucrat would follow him. They went round the back of the temple to a small office. There were no scanners there. There were no security checks.

"What is this office?"

"All will be revealed. Come."

They came to a concealed hole in the wall and the priest ushered him in.

"It is okay. Please enter."

It was a stuffy cabin with an old computer and some hanging lights. There were statues of many deities along the wall and different shades of tilak. The priest scanned Gandharva's DDs.

"Mahoday, this is not right for you. Your debts are not that bad," the priest was astonished.

"I'm sorry? What is not right for me—?"

"I was told you are interested in the programme and that—oh I see, you are auditing. Yes? You are not a volunteer. That makes a lot more sense. Sorry I got confused."

The priest clapped his hands and flashed a broad grin. Suddenly it all made sense to him.

"The Instant *Kashta* programme, has been in place for almost seven—no eight years now. I have been the administrator since the very beginning."

"What is the Instant Kashta programme?"

"Peet Gandharva ji did not tell you?"

Gandharva was growing impatient. He did not wish to show it though. The man he was speaking to, was a Santri kalaava. One false or disrespectful move and his promotion could be in jeopardy.

"No, *Maharaj*, please tell me . . ."

He showed him a brochure and started what sounded almost like a sales pitch.

"The Instant Kashta Programme or IKP is great for people who are born with very heavy debts. More than 50,00,000 PBs. For them, the activities on earth, that we provide as per the normal gene-tags and jobs are inadequate. They are too slow and ineffectual. IKP is an accelerated way for them to receive a large number of points very quickly."

"How does one do this?"

"Well, it is sort of like *samaadhi*—it is like taking early leave and giving up your life in the right circumstances, to earn the maximum Punya possible. Do you understand?"

"What circumstances?"

"Whatever the State needs. It could be defence-related, it could be for science, there are quite a few circumstances wherein one's death can benefit society. You accept a large amount of pain, by choice. You accelerate your Punya. Mind you, this is only made available to a chosen few who have extreme debts. Even for them, it is their choice."

"How many take this option? In my metrics I saw that there were quite a few who did so recently."

"So far there have been very few who reject the offer. We reach out to them at the age of 15. The option is always on the table and they can choose to exercise it at any time in their lives."

"But other people can only take samaadhi after the age of 85 years—"

"Yes of course, never before. There is so much for them to do here. There is a world to build and maintain."

Gandharva tried to understand the logic. "Who creates the circumstances for them to die, in a good or useful way?"

The priest raised his hands to the heavens.

"It is not so hard, Gandharva. One can give up this world easily, when one knows it is not the only one. It is all in service of the Creator. It is a grand submission." He put a tilak on him and bent down in obeisance to the deities.

"Let us pray that we may do good every day. Let us shepherd more souls to their divine destination. Do remember that the IKP is a programme not be trifled with, it is not something you can ever mention to a person of a lower kalaava than you. Understood?"

Gandharva nodded as his DDs lit up with a message. He had just been promoted to a Hara kalaava.

# 44
# FINAL GOODBYES

The Centre for Veteran Affairs was a huge circular structure with a wide dome on top. They had broken it down and rebuilt it a few times. One had to endure numerous rounds of clearance at each storey and all the offices were on the top floor. The long walks and cumbersome engagement were designed to make senior citizens reconsider the expedition.

The whole family accompanied Baba. Understandably, they were not eager and no one dared to lead the way. The old man walked in front of them.

"Isn't this empowering? You get to say goodbye on your own terms." He was chattier than usual, smiling at the guards and sentries along the way. The T100s clarified his purpose of visit at every checkpoint.

Mira wept and hugged her mother. She was old enough to understand what was happening. She had not spoken to Baba about it and he had not bothered to explain it to her either. His advice to her had become more drawn-out and repetitive. All the talk about being a better daughter, learning to be a good mother, and protecting her future children flooded her mind. She thought about what she might remember. His bushy eyebrows? His hairy knuckles? His love for walnuts?

She loved him. She had never been able to express it, other than through subdued everyday actions. She wondered if the daft old man had noticed. She pulled away from her very pregnant mother and ran ahead to hug him. He was surprised by this display of emotion and stopped to hug and kiss her.

"You are a good girl, Mira. Please don't cry."

"I am not crying," she said, with bulbous drops of salty tears and snot streaming down her face. He took her by the hand and they walked together.

Hara Gandharva was checking messages on his DDs. He carried the bag of cremation supplies with him. The box of camphor, a vial of water from the Ganga, some *samagri* and tulsi leaves. The new tax papers had been put out and he was on the team to assess the impact on different kalaavas and functions. Some early reports had been circulated, but they were rejected by their Lal Gandharva. Everyone had been called back to redo the analysis. He was distracting himself from having to send his father away forever.

To the casual observer, he looked like he was immersed in deep thought, walking with his head down and his hands folded behind his back. But to Jyoti, it was clear that he was reading his mails. His posture always changed when he walked around the house, trying to catch up on work, while others thought that he was present. He was never present, even when he was there. It was a wall that he preferred, a wall of 'work' that saved him from having to be where he was, with her, with the family.

It was a common affliction that they had seen in a documentary once, on the *Hour of Honour.* It was about the people of Hedonesia and their overdependence on technology to keep them happy and entertained. It was a bit ironic that they saw it on a television through DDs with constant updates and messages, but nevertheless, it spoke about a specific disorder. They called it Displatia: the inability to remain in the present. In some of the extreme cases shown on the programme, Hedonesian children were so enslaved by screens that they were incapable of talking to a person without turning to their devices every few seconds.

The material images or videos that they were accessing on their devices, rarely had anything to do with the 'real world' conversation they were supposedly having. They needed to watch cartoons or look at nude pictures while at dinner with their parents. They all had some escape from the present. Jyoti saw this in her husband and watched him scowl, fidget, and pace for reasons unknown. He was with everyone and yet not. She was not sure if she missed him.

They finally reached the sixth level. Baba went in for an exit interview with five wise men. The family waited outside. No one could know what the final conversation entailed. If all went well, he would be able to come out, bid them farewell and then be taken to a samaadhi hall. They sat down in the waiting area. Vidur had been kicking all day long, and even his sister could feel his enthusiasm when she embraced their mother.

"Should you even be here, Ma?"

"Some things are too important to not do, Mira. You will learn that someday."

"Why is he kicking so much? Do you think he is protesting?"

Jyoti did not answer. An old woman down the corridor was saying goodbye to her family. Her interview must have gone well.

"If Baba takes samaadhi today, do we know when he will be reborn?"

"I don't know, beta."

"Do we know where he will be reborn?"

She shrugged.

"Will he be human? Will he remember me? Will I ever speak to him again?"

"He will be human. He has done so many good things, he will be rewarded for them. He may not remember you as his granddaughter, but he will be nice to you when he sees you. Every Dvarcan stranger, could once have been family."

The doors opened and he was escorted out. He had a silly grin on his face and he raised his arms to greet them all.

"Come, this is the last time, I promise!"

The girls went to him and Gandharva reached out, placing his hand on his father's shoulder. They hugged.

"I am a cloud. I have rained and given all that I could. Now I must pass on, waft to new places and benefit others. I will still be a cloud, just different in shape and size. I will rub shoulders with new kin, swell, and shrink with them. In this life, I have given all that I could, and I am proud to have known you."

They said a prayer together, one last time as a family.

They watched as the sentries took him away. They crossed through another set of portals at the end of the long curved corridor and the doors flapped behind them.

"Be brave Mira. Be brave. He chose this. Not all of us have the luxury of taking samaadhi. Be proud of him," Jyoti spoke softly to her inconsolable daughter.

It was a peaceful death by lethal injection, followed by cremation. Gandharva was issued a slip, to return the next day for a final prayer, before the ashes were shipped off to Haridwar for immersion.

"Can I come in, after 6:30 p.m.? I won't be able to leave work sooner."

"We shut at 6:00 p.m. Mahoday. Would you like to request for a Grief and Mourning time allowance? Most people do."

"Sure, yes."

# 45
# PUSH ME, PULL ME

"Are we pushing or pulling?"

"Pulling now, pushing later."

"Keep straight and lean back, hold on tight."

It was impossible. Just the thought of grasping the slippery surface in the middle of the ocean was unfathomable. It moved at will, shivering and contorting without warning. The line moved with it and some of the volunteers fell. He tasted the bitter-salty water again as it splashed up into his mouth and nostrils. Some of it entered his eyes, despite the DDs. They could see the mountain top in the distance, and the long snaking rope that wrapped around it. Every tug was followed by a rumbling noise as they ran back to the boy with the red flag. Before he could catch his breath, Gandharva was pushed along to the front.

The men bumped into each other clumsily. They'd had a few dry runs, but those had proved to be quite useless. They were dry. Standing in the drink to churn it by hand, was very different from listening to process-guides and lectures about momentum in the tents on the shore. The great serpent, Vasuki, who served as their churning belt started to slacken and come loose.

"What happened?"

"Mount Mandara is sinking!"

It was true. The engineers used their sextants to confirm that there had been an unplanned drop in the height of their churning block. They were inadvertently driving it into the ocean bed. Divers at the base resurfaced and described the damage to the igneous rocks below.

"It looks like we have to stop."

"What?"

"Can't we just keep trying? Maybe with another mountain?" Gandharva suggested.

Moving Mandara had not been easy. It had taken months to drag the great peak all the way to the middle of the water. The Devas had lost their powers, but not their influence. They had rounded up the volunteers for their help. It was for a good cause. They had to restore the glory of their gods and that was worth any and every sacrifice. Gandharva stood with them, awaiting directions. The water lapped at his waist, as the hot sun baked the rest of him. He lowered himself into the brine all the way to cool off.

They strained to hear the new set of instructions and started asking the people around them.

"What about the demons? Have they no suggestions?"

"What can you expect from them?"

They had been asked to join the cause too, in exchange for some *Amrit*. The holy nectar of the ocean would cure the gods and appease their enemies. It was a rare truce that was unlikely to last. They refused to stand together on the same side of Vasuki, transforming the churn into some sort of competition. It felt like a tug-of-war at times. The Devas refused to be anywhere near the rear of the snake, seeing as how it was not becoming of gods and their volunteers.

They had chosen the head and neck of Vasuki. It took great pleading and coercion to get the demons to take the tail. No one really asked Vasuki what he felt about all of this. He was just a means to an end. Like the volunteers, he too had put his body on the line for the great cause. He lay there, breathing heavily, tired from all the commotion. Gandharva sensed his aggravation and tried to pet the scaled yellow-and-black skin that gleamed just a few inches away from him. He could hear Vasuki's thoughts.

"It will be okay, Gandharva. You and I understand. You and I know what it takes."

A small black dot appeared on the sun. It grew larger and larger, until it darkened the sky like a thick veil.

The volunteers panicked and some of them started to run or swim away. Vasuki and Gandharva stood still. The extra-terrestrial figure that had blotted the sky, started to reveal its form and shape to the bystanders. It had a head, four stubby legs and an oblong body that shone, just like the snake. It was a giant turtle descending towards them. It hovered at a great height, moving slowly but with purpose. Its heavy legs, like paws, waded in the air unhurriedly. The celestial half-shell wafted through the clouds and stopped near the top of the mountain.

It turned gradually and came to a stop. It appeared to be smiling with its gentle beak and cavernous nostrils. The colossal shell on its back was smooth and flat. Its eyes, like enormous black almonds, dripped with kindness. The Devas recognized Him. Gandharva too, was privy to the realization and he bowed down with the rest of the volunteers. They looked up at the gorgeous giant above them. He had come to save them. It was Lord Vishnu himself.

The turtle opened its wide mouth and let out a sound. With the strength of a typhoon, it lifted waves and carried them across miles, splattering in every direction. It was the innocent and pure song of love. Gandharva welled up and let it wash over him. He felt reborn. He felt cleansed. He threw his hands up in jubilation. The Lord had spoken. Thousands upon thousands of sea creatures came to the surface.

Dolphins danced acrobatically, whales spouted high fountains from their blowholes. Glowing jellyfish basked in the sun giving the shining surface of the water patches of red, orange, yellow, and pink. He looked down and saw schools of tiny fish rushing towards the great mountain in the centre. The turtle glided down, towards the surface of the water, as the Devas sang praises. Music filled the atmosphere spreading hope and expressing admiration for the *Avatar.* In their song they named him '*Kurma*'. Gandharva had a sense of déjà vu and he wept. He had been there before. He had heard the incantation before. Lord Kurma dived into the ocean. He raised the mountain and placed it on the back of his shell. Vasuki tightened his grip and the churning began again.

Both sides pushed and pulled for hours. There were rumblings under the surface of the water. Thunderous booms followed by shocks and claps.

"It must be working! The water is churning, we have disturbed it."

The Devas appeared again, to check on the work of the volunteers.

"How are you, men of valour, men of strength and conviction? Do you think the nectar will be found soon?"

"Any moment now—"

They cheered and sang songs from their vantage position as the turbulent waters jerked and curled clockwise and anticlockwise. The whirlpool was deep and wide, and they had managed to turn the ocean on itself. It splashed and rose with giant waves in a cone of rapid currents.

Gandharva woke up. He sulked and tears streamed down his face as he rose slowly in the V-lab's tank. The lab assistant came in.

"What happened? Why are you upset, Gandharva?"

"I will never see the light."

"What do you mean?"

"I woke up too soon. I have had this vision for years now, but I have never gotten past the journey to receive the prize."

A nurse marched in and pulled the lab assistant out of her way. She was very worried by something. "Are you alright, Mahoday?"

"He is fine, he is just upset that he did not make it far enough."

"You had a sudden neural spike during your vision."

"What does it matter? I am just a volunteer who does not get the *Amrit*."

"Did you hear Lord Kurma speak?"

"There was an invocation of some kind . . . he said something, yes."

"That's it! Have you ever experienced that before?"

"I—I don't know. I can't say."

"I believe that the sound you heard has charged and energized you to an unprecedented level."

He covered his face with his hands. He pulled them off slowly, and looked at the nurse and the lab assistant gaping at him, with hope and expectation in their eyes.

"Blessings come in many forms, Gandharva."

# 46
# THE MISSION BEGINS

The new apartment came with all the necessary pleasures and comforts of the new kalaava. Jyoti was still getting used to the upgrade. The brand-new television reminded her of Nakul, it would have given him a lot of joy to watch the *Hour of Honour* on it. The soft carpets might have pleased Baba the most, with their ornate designs and ergonomic texture. She locked the door as she left with young Vidur in her arms. Mira was at school giving a Home Science exam. Gandharva had left for his mysterious new assignment that morning. She knew very little about it and did not care to find out. She was told that it was a great chance for him to serve the Nation. It was an opportunity for the patriarch of a shamed family to undo the sins of his offspring.

She boarded a bus and sat at a window seat, nestling the new-born in her hands. She could feel his heart beating as he breathed peacefully. She felt the soft skin of his plump, ruddy cheeks. She thanked Goddess Durga that they were both safe and well. She took a blanket from her bag and wrapped him up in it. His tiny black eyes stared back at her, as if to say, 'Thank you, Ma!' The rattle of the bus was disorienting at first, but the young genius-to-be got used to it. She sang to him and rocked him a bit, to put him to sleep. It was a sweet psalm and the other travellers on the bus turned to her in admiration.

Many would argue that he was their son as much as hers. He would be a great man someday, unlike his brother. As much as she was taken by the serene beauty of the infant in her arms, she couldn't help but think of Nakul. She had not allowed herself to cry for him. She had no idea if he was alive or dead. How did he spend his days? Could he not find his way home? Could he not confess, be treated, be punished, and be pure again?

The bus dropped them at the temple district. She walked up the steps, past the *prasadalaya*, straight to the water fountains. Two jets emerged at hand and foot level. She washed her feet and rinsed her mouth, before carrying Vidur up the last flight of stairs to the bright white marble entrance to the Dvarcadheesh Krishna temple. A small display declared the completion of another moon with the word ***'PURANMASHI'*** in large bold font. The hour was auspicious.

The temple was the largest and most ornate shrine in all the land. It had been built on an ancient hillock, where deities and idols had been worshipped for centuries. The State had preserved the site in its original glory and built an enormous modern structure around it. She went to the Hanuman temple and read the *chaalisa.* She walked over to the *Shiva-lingam* and completed a few *parikramas.* She made an offering of milk and honey, chanting her favourite prayers again and again.

Tiny Vidur was the perfect little trainee. He was at ease in the quiet environment. His eyes were transfixed on his doting mother as she went all around the temple, to every individual deity. She felt a bit tired. Her strength had not been the same after bringing Vidur into the world. She was still recovering and sat down by a pillar, pulling her son closer to her bosom. A priest came by and offered everyone some *charnamrit* and sweet *boondi.*

The religion and its teachings had changed and taken many forms over the years. It had gone from the simple *Rig Vedic* traditions, wherein the main question asked by mankind was, 'How will we survive?' The answer came in the form of the elements. Man worshipped the elements as he wandered the earth in search of sustenance.

With the advent of agriculture and some scientific advancements, man's questions evolved. 'Who am I?' The answer came in the form of the *Upanishads* and man was able to learn more about how to exist in a family, with friends, with the knowledge of birth, and death. The cycle of rebirth was uncovered and it led to the quest for salvation or moksha. Paths were charted and *yogas* were developed. Karma, *Dhyana, Jnana,* and *Bhakti.* There were ways to attain eternal peace.

Science evolved further. Man grew more impatient and his world started to crumble. His great query now became, 'How do I perfect myself to achieve salvation?' The answer to this, came through the great revelation at Mahajageshwar, to which Shastri ji himself was a witness. The answer was Navmarg.

She sat under the arches thinking about how helpless she still was. In spite of all the directives, constant updates and policing, she still felt lost. She felt betrayed. The glorious marble pillars shone in the pale light and she touched them. They felt new. The deities and their chambers, however, had been there much longer. For 30 centuries men, women, and children had visited the peaceful grounds of the great temple with their hopes and wishes, their fears and complaints, their pain and their loss. She was just like all of them.

She tried to imagine the number of intentions, promises, and requests that had been expressed in front of the gods. She hoped that they were all for good. The thought comforted her and for a moment, she felt just a little bit less lonely. She wiped a tear from her eye.

Her DDs lit up with a message from XX.

"I HAVE MET THE MOST INTERESTING PERSON. YOU MIGHT KNOW HIM."

"Who?"

"HE IS A FAMOUS NAKUL. BUT NOW HE GOES BY THE NAME, PARSHURAM."

# SELECTED GLOSSARY

| | |
|---|---|
| *Aasmani:* | *Blue* |
| *Aatma:* | *Soul* |
| *Acharya:* | *Teacher* |
| *Adarniya:* | *Honourable* |
| *Aloo:* | *Potato* |
| *Ashramas:* | *Stages* |
| *Ajvain:* | *Seeds of bishop's weed* |
| *Amma:* | *Mother* |
| *Amrut-dhaara:* | *A medicine (literally stream of nectar)* |
| *Anjeer:* | *Fig* |
| *Antim yatra pujan:* | *Ritual regarding the final journey (death)* |
| *Apchaaram:* | *Disgusting behaviour* |
| *Baba:* | *Father* |
| *Babu:* | *A term of endearment for boys* |
| *Badaam:* | *Almond* |
| *Baingani:* | *Violet* |
| *Barfi:* | *An Indian sweet* |
| *Beta:* | *Son* |
| *Bhajan:* | *Devotional song* |
| *Bhakti:* | *Devotion* |
| *Bharta:* | *Roasted mish-mash of brinjals* |
| *Bindi:* | *A traditional dot between women's eyebrows* |
| *Boondi:* | *An Indian sweet* |
| *Brahmacharya:* | *Bachelorhood* |
| *Chameli:* | *A fragrant variety of jasmine* |
| *Chandan:* | *Sandalwood* |
| *Charnamrit:* | *Milk-based offering* |
| *Charhava:* | *Offering* |
| *Chaturgrah:* | *Smart home* |

| | |
|---|---|
| *Chaturpad:* | *Smart tablet* |
| *Chokha:* | *Potato mash* |
| *Daal:* | *Lentils* |
| *Devabhoomi:* | *Holy ground* |
| *Dharma:* | *Religion/ duty* |
| *Dhoti:* | *A rectangular piece of unstitched cloth worn by men* |
| *Dhyana:* | *Meditation* |
| *Divya:* | *Divine* |
| *Drishtikon:* | *Perspective* |
| *Gajar:* | *Carrot* |
| *Grihastha:* | *Householder* |
| *Halwa:* | *A popular Indian sweet* |
| *Har:* | *Liberation from the vicious cycle of births and deaths* |
| *Hara/ Hari:* | *Green (male/ female)* |
| *Indradhanush:* | *Rainbow* |
| *Jaivik:* | *Of life* |
| *Ji:* | *An honorific used as a suffix in Hindi* |
| *Jnana:* | *Wisdom* |
| *Kaddoo:* | *Pumpkin* |
| *Kakdi:* | *A variety of skinny cucumber* |
| *Kalaava:* | *A holy band worn around one's right wrist* |
| *Kalaripayattu:* | *A martial art from kerala* |
| *Kalash:* | *An urn/ pot for water* |
| *Karma:* | *Action* |
| *Kashta:* | *Pain, suffering* |
| *Kathal:* | *Jackfruit* |
| *Keffiyeh:* | *A headdress worn by Arab men* |
| *Kela:* | *Banana* |

*Khaadi:* *Coarse hand-spun cotton*
*Khayali pulao:* *Pie in the sky*
*Kurta:* *A collarless shirt*

*Laddoo:* *Round Indian sweets*
*Lal:* *Red*

*Madira:* *Alcohol*
*Mahadev:* *Shiva*
*Mahoday:* *Mister*
*Mandap:* *Specially-designed layered prayer area with a fire pit at its centre*
*Mata:* *Mother*
*Munshi:* *Clerk/writer*

*Nagada:* *A large traditional bass drum*
*Namaskar:* *Traditional Indian greeting with palms pressed together*
*Naraayani:* *Mother Goddess*
*Narangi:* *Orange*
*Navmarg:* *New Path*
*Navmargi:* *One who follows Navmarg*
*Navrasa:* *Nine chief emotions associated with a dance performance*
*Neel:* *Indigo*

*Paap:* *Sin*
*Parikrama:* *Circumambulation*
*Peet:* *Yellow*
*Poha:* *A breakfast savoury*
*Prasadalaya:* *A place where holy food offerings are prepared*

*Rahu:* *A malefic planet in Vedic astrology*
*Rati:* *Wife of the god of love/pleasure*

| | |
|---|---|
| *Sabzi:* | *Vegetable (curry)* |
| *Salwar kameez:* | *A type of loose trousers and long shirt worn by women* |
| *Santoor:* | *Stringed classical instrument* |
| *Sankat:* | *Trouble* |
| *Santri:* | *Orange* |
| *Sanyasa:* | *Asceticism* |
| *Sarson:* | *Mustard* |
| *Satvik:* | *Pure* |
| *Sena:* | *Army* |
| *Sevika:* | *Female servant* |
| *Shahtoot:* | *Mulberry* |
| *Shakarkand:* | *Sweet potato* |
| *Shakha:* | *Legion* |
| *Shani:* | *Saturn* |
| *Shringaar:* | *Beauty ritual* |
| *Shubh-shubh bolo:* | *Say Only Auspicious Things* |
| *Sindoor:* | *Vermilion* |
| *Sriman:* | *Mr. (honorific for a man)* |
| *Srimati:* | *Mrs. (honorific for a married woman)* |
| *Sthaapan:* | *Establishment/installation* |
| *Suji:* | *Semolina* |
| *Tadka:* | *Tempering* |
| *Thaalis:* | *Plates* |
| *Tilak:* | *An auspicious mark worn on the forehead* |
| *Trishul:* | *A long-handled trident* |
| *Uchchaaran:* | *Recitation* |
| *Vaanar:* | *Monkey* |
| *Vaig (short for Vaigyanik):* | *Scientist* |
| *Vanaprasthi:* | *Forest-retired* |

| | |
|---|---|
| *Vandana:* | *Devotional song* |
| *Varaha:* | *Boar* |
| *Vidhi:* | *Way* |
| *Vidyalaya:* | *School* |
| *Vipada:* | *Distress* |
| *Yantra:* | *A geometrical design used as an aid for worship* |

## OTHERS

1. *Vakratunda mahakaya, suryakoti samaprabha,*
   *Nirvighnam kurume Deva sarva kaaryeshu sarvada.*
   Lord Ganesh, of curved trunk, large body, and with the brilliance of a million suns, please make all my works free of obstacles, always.

2. *Sarvamangal mangalye,*
   *Shivesarvaarth sadhikay,*
   *Sharanye trayambakey Gauri,*
   *Naraayani namostute.*
   The one who is auspiciousness Herself in all that is auspicious,
   Shive, who fulfils all the objectives of the devotees,
   Who is the Giver of Refuge, with three eyes and a shining face;
   Salutations to you, Oh Naraayani.

3. *Om namoh bhagvate Vasudevaay namaha.*
   Prostration to Lord Vasudeva

4. *Tvamevamata, chapita tvameva,*
   *Tvamevabandhush-cha sakhatvameva,*
   *Tvamevavidya, dravinamtvameva,*
   *Tvamevasarvam, mama Deva Deva.*
   Thou art my mother, and thou art my father
   Thou art my brother (or relative), and thou art my friend
   Thou art my knowledge, thou art my wealth
   Thou art my all-in-all, Oh God of gods.

5. *Jai Shri Krishna! Om namahShivaya!*
   Victory to Lord Krishna, Salutations to Lord Shiva!

6. *Yaa Devi sarva bhuteshu*
*Shakti roopen sansthita,*
*Namastasyay namastasyay namastasyay namo-namaha.*
Salutations again and again to the Devi (Goddess) who resides in all beings in the form of Shakti (power).

7. *Om bhur bhuvasvaha tatsavitur varenyam,*
*Bhargo-devasya dhimahi*
*Dhiyoyona-prachodayat.*
We meditate on the glory of the Creator;
Who has created the universe;
Who is worthy of worship;
Who is the embodiment of knowledge and light;
Who is the remover of sin and ignorance;
May He open our hearts and enlighten our intellect.

8. *Yaakundendu-tushaara-haara-dhavalaa*
*Yaashubhra-vastra-avrtaa,*
*Yaaveena-vara-danda-mandita-karaa*
*Yaashveta-padma-asanaa,*
*Yaa Brahma-Achyuta-Shankara-prabhrtibhir-Devahsadaapoojita*
*Samaampaatu Saraswati-Bhagavati nihshesha-yaaddya-apahaa.*
(Salutations to Devi Saraswati) Who is pure white like jasmine, with the coolness of the Moon, brightness of snow and who shines like a garland of pearls; and Who is covered with pure white garments,
Whose hands are adorned with the Veena (a stringed classical instrument) and the boon-giving staff; and Who is seated on a pure white lotus,
Who is always adored by Lord Brahma, Lord Achyuta (Lord Vishnu), Lord Shankara and other Devas, Oh Goddess Saraswati, please protect me and remove my ignorance completely.

9. *Anhonee ko honee kardein, honee ko anhonee*
*Ek jagah jab jama hon teenon, Brahma, Shankar, Pashupati . . .*
They can make the impossible possible and the possible impossible
When the three of them get together, Brahma, Shankar, Pashupati . . .

# ACKNOWLEDGMENTS

It has taken me seven years to complete the *Dvarca* trilogy. Sadly in this time, even though it is a work of futuristic dystopian fiction, I have seen parts of it come true.

Fiction exists because history stutters when it repeats itself. Through it, we live out our dreams and nightmares together.

There are many people to thank for making this book happen: my grandparents, for introducing the power of stories to me; my parents and sister without whom I would be lost; my wife, without whom I would have no reason to be found.

Also, the good people at Writer's Side and Fingerprint, for their patience, courage, and support.

And last but not least, all the authors, artists, comedians, and film-makers I admire and know only through their work: thank you for inspiring me.

Madhav Mathur was born and raised in Delhi. He lives in Singapore, where he works for an MNC by day and as a writer–film-maker by night. His first novel, *The Diary of an Unreasonable Man* was published in 2009. His award winning films, *The Insomniac* and *The Outsiders* have been screened at numerous festivals. He hopes he is getting better at doing the things he loves.